CW01659485

WOMEN'

From beyond the trees th

'Go on, Hansi,' a voice sl

'Hurry up. It's my turn n

They killed Dieter. Go on

And the ring of soldiers closed in on the women in the midst, the tired dejected women, the beaten women who would pay the age-old price of defeat.

'Nitchevo,' a sulky Ukrainian girl mouthed.

'Nitchevo.'

But as a hand seized her, Katrina Semoyovna saw an incredulous light come suddenly into Vyora Pekare's eyes.

'Rudi!' she gasped. 'Rudi...'

But her voice was drowned in the hungry mutter of the men as they seized their prey, as their hands grappled and fumbled fiercely, dragging at tunics, ripping at the rough fabric of the uniform trousers...

W. A. BALLINGER

Women's Battalion

A MAYFLOWER BOOK

GRANADA

London Toronto Sydney New York

Published by Granada Publishing Limited in 1967
Reprinted 1967 (twice), 1968, 1969, 1972, 1973, 1978, 1982

ISBN 0 583 11092 4

A Granada Paperback Original
Copyright © Press Editorial Syndicate 1967

Granada Publishing Limited
Frogmore, St Albans, Herts AL2 2NF
and
36 Golden Square, London W1R 4AH
866 United Nations Plaza, New York, NY 10017, USA
117 York Street, Sydney, NSW 2000, Australia
100 Skyway Avenue, Rexdale, Ontario, M9W 3A6, Canada
61 Beach Road, Auckland, New Zealand

Printed and bound in Great Britain by
Cox & Wyman Ltd, Reading
Set in Monotype Times

This book is sold subject to the condition that it shall not, by way of trade or otherwise, be lent, re-sold, hired out or otherwise circulated without the publisher's prior consent in any form of binding or cover other than that in which it is published and without a similar condition including this condition being imposed on the subsequent purchaser.

Granada ®
Granada Publishing ®

Women's Battalion

CHAPTER 1

The soft, lazy balloons of smoke were rising here and there across the face of Misgorod, sometimes showing for an instant in their hearts the intense heat of the explosions that brought them into being. Beyond the town the River Don swung in a slow, polished arc, both guardian and threat to the town within its curve.

It didn't look too bad, Colonel Andrienko thought as the staff car breasted the gentle rise and passed through the last clump of trees. It didn't look nearly as bad as most of the cities he had passed through since last he saw Misgorod. There was a lot more of Misgorod left than he had expected to see. And if this little battle could be finished quickly then Misgorod would make a very nice little winter quarters for his green and untried regiment, newly arrived from the Urals.

Corps headquarters should be somewhere about here, he thought as he motioned Sergeant Sychev to pull the big Mercedes to the side of the rutted road. Old Long-Lug always liked to be in sight of his troops in an action – if not actually in the firing line.

The big car, carefully preserved loot from earlier fighting, slid to a smooth stop.

"Do you see the general, Pyotr? He should be about here if he's anywhere."

"Unless he's down there, Comrade Colonel . . ."

The driver thumbed towards the broad, waving field of rye that lay between them and the town.

Some tractors were moving through the rye and the colonel gave a little barked laugh of delight.

"Trust Gnotke," he chuckled. "The city might be ruined but Gnotke still gets his harvest in. But you don't know Gnotke, I think. He was rayon chairman when I was here before. The apple of his eye was that kolkhoz. He took over the district in very poor shape. The collective had never fulfilled its norm. And, my word, he really made them work, men and women together, sweating it out in those fields. It seems a long time ago."

He pulled himself from the car, a tall, lean man with a stiffness in one hip and the Order of Lenin about his neck.

"I suppose the old peasant lies deep in all of us; just moujiks at heart."

He sniffed at the air, at the mingled scents of growing crops and distant battle.

"I think I enjoyed that spell with the kolkhozniki as much as anything I have ever done. The feeling that something useful was being achieved. And the girls, too. Ah, Pyotr, those were the girls."

He was leaning on the door, taking in the fields, the life that was visibly rising from the earth, making a sharp contrast with the death that was visibly and audibly taking place in the town.

"I wonder how Gnotke did it," said Colonel Andrienko. "How did he keep these crops undestroyed? Of course, he was always as sharp as a monkey that one . . . But how long is it since we saw a field with a growing crop?"

"Many months, Comrade Colonel," Sychev answered. He could have called the colonel Nikolai but he sensed that this was a mood of formality. There were times when there was no formality between these two who had soldiered so long together, in Finland first and then in Poland and now in the Motherland itself. There were times when it was "Nikolai" and "Pyotr" and times when it was "Comrade Colonel" and "Sergeant." In knowing and interpreting the colonel's moods and needs lay the sergeant's particular genius.

He had no greater ambition than this, to be the colonel's driver, to take him where he willed to go, to get for him whatever the needs of the moment might be, vodka, women, food or ammunition for his battalion. It was a good job, his, and he hoped to keep it until at last peace came.

"Burned fields, Pyotr, we have seen too many burned fields. Burned fields and burned towns and burned people. I find myself moved by the sight of a crop that has not been burned. Perhaps, Pyotr, it is a symbol. Perhaps, after all, the retreating is over. If fields are left unburned there must be some hope that we will harvest the crop. Or perhaps it means only that the commissars have been careless."

The colonel had a lean, chiselled face, a Georgian face rather than Russian. There was a hint of satirical humour about the mouth and eyes and Sychev knew well how swiftly his devastating wit could be unleashed – even on the commissars.

Agonised, Sychev had heard him more than once let loose his mordant humour on the commissars, on the Party, even on the Hozyain himself, on Joseph Vissarionovitch Stalin. Only the Order of Lenin on his breast protected him, for not even the commissars or the NKVD lightly crossed a holder of such a decoration.

"Destruction beyond," mused Colonel Andrienko again. "And yet the fields still give up their harvest . . . Yet, correct me if I am wrong, Pyotr, is it not early for harvesting?"

Himself reared on a kolkhoz, Sychev nodded.

"On our collective we would not harvest for another month."

"And yet the tractors are in the fields," said the colonel. "Strange – as a city man I find it strange."

He had in fact, been a Professor of Literature before war snatched him from his desk and his lectures, made him an officer and used his brain's keen edge for the destruction of men instead of their instruction.

The tractors were half-hidden in the rye, mechanical monsters trudging across the fields.

"This I find most peculiar indeed. And the peculiar should be investigated at all times, Pyotr."

"The regiment," his driver pointed out. "They are coming."

"Not for an hour. More than an hour if Kuznetsov halts for a meal break. We will discover the reason for these tractors."

Fives miles behind his regiment would be plodding along through the dust – his new, untried regiment, raised in the Urals, trained and equipped in frantic haste and sent here as part of the spearhead of the new counter-attack, the overwhelming drive that would smash the German army and send it fleeing in terror back to the Reich and the mad figure of its Führer. Or so they said in Moscow at least. But then, they did not have to fight the battles.

The two men left their battered car and waded across the waving fields of rye towards the mighty machines that were reaping such an early harvest.

And such a strange harvest.

There had been a battle here. Amid the rye, the Germans had held a strong position and their gun emplacements had been well sited to give all-round fire cover.

But, plainly, they had not been well enough sited. For they had been over-run. Machine guns and mortars still reared minatory muzzles, though now their crews lay dead in the pits and slit trenches.

This was the battle of the day before, Colonel Andrienko thought. The battle that had cleared the approach to Misgorod and driven the Germans back across the Don.

A costly battle, he thought. Swathes of the attacking troops had been cut down as they charged, swathes of dead amid the rye.

And this was the harvest that the tractors were reaping.

Bulldozer blades were fitted to the front of the tractors and they were pushing the piled bodies towards a great waiting pit that had already been excavated.

"We are become mightily tidy," Andrienko smiled quizzically at his driver. "I never remember seeing a battlefield cleaned up so quickly."

"NKVD," Sychev murmured. "The drivers . . ."

And indeed each tractor was manned by a man in the purple-epauletted secret police uniform.

"A strange harvest indeed . . ."

A stocky NKVD lieutenant came blustering towards them, hand on his holster.

"This is forbidden, Comrade Colonel. No one is to come here."

Andrienko's pale eyes surveyed him, noting the new, clean uniform, the well-trimmed hair, the evidence that he had lived in comfort. Even his boots were polished.

The contempt of the fighting soldier for the rear echelon was in Andrienko's voice:

"I am not accustomed to orders from junior officers," he said frostily.

His hand, by accident or design, flipped the Order of Lenin on his breast.

"My regiment is on the road. Shortly it will be in action here. It is my duty to examine the ground."

Sychev saw the lieutenant's eyes darken with anger. The NKVD were not accustomed to having their orders questioned.

"Your regiment will not fight here," said the lieutenant shortly. "The Germans are all across the river – the live Germans."

Andrienko was walking forward, long legs striding easily, making the pudgy lieutenant trot to keep level with him.

"This is a matter of State security," the lieutenant threatened. "You must go no further . . ."

Andrienko ignored him.

Now he was at the edge of the pit, seeing the piled conglomeration of bodies beneath him.

And now at last he knew the cause of the lieutenant's anxiety. Now he knew why the NKVD were doing this rare, urgent battlefield clean-up.

And now he knew why, above all, they did not want any young, raw troops to see the evidence that he saw. This was a sight to shatter the morale of any young soldier.

So the rumour was true. He had heard it and had not believed. Now the evidence was there in the shattered bodies in the uniform of the Red Army.

For this was the Zhenski Battalion.

Here and there a tunic had been ripped or trousers torn from a shattered body by the blade of the bulldozers.

And instead of the hairy chests of men the full bosoms of women were revealed.

The Zhenski Battalion. The women's battalion. It was true then. Mother Russia had sent her daughters out to fight – and to die.

On the edge of the pit a body sprawled face downwards, one hand and arm dangling over the edge of the raw earth. Andrienko saw a silvery gleam at the wrist and he stepped forward abruptly to stoop and examine.

The little silver links held a flat, oval plaque. Andrienko had no need to examine it closely. It was the exact duplicate of one on his own left wrist. There was one word engraved on each: Pamyat.

"Memory."

Gently the colonel turned the body over. Machine gun bullets had stitched a line of blue-edged dots across the breasts where once he had lain. And the lips he had kissed so often were muddied with the clay of Mother Russia.

"Vyora," he said softly. "Oh, Vyora . . ."

And deliberately, as the NKVD lieutenant fumed behind him, he stooped lower and placed a last long kiss on the dead, cold lips.

"I will have to make a report. This is not proper. There are orders from Moscow . . ."

Bleakly the colonel surveyed him and Sychev held his breath, waiting for the explosion. But Andrienko's voice was in gentle contrast to his words.

"You can take your orders from Moscow, my good lieutenant, and you can stuff them up your fundamental orifice. Or, since plainly you have had no education, up your backside."

With a raging sorrow within him, Andrienko stalked back across the waving rye to the battered, bullet-holed staff car.

The Zhenski Battalion, he thought. The Women's Battalion. Poor Vyora . . .

A woman was walking through the trees, though it was only at second glance that Andrienko knew her for a woman, for she was in man's uniform, with a too-big greatcoat slung over her shoulders.

"Hey! Wait there a second."

Andrienko ran towards her. At least then there was one survivor of the Zhenski Battalion. Now perhaps he would learn the truth of what had happened here.

The other figure paused only imperceptibly then walked on in a dazed, unsteady way.

"Comrada Baba, I would be obliged for some information on the battle . . ."

He fell silent as he looked again at the face. "Baba" he had said, for she had seemed like an old woman as she walked, stiff and somnambulistic.

But there were no lines of age on the face when he gazed into it, holding an arm to halt the woman. The only lines were of suffering.

"About the battle – " he began, while she stared at him apathetically.

Then his mouth opened wide in sheer surprise.

"Boge moy," he breathed unideologically. "My God, it's Katrina Semyonovna. Don't you remember me?"

What had they done to her, he wondered wildly. What had they done to the famous authoress, the holder of a host of awards? The darling of the critics? How had they reduced her to this helpless, ageing woman?

The woman did not speak but began, still silently, to turn away. His hand was still on her arm, laid there lightly. But as she turned his grip closed . . . on nothing.

He began, with a terrible, cold rage, to understand some of the things that had happened here, to Vyora Pekare, to Katrina Semyonovna; to the Zhenski Battalion.

CHAPTER 2

"Zhenski Battalion? What the hell do you mean, Anna? There isn't any women's battalion here – or anywhere else as far as I know. Zhenski Battalion indeed! You've been out in the sun too long."

Katrina Semyonovna returned to her notes, scribbling, altering, punctuating. She was a thin-faced woman with long, black hair that hung to her shoulders and had a bluish glint when she washed it and brushed it well. She did this about as often as she put make-up on that long, well-moulded but undeniably thin face. Which is to say perhaps once a year.

Down the river they could both hear the mutter of the guns as the Red Army drove back the invader, smashed the bright point of his armoured spear, gave him exactly what he deserved for daring to set foot on the sacred soil of Russia. He might have raced across the Ukraine but he would find it different here. The Red Army was smashing him, holding him, driving him back. Or so the communiques said. But the sound of the guns was undeniably louder today than it had been the day before.

"I don't know how you can sit there, Katrina Semyonovna. How can you sit and scribble when I bring you such exciting news! If I had told you the sky had fallen you would only say, 'Well, put it back.'"

Anna Turuchin was about twenty then, a well-made girl with short, tousled fair hair and a round chubby face. When she was excited as now she did not look more than fourteen, an excited schoolgirl with less sense than most schoolgirls.

"Listen," said Katrina. "I have a chapter to finish to achieve my norm. Leave me alone. You don't want me sent to Siberia."

She spoke only partly in jest. Of course writers did not have norms to fulfil like factory workers or kolkhozniks. But still there was the unwritten, tacit assumption that a writer paid for his or her privileges, freedom from manual labour, freedom to travel through the U.S.S.R., freedom even for a distinguished writer like Katrina Semyonovna to have a secretarial assistant to help with research, run messages and perform all the other petty tasks of day-to-day living that liberated a writer for the writer's prime and only justification – to write.

Katrina felt no shame at all in the privileges she had been accorded; her comfortable flat in Moscow, her dacha in the country, the money she could draw almost at will. All these were, she felt, fully justified by her work. The people needed not only organization, economic sufficiency, freedom within the proletarian framework. They needed also food for the spirit, for the mind.

A manager of a factory, a party official had as much as she, and did no more for the country and the people. A writer was, she liked to say when the various intellectual societies of which she was a member met, at the same time factory manager and factory itself. The manager part of the writer saw that the body was fed, the mind supplied with the natural food of its kind, facts, news, impressions. And the mind, the factory, turned this food, this raw material, into words, into books, stories, plays, films.

And all of them devoted to the furthering of the great cause, to bringing nearer the day when all the little snags and flaws that were bound to occur when a great machine first began to turn would be smoothed away. To the Party.

If she tried, Katrina Semyonovna could just remember the days in Moscow before the Revolution. She could remember a great house with brilliantly clad guests, rich foods, wonderful wines.

She could remember her father, too, gorgeous in a glowing uniform. Sometimes, for the special benefit of very young and new members of some group she would recall those days – and recall them without the slightest fear of being called a revisionist.

"For that splendid uniform of my father which I used to so admire – that was only the livery of a servant, the badge of slavery. All those rich foods – we never tasted them, not we servants and children of servants.

"But despite his livery, my father was no slave. He fought the fight for liberty. He was a hero of the Revolution. They lashed him like a dog in the yard of that great house, lashed him until he died, bloody but not broken, defying them to the last."

In fact, she had been sent out of Moscow just before the Revolution and her father had been shot by White troops while he looted his master's money boxes and pulled and hacked the rings from his mistress's fingers. But this of course was not known to one who was only a child.

And a child of the Revolution. Everything that the new state had to offer in the way of education was thrust on Katrina Semyonovna, daughter of a Hero of the Revolution. Equally, she absorbed everything that the state had to offer in the way of indoctrination. If she had not been designed so by nature and history she certainly became a most fervid Communist. And a writer.

She was still a student when her first book was published,

a glowing novel of life on a collective farm. "A book," as an "Izvestia" critic remarked, "that for its constructivist and forward-looking realism marks down its author as both mature in political judgement and wealthy in the knowledge of the deep springs of human nature."

That had been ten years before. She was still writing and still getting the blessing of the authorities for her work.

There were other authors who could stray from the path of Lenin-Marxist realism – or who found the path had suddenly been yanked from beneath their feet – but Katrina seemed always to be completely abreast of the latest trend in top-level thinking.

There were times when she herself wondered if she actually created the imperceptible changes that went on at all times in the level of the highest thinking. Did the Hozyain, she even dared to wonder at times, get some little fraction of his ideas from her? It was possible. But it was more likely that as a child of the Revolution, and one who moved in increasingly more rarefied circles, she was simply attuned to the mood of the Party, absorbing it as she breathed.

Certainly she had maintained a dominating position as a younger Soviet novelist – as the younger Soviet novelist – for an amazing length of time. Other leaders in the race struck their sour notes and fell from grace, went for re-education in fundamental thinking under the aegis of the NKVD, but Katrina Semyonovna never. She had become a sort of literary aparatchik.

Even when Sasha, poor, brilliant, beautiful, lovable Sasha, fell from grace she was not affected. Sasha had been the comet who dazzled the whole Soviet literary scene for a season. His brilliance drew even the commendation of Comrade Molotov, who remarked, "Sasha Ryevsky can say more in a sentence than most of our writers in a whole book."

It was only natural that Katrina should marry him. She loved him devotedly, his long, waving hair, his deep, lucid eyes, his tender, humorous mouth. She adored making love with him and their married life was almost bourgeois in its romantic intensity.

Nevertheless it was Katrina too who noted his first tendency to deviationism and revisionism. And when, in "Reappraisals from Afar", he showed signs of unregenerate Trotskyism, she saw where her duty lay.

No doubt his faults would have been found out soon enough, detected by the ever-moving finger of the censorship bureaux. But it was Katrina's letter of condemnation of modern trends which led first to his trial. Naturally by that time she had divorced him and her own good name remained unsullied.

Sometimes, but not very often, she thought of him. By now, of course, he would have seen where he erred. Patiently the teachers at the school for re-education would have pointed out how fundamental wrong thinking could lead to errors of deduction; how a new approach had to be formulated in order to recapture the basic truths.

She saw this college of re-education as a pleasant, quiet place, far from any distractions, where teacher and pupil would walk slowly in shadowy cloisters, going over each subject with patient, kindly care until at last error had been extirpated and right thinking took its place.

Sometimes, she almost wished for a spell there herself, for peace and rest from work and thought. There would not be quite the same bustle as in the university where she had herself been educated. But the spirit would be there.

Katrina Semyonovna had an almost infinite capacity for rationalism. But she was, after all, a child of the Revolution.

Anna Turuchin was still buzzing like a bee about the room. "She said I will be a sergeant. Of course I was in the Osaviakhim. I even have the 'Voroshilov Sharpshooter's' badge. And I marched in the May Day Parade when I was only fifteen."

She thrust her chest out proudly, gazing eagerly across the river towards the sound of gunfire.

The Osaviakhim, she was thinking, the happiest days of her life. The Society for the Promotion of Aviation and Chemical Defence. The best club in the world. The shooting, the swimming, the athletics . . . and the drill, above all the drill.

To feel herself one with ten thousand other women or

sometimes men and women, marching and counter-marching with split-second timing across the vast barrack squares. To drown her personality in the mass of all the others. That was real Communism, she had thought afterwards, true Communism. Not an individual. A part of a greater whole.

Then it had been fun only, the greatest fun in the world. But now at last she would have the chance to prove its real purpose.

The Zhenski Battalion. And she would be a sergeant. Life could hold nothing more.

Katrina sat up at last, rubbed her eyes wearily and turned to the girl.

"Now – what were you talking about, Anna? No. You'd better get this typed first. I'd like three copies for I think there's going to be quite a lot of revision."

It was not going well, she admitted to herself, this novel that had been suggested to her in Moscow – that is, which she had been instructed to write.

The book was about a poor fisherman's community, a co-operative fishing village on the Don. It was to tell about their sufferings under the old regime and how the Revolution had brought a new dawn of hope.

Through two or three generations, the story was to tell how, through the co-operation of the group, they were able to buy and make better nets, build better and bigger boats, enjoy a better life.

Misgorod had been suggested as a place where there was such a community and where she could draw on actual experience of the fishermen themselves as material for this book which the head of the publishing syndicate was quite sure would be a great solace to the army of workers and peasants fighting the German invader.

When she reached Misgorod and found that the community consisted actually of a few decaying huts and some almost as decayed fishermen, Katrina wondered, uneasily, if the publisher had some particular knife to thrust in her back. To base a novel on the facts that she had seemed to learn would be an outright betrayal of the Revolution.

Anyone who wanted her to write such a book could wish her no good. And yet she had slept several times with the publisher and had thought they were good friends. Therefore the answer must lie elsewhere.

Plainly the whole fault lay with the fishermen themselves. They were uncouth, lazy, dirty, apathetic, the very antithesis of the Soviet proletariat. Still, they were material, though they should certainly be taken away and trained. And she had in fact been using them in her book, using them as the contrast to an upright, bright, forward-looking and imaginary co-operative prospering on another part of the river. They were the contrast that proved the truth of the Revolution.

Yet the work had depressed her so far. She was not pleased with it. It did not have to her the forward-looking flavour she delighted to impart to all her work.

She was still so immersed in the depression of her thoughts that she had not absorbed anything at all that the silly girl was saying.

Now as the words sank in she stared incredulously at Anna.

"You're not going to do any typing? What on earth do you mean?"

"It's over. I'm finished. I'm not going to be a secretarial assistant any more."

"You must be out of your poor little mind, child. You know you can't change your occupation in time of war." Or at any other time, she might have added.

She frowned, and there was a hint of asperity in her voice: "Of course, I could return you to the secretarial pool and look for a new assistant. But I don't think you'd really like that, would you, my dear?"

The threat had no effect whatever.

"Pool! The pool won't see my backside. I told you, I'm going to be a sergeant. In the Zhenski Battalion. I'm going to fight. Za rodinu, za Stalina . . . for Fatherland and Stalin."

Katrina felt a first icy stab of unease within her.

"What is all this? Who said you were to be a sergeant? Who's been filling your head with this nonsense about a woman's battalion?"

"The Comrade Major," the girl said pertly. "Shall I tell

her you said it's a lot of nonsense? Comrade Major Kroup!"

Now there was a whole iceberg within Katrina Semyonovna's heart. Now she knew it was true and not some wild joke. For Major Kroup of the NKVD never joked.

CHAPTER 3

"No," said Gnotke, "I won't do it. There is no precedent for it at all. Without direct orders from Moscow I cannot possibly permit you to proceed, Comrade Major."

From behind his desk he looked up at the towering, billowing figure of Major Natalya Kroup, at the huge, unmoving monolith of a face. In his heart he felt a little desperation.

"Comrade Zavedivayushchi Gnotke, in war there are no precedents. In areas of war also the civil power may be supplanted at any time when the military commander so deems it necessary. I refer you to the Code of Administration, section fifty-one, sub-section B(iii)c."

From her own desk in a corner of the room Vyora Pekare watched uncomprehendingly. This was the first time when she had ever seen Gnotke not in command of a situation. Even when high Party officers had come to Misgorod from Moscow he had seemed to her of a greater stature than they.

But they of course had been delighted at the progress he had made in the town, at the improved efficiency of the kolkhoz, at the undoubted general air of well-being amongst the people. Certainly there had been a wizened, sly-looking secretary who had questioned his authority for some actions. But he had been silenced very quickly by the others, who were only too glad to have someone making things move forward even if not in strict accordance with the rules.

But now, and she could sense it though his face seemed as composed as ever, now there was doubt in him and perhaps fear. And this woman had brought the doubt and fear, this huge, gross major of the NKVD. Already she felt she hated her.

"The interpretation of section fifty-one is that an area of war is to be deemed as thirty kilometres from the front line.

This morning's Corps communique indicates that the front line is still forty kilometres away. Therefore the civil power remains paramount, Comrade Major."

"That was this morning, Comrade. It is now midday. There have been advances and re-groupings."

Though her great, broad face with its hint of moustache at the corners of the mouth and the distinctive, hairy wart on the chin remained impassive, Major Natalya Kroup was exultant within.

For it was her particular joy to make men suffer, to see their little souls wriggle under the well-placed jabs of her words. And later, perhaps, to see their bodies wriggle.

As long as she could remember, Natalya Kroup had hated men. She had hated her father for a hundred reasons. Because he was her father. Because he was a drunken beast of a foundry labourer, who, in his orgies, beat the frail, helpless woman who was her mother until the blood scattered the earthen floor of their hovel. Because he had forced himself on her own immature body. Because he had sent her out to sell that body for a few kopeks and beaten her because men did not want to buy. Because he had starved her and beaten her and mocked at her ever-growing ugliness and gross body. Because he had killed her mother eventually by the cumulation of abuse and neglect and bearing of dead children. Because he was a man and all men were swine.

Her father had done only one good thing and that was to get himself killed in the Revolution in what seemed like circumstances of exceptional bravery at the head of a charge on a barricade. Unlike Katrina Semyonovna, she had no illusions about the death of her father. Undoubtedly he would have been drunk on looted vodka. And probably he was only after more vodka when he was killed. But his death had served her well.

She had had little difficulty in entering the NKVD and in rising swiftly from the rank of private. Yet even in her own service there had been men to hate, men who tried to stop her promotion because she was a woman, men whom she knew despised her for her sex.

Through all her career she had had to show herself twice

as efficient, twice as ruthless as a man in order to progress. She had volunteered for the Lyubyanka service and there for the first time had gained a sort of respect from the men about her.

She was the interrogator supreme behind the bright lights, emotionless as she drove deeper and deeper into the hidden places of a man's mind, devising ever more unnameable indignities and agonies for a man's body. She could extract sincere confessions from the utterly innocent, break down the spirit of even the toughest deviationist.

Even the hardened NKVD men had a sort of horror of her, a fear. In their messes she rarely joined in the drinking parties – or was invited, though there were other women in the service who did, who became, as it were, honorary men. Her rank was hardly earned. To become lieutenant she had to be twice as good as any of the men who were promoted over her head. It was even stiffer to reach the rank of captain.

Yet, once there, the path began to clear. By now her undoubted abilities were plain, not only as an interrogator but as an administrator and organiser. When she took charge of the messing arrangements and the food became eatable for the Lyubyanka officers, the tea hot – and costs down – a reluctant respect began to be accorded her. It may have been this regard of her fellow-officers for her efficiency that caused her transfer to the Forward Areas Control Section. Or it might solely have been a desire to get rid of her.

At any rate, she was in Poland, a captain, second in command of an Enforcement Company, when the German attack came and steam-rollered its way eastward through the crumbling resistance of a hopelessly ill-organized, under-armed and surprised Red Army.

It had been her company that manned the road blocks, turning back the routed Ivans against their foes. She had superintended demolitions, interrogated fleeing officers and either driven them back to their units or shot them out of hand.

Her reports had led to the stripping of rank of three corps commanders. Her finger had been on the trigger of the pistol that shot them.

And the rout had been stemmed. The NKVD division spread out behind the Russian troops had been more terrible to the Red Army than the advancing tanks and infantry of the Wehrmacht. The rout had been stemmed and ill-armed, unfed, disorganized Russian soldiers had at last clawed the German advance from a gallop to a crawl.

A majority had been Natalya Kroup's reward, a majority and transfer to another field of action.

And now she was in Misgorod with the Germans advancing again and a terrible hatred and contempt for all men in her heart.

Had the front already dropped back ten kilometres, Gnotke wondered. Was it possible? And in his heart he knew it was. Nonetheless he had heard enough about this grotesque woman to know that he must not seem indecisive. He must not let her know that, within, his resolution was crumbling.

"If I give permission, Comrade Major, what will be your procedure in forming your women's battalion?"

Kroup's great, greyish rock of a face showed no emotion but there was triumph behind it. She had won as she had known she would win, as a woman would always win.

"I will require the use of your files. All former Osaviakhims will be embodied. Also all women between the ages of fifteen and thirty not engaged in work of national importance. Also all women with past experience of firearms."

"This will mean an almost total denuding of my clerical staff. It will mean a break-down of civil administration."

"So will the German capture of Misgorod," she answered flatly.

She had walked heavily over to the window to gaze out.

"It is noted that the orders with regard to the scorched earth policy have not yet been carried out. There are crops standing in the fields."

This was the one Gnotke had been subconsciously waiting for. He had been stalling on his own orders to burn the fields, hoping against hope that it would not be necessary. The fruit of all his work in Misgorod would go up in smoke with those fields and he had delayed deliberately, hoping that at the last moment the tractors would still be able to harvest the rye and the wheat.

"Scorched earth policy, Comrade Major?" He feigned surprise.

"You must be aware of Comrade Stalin's directive. All fields to be burned, all crops destroyed. Nothing must be left that can be of any use to the enemy."

Gnotke shot a frantic glance at his secretary, Vyora Pekare.

"Not all directives from Moscow reach us as quickly as we would wish, Comrade Major. No doubt we will receive this one in due course – and act upon it."

"No matter. I am glad the crops are there. This is an open country. When my battalion attacks we will be glad of the cover of the crops."

For a moment Gnotke was startled from any thought of himself.

"Attack? But you're not going to use your women as combatant troops? That . . . it's unprecedented!"

"War breaks all precedents." She turned on him fiercely now. "You think women can't fight. Pah! You are like all men. You want women as comfortable slaves, for your use. Even in this great Soviet Union of ours this outmoded attitude still persists. Of course they can fight! A woman can press a trigger as easily as a man – she can die as easily. My battalion will be a fighting battalion. Fighting!"

The ferocity faded back into the carven stone of her face.

"Now. I shall require your office. Your files. The use of your secretary. Is she competent?"

"Very."

"Thank you, Comrade. In two hours I shall have finished. You may then return."

"I am happy to be able to facilitate the Comrade Major," Gnotke answered calmly as he made for the door. "I shall continue the administration of the district from my assistant's office."

Vyora, watching, could divine just what torrents of hate and humiliation were storming through his veins. But she had little more time to think of Gnotke. Major Kroup had stumped over to her own desk and laid a hand on her shoulder.

"Very well, child. Tell me about yourself. Everything."

Her heavy body leaned against the back of the chair and Vyora could feel the pressure of the massive mounds of her breasts against the back of her neck.

"There . . . there isn't much to tell," she faltered.

And yet her whole life story poured out swiftly in brief spurts of words, followed by the occasional shrewd question from the major.

While Kroup stood there, her big powerful hand was working slowly round Vyora's neck, savouring the smoothness of the skin, tracing with a finger the line of bone and sinew beneath.

Vyora felt herself tremble a little under the touch.

"You have no need to fear me, child," Kroup growled gently. "Only enemies of the state need fear me, enemies of the state and evil men . . . which means all men."

She tilted Vyora's chin up, tilted her head back until it seemed as if her neck would snap and all this with only the pressure of her fingers. Upside down they looked into each other's faces, the faces very close. Vyora had an overwhelming feeling that she was about to be kissed.

"All men are swine, little one," murmured the major. "But that I think you have learned, niet?"

Vyora's lips quivered a little, but she said nothing.

Abruptly the major's hands fell away and she turned and strode to Gnotke's desk.

"You will be on my personal staff," she snapped. "Your knowledge of German will be invaluable when we take prisoners."

"But the Comrade Gnotke? I am his personal assistant."

Calmly Kroup mouthed the foulest oath in the Russian language.

"The Comrade Manager will not be needing a personal assistant much longer . . . Did he make you his lover? His mistress?"

Dumbly Vyora nodded, the feeling in her heart that she could withhold nothing from this woman.

"As I said, all men are swine. Now to the files. We will see what we have here."

Personal details of every soul in the district were contained in the steel filing cabinet. Here they were in condensed form, letters and numbers giving classifications which would be amplified in the full files held in the main records office.

"All the Osaviakhims first," said the major, fingers already fluttering through the file cards with the deftness of a card-sharp. "Then we'll see what other categories can be of use."

The work proceeded in silence, the selected cards growing up in one pile, the rejects in another. A satisfaction began to grow in the Major's eyes.

"Good. We have a fine nucleus here," she declared as she fingered the last card. "Now you must type me a list of these names, in triplicate. And while you do that I will go through the cards again for the other categories. Tomorrow the Zhenski Battalion will be formed."

CHAPTER 4

Thankfully, Katrina Semyonovna closed her notebook for the last time and turned away from the filthy huddle of huts that were to be the nucleus for "In the Don – Ever a Fish". The old woman she had been questioning turned back equally thankfully to her pot of fish stew on top of a smoking fire of damp driftwood.

In the old days, the old woman thought, it had not been like this, questions, questions, questions. In the old days they caught their fish or starved and a woman had only to worry about what would be in the pot for the next day or if her man was really carrying on with that young minx from the Cossack stanitsa across the river.

God send the old days, she thought, and crossed herself furtively as she gazed to the westward where the sound of gunfire had grown still louder, where towering columns of black smoke rose here and there. Maybe the old days would still come back. Maybe they were coming now. At any rate, the city woman with her strange smells and her too elegant clothes was going and that was something.

It would have surprised Katrina to know that anyone thought her clothes elegant. Deliberately she had underdressed for this visit. And as to scent, all she used was soap. But then, soap was a luxury these fisherfolk had not known in a long time. They did indeed make a sort of soap of their own from home-made lye and the oil from fish livers. A little extra smell of fish did not disturb them.

Annoyed that Anna had not come back with the car, Katrina began to walk towards the town along the river's muddy bank. They would leave today, she decided. There was no point in hanging around any longer. She had all her notes. The typing could be done in Moscow. Perhaps even she would do a complete re-write in Moscow. She had not been satisfied with her output over the past few days. Misgorod was altogether too depressing a place for a creative artist. And in the last day or two with the army everywhere it had grown still more confusing.

Corps headquarters, trucks and guns clattering through the streets, horses, mules, even donkeys dragging wagons, mud-stained soldiers staggering through the streets . . . could anyone be expected to write in these circumstances?

She was second to none in her admiration for the deeds of the heroic Red Army. But she could praise better from a distance.

She halted once, frowning. For a moment or two it had seemed to her that the sounds of battle actually came from the east. But that of course was impossible. The front had been consolidated, the morning's communique said. The Germans were held on a broad front twenty kilometres west of Misgorod. Now the great Russian steam-roller would advance and crush the Fascist invader.

And yet, she thought again, the firing did sound as if it came from the east.

Then she had the answer. Training. A Red Army unit must be training, setting their sights or whatever it was they did.

She quickened her pace, determined that this time she would have some very strong words to say to Anna Turuchin. She had no right to keep the car so long. She should have been back long ago.

She could not know that in the sense she meant it, Anna Turuchin would never come back.

The old quartermaster gazed in astonishment at the women.

"Give you uniforms! Give you rifles! You must be out of your minds, comrades. These stores belong to the Red Army. No, no. You must be joking."

He began to roll a cigarette of mahorka in a month-old fragment of "Izvestia". Anna Turuchin glanced sideways at Major Kroup. Was this to be the end of it, then? Was there, after all, to be no Zhenski Battalion?

Irina Tsiganka threw herself forward, the only other of the women in uniform.

"Old pig! Old fool! Who do you think you are? Obey orders when you are told. Open your stores. Do as the major says."

Irina was a dark-eyed, dark-haired, fey-looking girl, slim and supple, and anger blasted from her like a visible force.

But the old quartermaster had guarded his stores for too long, against too many thieving privates and sergeants and officers even to be impressed.

"Due authorisation," he mumbled, licking the rough square of paper. "That's what you want. Due authorisation. I don't give out stores without due authorisation."

"What do you think these are?" Natalya Kroup snarled, flicking a finger across her badges of rank. "Laundry marks? I will sign any authorisation you require. Now, give me the stores."

The old man scratched a match into light with his thumbnail and luxuriously drew on the rank tobacco.

"Comrade Major, I've been caught that way before. The stores in this warehouse are in my charge. When the auditors come I am the one who has to say why there are so many boots missing, so many blankets. I am the one who stands court martial, not you, Comrade Major. You are far away then. But give me due authorisation from the Corps Commander so that my books are correct and then you may take what stores you will – what are authorised, that is."

He cackled softly, a lifetime of service behind him, a lifetime of denying troops their needs, of catching thieves, of working his own quiet little swindle on the black market.

"That's enough," Kroup growled like a man.

The quartermaster was not at all impressed by the sight of the pistol in the Major's hand. He could not remember how often he was threatened by furious officers. But they all holstered their guns at last and went off empty-handed. Not even the NKVD would dare infract the sanctity of Red Army stores.

He was still thinking this as he slumped back in his comfortable chair with a neat, bluish hole between his eyes. His cigarette crumbled on the desk and one of his precious files began to smoulder.

"Right," ordered Kroup. "Take what I have told you to take. Those clerks will help you."

And indeed the three clerks and a sergeant who had seen their master fall back dead in his own chair were not in the least reluctant to assist.

Bales of uniform, strings of boots, crates of rifles, were carried out to the lorries Kroup had already commandeered.

And calmly the Major noted down on a form the exact numbers of each article as they were drawn from the stores, loaded onto the lorries.

When all had gone she signed the form.

"Natalya Kroup, Major, NKVD."

And straight-faced she handed it to the sergeant.

"For your books," she said. "The books must be kept straight."

And she was not joking.

It was certainly a nightmare, Katrina Semyonovna thought. It must be a nightmare. She had been working too hard. Her mind had gone over the edge. That delightful Caucasian doctor from the Institute of Psychiatry had warned her that writers worked under abnormal strains.

For obviously it was quite impossible that she should be standing in the ill-fitting, coarse uniform of a private of the Red Army in the middle of a smelly kolkhoz while a man-like woman in the uniform of a NKVD Major hectored her and the three hundred other women and girls drawn up in two ranks, two straggling, untidy ranks.

"Now hear me," Kroup strutted slowly up and down, her great voice booming across the parade ground. "It takes three years to make a man a peace-time soldier. It takes three months to make him a soldier in war-time. But we are not men. It will take us three days. We all know that women are braver, cleverer and more enduring than men. Now we have the chance to prove it.

"The enemy are at the gates of Misgorod. They must be halted, driven back. And we are going to help to do this. In the brief time I have, I am going to weld you into the greatest fighting formation of the Red Army. Some of you will certainly die. Some will be terribly maimed. I offer you nothing easy. What I offer you is the chance to put your names firmly into the pages of history.

"When the war is at last over, when the German invaders crouch on their knees, the name of the Zhenski Battalion will be the one that is remembered. You will be remembered – and that may be your only reward."

She paused, jaw outthrust, still striding up and down before them.

"Now you are to be divided into squads. I have already appointed sergeants, those who were Osaviakhim members and have the best knowledge of arms and their use. They will instruct you in elementary drill – no more than this – and in the use of the arms. Those sergeants have full authority from me. You will obey them without question. Do you hear me? And the sergeants will obey me without question.

"Very good. Now divide into your squads as your names are called out."

With a feeling of inevitability Katrina heard Anna Turuchin call her own name and went to join the thirty other assorted women in her former assistant's squad.

CHAPTER 5

"Why is she not training with the others?"

Sulkily, Irina Tsiganka pointed to Vyora Pekare, now busily typing in Kroup's office, which had been the office of the president of the collective up until a few hours ago –

just as the barrack rooms taken over by the Zhenski Battalion had been the dormitories of the kolkhozniks.

Some of the collective's women had already been enrolled in the battalion and had been returned to their old quarters. The men, too old, unfit or stupid for military service, had been ejected mercilessly. Their president, with past experience of the NKVD – though of the mildest only – had not dared to protest. He had asked mildly: "Where are they to go, where are we to go, Comrade Major?"

"To hell for all I care," had been her brief, blunt answer.

And the president had wandered off unhappily. Someone should have orders for him. Surely someone could tell him what to do? He headed for Gnotke's office. The Zavedivayuschi would certainly have the answer.

But as Vyora Pekare could have told him, his journey was a fruitless one. One of Vyora's last tasks for her former boss had been to find in her files an urgent memorandum calling him to Stalingrad for an area conference on crop policy and kolkhoz norms for the following year.

There was an unexpected emotion in his eyes as he bade her farewell.

But: "One cannot fight the NKVD" was all he said as he patted her bottom for the last time.

That pat was all there was time for because already the train, packed tight with official refugees, was in Misgorod station. It was only being held for him because he had befriended the station master so often in the past. And after all, Gnotke had no real cause for gratitude for this favour.

Fifteen miles beyond Misgorod the train was dive-bombed by German Stukas and dissolved into an untidy heap of scrap iron, scrap wood and scrap bodies – including Gnotke's.

Vyora did not know this, of course. Already chaos and fear had begun the process of disintegration in the town. Rumours and counter-rumours swept the place. Food hoarding had intensified and no news at all could be relied on.

Significantly, if there had been anyone to notice, corps headquarters of the Red Army had already evacuated across the Don and were controlling, if that was the word, the battle from a village hidden in the forest beyond.

Vyora only knew that Gnotke was gone and she felt again the desolation she had known when Rudolph Küster left her for the Wehrmach. Rudi, she thought now unexpectedly, poor Rudi. What life had he had since their parting in Berlin? Was he indeed still alive or had he been found out as a secret Communist? Maybe already he had been shot as a traitor.

Thinking of Rudi, Vyora hardly heard Irina Tsiganka's complaint.

And Major Kroup, busy with the schedule for the next day's training, only raised her massive head for a minute to glower.

"Shut up, you little gypsy slut," she ordered quietly.

Irina's lips tightened and the skin became taut on her high cheekbones. "Gypsy" yes. Or half gypsy. Her father had been one of the wandering romanys who still trekked Russia, in defiance of order, in defiance of orders, nomads because that had been their life for a thousand years.

Her mother had been Ukrainian, though, pure Ukrainian. She had been charmed into bed – or more likely behind a haystack – by the handsome wandering romany with the magnetic eyes and the deft fingers on the strings of a balalaika. And though there was no real stigma on illegitimacy any more, still the fact remained that the gypsy was a foreigner and all her childhood Irina was "the gypsy brat" in the village.

And expected to be, because of her blood, what Kroup had called her. A slut.

She could remember her childhood vividly, without the slightest effort at recall. The boys in the village school: "Come on Tsiganka . . . let's have a go." Or: "Tsiganka – come to the barn by the three trees." Or: "Tsiganka, the other boys say they have seen you naked. Now let me see you."

And all this before even the first down of puberty had appeared between her thighs, while her breasts were still tiny, hard buttons.

All this because of her gypsy blood. Because the gypsies were a loose, fiery race, animals who cared for nothing but sex. Or so they said in the village. The boys even thought they were doing her a favour when they pinched her bottom or lifted her skirts.

Tsiganka! If even they had called her Irina. But no, it had to be Tsiganka. Contempt even in a name.

Yet, miraculously, she had kept her virginity in the village. The boys might contrive to feel their way up her legs, to lift her skirts, even once to get her naked. But somehow she had kept them from going further. Somehow . . . perhaps because she had the tigerish gypsy spirit in her, because when she fought she fought with everything, with nails and teeth and feet, a little whirlwind of fury.

She had learned then every trick of in-fighting; she knew a boy's tenderest parts, she learned wiles. She learned ruthlessness. And she learned these virtues alone. Her mother was no protection, no comfort. When she ran sobbing to the woman who should have taken her in her arms and brought some balm to her spirit, she was rejected. It was: "Get out of here, you brat, and don't come bothering me."

Indeed she was a grave embarrassment to her mother, especially when she had married the village storekeeper – a twisted little man who had always desired her but had no hope of courting her when she was single and unblemished. Now there was a new brood of flaxen-haired little Ukrainians amongst whom Irina stood out like a bad penny.

Even so, she might still have been there in that dreary little village in the Ukraine save for her stepfather. He had a twisted mind to suit his twisted body and he heard exciting rumours about this hot little step-daughter of his. He decided to put them to the test.

And, in the kitchen of her own home, Irina found herself in the arms of her mother's husband, felt the urgent probing of his body against hers.

In true gypsy style she lifted a knife from the table and even while he pulled at her underclothes she thrust it deep into his back.

Her last shred of respect for the male sex fled as she saw him lying, dying, praying, bleeding profusely with his trousers down about his ankles. Men were not only cruel bullies. They were cowards, too – and absurd.

She had fled then, obeying the first instinct of her gypsy

blood. But she had stolen everything of value she could reasonably carry as well as food, obeying the second gypsy instinct.

West and south she had fled, for no particular reason, a waif who stole into villages, robbed, and stole out again. For two years she wandered until she came at last toward the Polish frontier – at the very time it erupted into new war.

And that was when she met Kroup – or Kroup found her.

She found her about twenty-four hours too late. An advancing German platoon had found her first.

And now at last her agility and her teeth and her speed availed her nothing.

There were twenty-three men in the platoon and each of them had taken her. Holding her down at first, laughing at the sport as her slim brown body jerked and twisted in its efforts to escape their piercing organs while they held her by wrist and ankle. And at last she had struggled no more but lay in a smouldering, withdrawn anger while they violated her as they pleased, some of them coming to her for a second time for it was long since they had seen a woman.

Afterwards she lay, broken-seeming, in a corner of their dug-out. And when they slept she cut the throats of four and made her escape into the cold autumn night, naked, a brown wraith.

Kroup's platoon had found her and Kroup herself took her into the bedroom she had commandeered, put her to bed and sung her gently to sleep, her head on the Major's great bosom, her ears hearing for the first time the kindly words of another woman. It was as if she had found her mother at last.

No one who knew the NKVD major could have believed she would be so gentle. And yet Kroup had the same need as Irina Tsiganka. She needed, somewhere in the core of her being, something that not even the State or the Party could give her. She needed something to love and be loved by.

Though she had taken many women as lovers before, it had been in a cold, clinical physical way to supply a physical need. And though there were plenty willing to pleasure her they did it from a sense of duty, a sense of fear perhaps. She sensed always a momentary withdrawal when her hands first fell on a woman's skin and the caressing began.

With Irina, though, it would be different. It was different.

They had been together a long time now – or it seemed a long time – from the start of the invasion. Irina had become a part of Kroup and Kroup of Irina. Which was why "slut" rankled so.

"I'm no slut, Comrade Major," Irina said now.

Kroup raised her massive head again and gazed at the girl, looking into her mind, understanding what she saw there.

"Pekare," she ordered. "Go to Number Four Platoon. Bring me their ammunition state."

And when Vyora Pekare had gone Kroup beckoned the little gypsy closer.

"You are jealous, Irina," she said.

"Why should she not train with the others?" Irina demanded.

"Because she is my assistant."

"I was always your assistant before. You never needed anyone else."

Kroup sighed. To no one else would she have explained herself, for in all armies it is the same. An officer does not apologise. An officer does not explain. An officer does not regret . . . not to lower ranks.

"Irina Tsiganka, this is a military operation. There are things to be done. Can you work a typewriter? Can you prepare me lists? Can you help me with the organisation? No. These things you cannot do. Other things you can do. You can do them superbly. You can steal. You can cook. You can play tsigane tunes on a balalaika. For these I love you and also because I love you. But you cannot do everything. I need this girl."

"You love her," Irina hissed through clenched teeth. "You will have her in bed very soon. I know you. There have been others. You are not faithful."

Without apparent emotion, Kroup rose a little in her seat and swung a huge, flailing slap at the girl's cheek. Irina rocked to it and almost fell. She could have dodged the blow but deliberately did not.

"Irina golupchik, you will make me angry. Pekare is my assistant. If I decide I want to take more from her than that,

I will do so. If I do not then I will not. Either way it is not your business. Not, you understand?"

Her mouth clamped tight like a rat trap.

"And there will be none of your little tricks with knives, you hear me? Not like the girl at Dnepropetrousk. You understand? Oh yes. I knew . . . I will tell you this. I need this girl for her work. If anything happens to her you will suffer also."

"Beat me then," cried Irina. "Flog me!"

"No. That would be too easy. I tell you now – if you touch Vyora Pekare I will give you to the men. I will have every man in Misgorod through you, if I have to march them to you at gun-point. The men, Irina darling, that will be your fate. You understand?"

Miserably, the gypsy girl hung her head.

"I am sorry, Natalya. I am most humbly sorry. I kiss your feet."

"You can kiss my arse if you like – just remember what I say."

CHAPTER 6

The penal battalion slogged slowly through the streets of Misgorod, a tattered army without banners. They marched past the gates of the kolkhoz where Katrina Semyonovna stood on sentry duty, still not believing the weight of the rifle in her hand or the coarse feel of the uniform against her skin.

They were like an army of ghosts marching past, shuffling grey-faced ghosts in the ragged remnants of uniform.

And though she knew they were paying for their crimes against the state, Katrina could not hold back her pity from them. They were victims, as she was a victim, of this terrible war, of the brutal invasion by Hitler's Huns. But for the war they would have been in their re-education centres, re-thinking their approach to life, being guided back gently but firmly to true Stalinist-Leninism.

And but for the war she would have been continuing with her work, writing, developing artistically, helping the

Revolution through art, helping art through the Revolution.

Even now, despite the weight of the rifle in her hand, despite the tenderness on the inside of her thighs where the rough cloth was chafing her, Katrina Semyonovna could not quite accept that this was happening to her. It was still a nightmare from which at last she would awake.

Simply, it was impossible, it was ludicrous, it was laughable that she, Katrina Semyonovna, darling of the critics, holder of a Stalin award for Literature, precious cultural asset of the Soviet Union should be expected to act the part of a woman soldier.

With a brittle laugh she had pointed out the obvious misunderstanding to That Woman – for she could not even begin to think of Major Kroup as anything else. She had showed her her papers, those precious documents with all the Cultural Ministry stamps on them, papers good enough to take her into any company in the whole Soviet Union.

And that creature had laughed. That Woman had said that she could, if she liked, use the documents for toilet paper – in fact, the expression had been even coarser. That Woman would have a rude awakening one day. Not even the NKVD badges would protect her when Katrina Semyonovna got back to civilisation and started pulling strings. This she promised herself. This would be a real and complete revenge.

Most humiliating of all was not to have been made a sergeant. This she could not understand. Plainly if this ridiculous Zhenski Battalion was to have any chance of success those who commanded must be those used to command.

Instead That Woman had made Katrina's own personal assistant into a sergeant, a chit of a girl with no knowledge of the world, hardly sense enough to organise a railway ticket. It had been bitter, very bitter.

And yet at the same time, of course, it had been useful too. Her novelist's mind, which was divorced from her woman's mind, saw all the possibilities of this women's battalion.

What a novel was here, that part of her mind thought. What life, what ardours, what experience.

And the woman's part of her mind promised that when

the writing came That Woman would be shown up in her true colours. The world, or at least the Soviet world, would know what a monster could come to fruition in the NKVD.

She was toying with phrases in her mind, watching the penal battalion trudge slowly past, wondering a little why only one in three of them seemed to have rifles. What did the others do? How did they fight the enemy without rifles?

It was then that the face swam across her vision. It swam into focus and out and became just a head amongst the other heads marching up the dusty road towards the enemy.

And yet, for an instant, she recognised it.

The long, wavy hair was prematurely grey, the cheeks had fallen in. The eyes were in deep, hungry sockets. But they still had that lucid, liquid quality. And there was still tenderness in the mouth.

Sasha! The time-lag of recognition snapped close. Sasha. It had been Sasha. Sasha her love. And yet it could not have been Sasha. Surely long ago Sasha must have left the re-education centre. Sasha would never be a recidivist. No, it could not have been Sasha. They would never have put Sasha in a penal battalion. Not Sasha, who had been such a bright star across the firmament. The Soviet would never have put such a man into the uniform of a convict soldier.

Then she felt the itch of her own coarse trousers and knew that it was true.

"Sasha!" she cried aloud and started to run from the gate, down the column.

A bellow from behind halted her.

"Katrina Semyonovna! Halt! Return to your post!"

Sergeant Anna Turuchin was coming to inspect her sentries, marching with quick precise strides, a little clockwork soldier.

Despite herself Katrina came to a halt. And as she did so she saw a face turn in the grey, anonymous, marching column. Sasha had heard his name called and for an instant he swung his head round. For the briefest instant their eyes met and he smiled.

Then other heads were between them and Anna Turuchin had reached her side.

"For a sentry to leave her post in time of war is an offence punishable by death," the sergeant parroted. "Katrina Semyonovna, this time I will overlook the matter since you have so little experience. Next time I will make a report. Now, return to your post."

CHAPTER 7

The point squadron of the Waffen SS division had come a long way. It had come fast, too fast really. There had been no time for proper maintenance. The squadron's Mk III and Mk IV tanks were weary with miles. Bearings were worn and screamed for oil. Engines kept going more by faith than by design.

The dusty, dry air was playing havoc with every piece of machinery. Grit got in and wore and wore, scoring surfaces that should have been mirror smooth. Engine bearings were burning the oil that the pumps forced through them. Cylinder linings were roughened by the grit that the air intakes let through. Even the very tracks slapped round their idler pulleys, the pins worn in the surface plates until it was a wonder that the tanks could move at all.

Yet still they drove onward, taking objective after objective in a heady catalogue of success. Nothing could stop them. Nothing could stop this new blitzkrieg across the dusty plains of Russia.

The tanks might be dirty – but they still kept their insignia clean. The Runic double "S". The insignia of the Waffen SS, the crack troops of the German advance. The hammer of the Slavs.

The column was swinging in a quick pincer movement, cutting behind the lines of the main Russian force that now held their own corps at bay. Or that, rather, had been allowed to commit itself piecemeal into a set-piece battle, tying up its whole force, skimpy armour, inadequate artillery, exhausted infantry, while the Waffen SS Division moved swiftly round the flank, thundered unhampered towards Misgorod, to the crossing of the Don . . . and all stops east.

And who could halt them? Who could delay them?

The voice of the leading tank commander crackled over the radio.

"Herr Leutnant, it's true I tell you, true. Cavalry. There's cavalry ahead . . . On horseback . . . On horseback. The Cossacks. These must be the Cossacks."

The first of their kind. The Cossacks. The qussaqs; the adventurers.

For in the dim mists of time these mercenaries had been hired for the defence of Holy Russia. To each stanitsa, each village group, had been given a grant of land which was owned in common, farmed in common. And in return the men of the stanitsa gave their years from eighteen to forty-eight to defend the realm.

War was their trade, war was their life. It was for war they mated, bred children, farmed, trained their superb little horses.

There had been the bad years when loyalty was divided, when they did not know their master. When the Revolution came and they had not protected the Romanovs, many of them left the land of their birth. But the Bolsheviks saw their potentialities. The Chervonny Cossacks, the Red Cossacks, were the scourge of the kulaks whom they hated since the kulaks had always their eyes on the Cossack lands.

And the Soviet provided a system they understood, a system they had lived by before Marx was born, or Lenin.

Again their little horses swept across the plains, harassing German lines of communication, driving swift raids into the under-belly of the enemy.

And performing other functions.

There were no heroes in the penal battalion. They had been heroes once, maybe, heroes of the spirit, perhaps. But now they were broken, empty men, drained of everything by the long, empty, starved years of prison. And ahead lay German tanks and German guns.

Their rag-bound feet had marched long enough. There was only one rifle between three of them. It was a time for surrender, for breaking back towards the town, for flight.

And suddenly between them and Misgorod were the Cossacks with their long, curved sabres.

The devil and the deep sea.

The Waffen SS were not picked for softness of fibre.

But when the tanks began to plunge into the lines of men, when the tracks slipped on human flesh something turned in the hearts of these men. Along the line of the advance tank after tank slowed to a halt, as if the very metal of their fabric was disgusted with the brutal slaughter.

The harmless ping of rifle bullets sang off the armour and here and there was an occasional burst of flame as a petrol bomb burst harmlessly from an armour flank.

It was murder; sheer, bloody murder.

And paradoxically it slowed down the Waffen SS as real opposition would never have done.

With Misgorod at their mercy the leading squadron halted and laagered for the night. There was in any case plenty of time.

In ones and twos the pathetic fragments of the penal battalion straggled back into Misgorod, those who had escaped the guns and tracks of the German tanks, those who had escaped the swords of the Cossacks.

For the Zhenski Battalion, in Misgorod, training had ended for the day. Only the sentries were on duty.

And at the gate Katrina Semyonovna waited as the doleful procession of shattered men straggled past to whatever fate awaited them. Already Major Kroups' NKVD detachment was rounding up the stragglers, re-forming them in the middle of the town, preparing them for another hopeless advance in the morning.

Frantically Katrina watched for a familiar face, watched for Sasha. And every now and again she would dart out into the dusty road, seize a dazed man's arm.

"Sasha Ryevsky . . . You know him? Where is he?"

Blank eyes gazed at her. Shaggy, lice-laden heads shook negatively.

"Niet . . . niet . . . Niet . . . "

Then at last a familiar face above a limping body hove painfully into sight.

"Ilya . . . Ilya Rokossov . . ."

The name sprang to her tongue as she darted forward and then halted, unsure of herself. Could this in fact be Ilya Rokossov? The brisk, dapper little Ilya who had had such a success with his poems for a season until he mistook popularity for omnipotence and had to be sent to re-learn his lessons.

No. It had been a mere coincidence. A faint similarity in the carriage of the head. Ilya was younger than herself. And this was an old man, old, crippled, hopeless.

Then, as she started to turn away, a little life came into the grey eyes.

"It is Katrina . . . Katrina Semyonovna! Oh, Katrina . . . "

She was thankful for the shadows, as his arms went round her in a hug that had no strength. It would not further her career to be seen on intimate terms with a man from a penal battalion.

His lips twitched into a terrible, hopeful smile that showed blackened teeth, blackened in the mouth of the man who had always been so very, almost decadently, particular.

"Oh, Katrina! Have . . . have you a cigarette? Mahorka?"

The infinite longing in his voice moved her more than anything could have done. She fumbled through her pockets and found a packet of her own special blend, one of the last packets she had brought from Moscow.

Only two fingers were left on the hand that fumbled with the packet. Old scar tissue covered the stumps of the others, a terrible, shapeless tissue, rough mounds of skin and scab.

"Frostbite," he said as he saw her eyes on the hand. "Frostbite . . . "

He swayed a little as she lit his cigarette and they both moved to the bank at the side of the road.

Wearily, making an effort of the job as if his knees were locked solid, Rokossov sat down, cigarette cupped in the palm of his hand, drawing in great lungfuls of the smoke.

"The Number Seventeen blend," he breathed. "And just the same. After all these years . . . just the same. I used to wake sometimes, up there, with the smell of it in my nose – and then it would be someone else's filthy feet in my face. You want to know about Sasha?"

"He's dead?" she asked with a terrible certainty.

"He's dead. He's as dead as any man can be whose bowels are wound like string round the wheels of a tank. But then, Sasha was always the lucky one . . . always the lucky one."

"Lucky?"

The tears were coursing down her cheeks but she was not sobbing.

"With us, it is lucky to be dead . . . Oh, Katrina, that cigarette was like a breath from Heaven – if you'll forgive my mentioning a mythical and forbidden subject."

"Take them all. Keep the packet. And my lighter. Keep it. Ilya, tell me . . . Tell me about Sasha."

"One rifle between three of us . . . the tanks before us and the damn Cossacks behind to drive us on. What more is there to tell? Bare hands against armoured plate. Rifle against cannon. Twice I threw myself in front of a tank's tracks to die and each time it turned away. But I was never lucky. Sasha at my side had better luck . . . You are really giving me these cigarettes? Giving them? You can't know – "

"Not the battle. Don't tell me about the battle. Tell me about . . . before. About the re-education."

He looked at her strangely.

"You are wondering now a little? You who sent him there . . . "

"It – it was my duty." There was no conviction in her voice. Carefully Ilya Rokossov stowed away the cigarettes and the lighter in some recess of his foul rags. The smell of him was strong in her nostrils, the smell of sweat and dirt and urine and decay, the smell of everything that the State fought against.

"I will tell you, Katrina Semyonovna," he said fiercely. "I will tell you what you did to the man you loved."

"He was guilty . . . guilty," she moaned. "He wrote against the State – No! – don't tell me. I don't want to hear now."

"But you're going to hear."

Despite his emaciation his hand was suddenly like a vice on her arm. The rank stench that came from every part of him grew stronger.

"This is something for one of those nice books of yours. Something for all the Party to hear, all the people. You shall hear about the re-education centre. You shall hear about Sasha."

The coldness of the bleak north sank into Katrina as she heard about Vorkuta and the camps beyond. There had been the long train journey first, in open cattle trucks, fifty and sixty men and women to each truck. Some days they were fed – if a bowl of thin cabbage soup and a slice of black bread could be called food.

But that had been a joy and pleasure compared with what was to come, with the camp itself.

Detail after detail sank reluctantly into Katrina's incredulous mind. The sparse, filthy huts, the brutal, callous guards, the bunks that had to take two men to each because there were more prisoners than room for them. The filthy, inadequate food.

Then there were the criminals, the real criminals, the sweepings of the gutters of the whole Soviet Union.

They now became the aristocrats of the camp, the rulers more even than the guards. These were hardened men and women who would be the dross of any society, who would kill and torture for the pleasure of it if they could not devise a way of profit.

The way in which these criminals had seized the upper hand was the ultimate degradation for the intellectuals and politicals. The criminals had no difficulty adapting their continual war against law into a new war in which they were the law, far more the law than the guards who came into the camp as little as possible.

Ilya had seen women raped – and men, too. He had seen throats cut for a crust of black bread. He had seen – and suffered – the frostbite of neglect.

There seemed no end to the long threnody of despair.

And of everything despair had been the worst affliction in the camp. Letters were rarely if ever delivered. Parcels almost never. The world outside might have ceased to exist. In winter they were grey specks of life in a world of ice. In summer the mosquitoes came as they were driven out to cut timber or perform other labour. And the mosquitoes made them long for the winter. The cold made them long for the mosquitoes.

The unending cycle went on and on. Men were no longer sure when their release would come, when their "re-education" would be complete. Perhaps release date had passed. Perhaps it was tomorrow. A sodden apathy gripped every soul by the end of their first year in the camp. And there were some prisoners who had been there for fifteen years, living corpses who survived, drew their tiny rations and existed solely as animated aggregations of flesh and blood and bone. But not as people. Not as human beings.

If she could have stopped Ilya then, Katrina would have done so. Every word he spoke drove direct at the heart of her belief, cutting it away, breaking it into ever smaller fragments.

Twice she tried to wriggle free. But each time he held her until at last everything had been said that could be said.

"And that is all," he concluded. "That is all, Katrina Semyonovna. That is why I said Sasha was lucky. That was re-education. That was Vorkuta. Nice, eh?"

She gave a low sigh.

"Oh, Ilya . . . "

She forced herself to be practical, to put the thoughts he had engendered from her mind.

"Come with me. At least I can get you some food from our kitchen. Afterwards . . . "

She gulped and made a supreme sacrifice. "Afterwards if you like you can sleep with me."

The thought revolted her, the idea of his filthy body with its stenches and decay, in the same bed as herself was infinitely disgusting. But as she made the offer she knew it was not really to Ilya she made it, but to Sasha. Somehow she must atone for what she had done, for what the state had done. She wanted her own person to suffer in atonement.

Ilya laughed harshly.

"Bed! With a woman! After these years do you suppose there is anything left in me to give to a woman? I am a raisin, Katrina, a dried-up prune of a man."

"Some food at least . . . Come, Ilya. I will get you some bread and soup . . . "

She tugged at his arm, trying to take him with her.

And from a little way behind there came the sound of a pistol shot. Ilya Rokossov jerked galvanically as the bullet hit him. Then he sagged gently to the ground.

"After all," he panted, "I'm a lucky one too."

He was dead as Major Kroup strode up, thrusting the pistol back into her holster.

"Just in time!" she growled. "I saw you struggling."

She spurned the body with her toe.

"Penal battalion scum. And like all men. Always trying to force a girl. Always trying . . . Filthy swine that they are."

Katrina was sobbing hysterically as the Major helped her back towards the barracks, a consoling arm about her, an arm that grew ever protectively tighter as they passed the sentries and passed the door of Katrina's barrack room and came at last to the Major's own door.

CHAPTER 8

It was still the middle of the night when Major Kroup called her conference. All the sergeants were there, Irina Tsiganka and Vyora Pekare, notebook at the ready.

In the barrack rooms there was chaos as sleepy women rose, fumbled for their clothes, complained . . . and wondered.

Kroup waited until silence had fallen on the group in her office.

"Our chance is coming even sooner than we had hoped," she said harshly, eyes alight with the first show of real emotion any of them had seen on that great tombstone of a face. "Our chance to serve the State, our chance to prove ourselves. This very night the Zhenski Battalion goes into action."

There was a low murmur which Kroup was pleased to take as wondering delight.

"Time is short," Kroup went on, "but the chance is there, the chance to strike such a blow as will make the name of the Zhenski Battalion remembered for ever.

"Less than five miles from where we stand an advancing

column of the German Army has halted for the night. Cossack scouts have already reported that their sentries are slack. They think they are dealing with a beaten nation. They think we will never strike at them as they have struck at us.

"Before dawn this day we will fall on them. We will destroy them. We will send them back shattered, to make the name of the Zhenski Battalion a name of terror like their own."

She glared round their faces, jaw jutting pugilistically.

"There will be no mercy for any of them. There will be no prisoners. And your task will be easier when I tell you who they are. For these are men of the Waffen SS, the baby-killers. We are going to destroy the baby-killers."

Her voice, the sheer force of her huge personality, had them all in its grip. And her last words had been the key to unlock their fervour.

For who had not heard of the baby-killers, the brutes who had marched through a maternity hospital, seizing babies by the legs, smashing their heads against the walls. The mothers had, of course, been raped and bayoneted. But this was part of war. It was the thought of the babies that really stirred the women, babies brought to life after the nine long months of pain and discomfort only to have their brains dashed out against a wall.

Of the truth of the story they did not doubt. Had Moscow radio not given it out? Had there not even been eyewitnesses who miraculously survived to be interviewed at the microphone?

The sergeants listened intently as Major Kroup detailed her plan.

As a plan it could scarcely have been simpler. The three companies of the Zhenski Battalion were to approach the enemy camp from two sides, one company to the north and the other two to the south.

The approach would be made in complete silence until the northern company was well within rifle range. Then that company was to open up a withering fire on the sleeping Germans. As soon as the enemy replied, the first of the other companies was to charge them in the rear. And the remaining company would make for the tanks and vehicles, attacking with Molotov cocktails, sending the blazing rain of fire into the vehicles before the drivers could start up and move off.

It was a simple plan and it could have been effective:

If the women's battalion had been fully-trained soldiers accustomed to the most difficult of all manoeuvres, moving by night over not wholly familiar terrain.

If there had been an effective system of signals.

If, in fact, the German sentries had been slack. But these were the Waffen SS. These were men who had been fighting across Europe. They did not set sentries which could be seen and knocked out easily.

And if the battalion had not been women.

But the "ifs" were there. And for all the spirit Major Kroup had instilled into them, the women were moving inevitably to disaster.

The Zhenski Battalion formed up in the starlight in the open square before their barracks.

"Za Rodinu . . . za Stalina," Major Kroup said briefly. "Left turn! Quick march!"

"For Fatherland, for Stalin," she had said. But she might as well have said with the gladiators of ancient Rome: "*Morituri te salutant*" . . . "We about to die salute you, O Caesar . . ."

Within the belt of trees the shapes of the tanks were only long-snouted grotesques in the starlight, big, implacable monsters who crouched ready to pounce outward from their concealment, frightening yet unreal to the women who had seen such things only at the cinema or on a May Day parade.

Number One Company crept forward on its diversionary task, a strange wonder in the hearts of the women at the deadly steel in their grasp, at the deadly task that was soon to be theirs. Yet no one faltered, no one dallied. Ahead lay the baby-killers.

With amazing silence for untrained troops they took up their positions, ready to pour fire into the enemy camp where no light could be seen and where no one seemed to live. The baby-killers would soon feel the lead of Nemesis blazing through them.

And at the other side of the wood Two Company and Three moved up, ready for the moment when their own fire would pour into the enemy position, when they would charge forward with their bottle bombs and send the obscene monsters of steel into a roaring pyre of flame.

Silence, utter silence as they moved forward.

In Major Kroup a mighty surge of thankfulness was welling up.

It was going well. It was going perfectly. The Zhenski Battalion was moving into history.

She was leading Number Three Company, between it and Number Two so that she could control both. Her own pistol was in her hand and even her imperturbable spirit was moved to a silent breathlessness at the daring of their task.

A little farther and they would be in position. A little farther and they would be out of the open ground and into cover. A little farther and success would surely be with them.

And suddenly the long silence was shattered.

"A-a-agh!"

A woman's scream burst through the night.

"Akh . . . Akh . . . "

An owl. A low-flying owl whose silent wings had brushed her face. A small, harmless creature of the night, or harmful only to mice and little birds.

But because it was a creature of the night, because this was a land of old, dark superstition and because she was a woman and because she had had so pitifully little training, she screamed.

And the German guns replied.

For there were sentries and they were hidden behind the boles of trees and in slit trenches all round the perimeter of the wood.

And as they heard the scream they fired.

The scream was drowned by the new scream of bullets streaming out from the wood, howling over the attackers' heads, cutting them down in swathes as the range was shortened.

Yet still the charge went on.

Still some of the women went running forward with their bottles of petrol and phosphorus, firing their rifles and screaming to a new tune, screaming with rage, with exhilarating, mind-dazed anger.

The baby-killers, was the thought in their mind, ahead lay the baby-killers.

And against all odds, against the possibilities let alone the probabilities, some of them broke through the outer ring of defenders.

Here and there in the wood the fires began to flare up.

Now the defenders' positions were outlined against the increasing flames.

And now if ever the last faint chance of success existed. Now, if the attack had been pressed home, the proud Waffen SS might have been defeated . . . by women.

But now the one person who could have seized the instant was not there to realize it.

For Natalya Kroup lay motionless on the ground with Irina Tsiganka crouched over her, crying out her name, feeling desperately for her heart, for any sign of life. There was blood on Kroup's face and a gash along her head. But she was alive.

"Quick!" Irina commandeered a stretcher party, or what passed for one. There were no stretchers and the women bore off the massive body of their commander cradled in their arms.

And the attack of the Zhenski Battalion dissolved into chaos, retreat and rout.

For some death. And for others only a longing for death. All told there were only a dozen prisoners alive and unwounded from the Zhenski Battalion, huddled together under the astounded gaze of their captors.

"Women, by God! Women. They're fighting us with women!"

"Well, we know what to fight *them* with!"

Katrina Semyonovna felt an ultimate hopelessness as she gazed round the hungry, pitiless faces. Of all her fellow prisoners the only one she knew was her own sergeant,

Anna Turuchin. Turuchin, who had been her assistant, and then become her sergeant and was now her fellow prisoner.

Oh, and there was that blonde girl who had worked in Gnotke's office. She knew her by sight. She had seen her with Kroup. Vyora something-or-other.

Kroup, she thought with revulsion. Kroup! Her belly heaved when she remembered what Kroup had done. She remembered the shot that had killed poor Ilya. And she remembered the terrible hour in the major's room before the news had come that had sent them all out to be killed or...

But no matter what they did, she thought, it could be no worse with the Germans than with Kroup. That gross body that was a woman's and yet not a woman's. That terrible, overpowering presence.

She could still remember the harsh smell of Kroup's body, the hungry fierceness of her thick fingers. She hoped that Kroup was dead.

From beyond the trees there was a long scream of agony.

"Go on, Hansi," a voice shouted hoarsely from out of sight. "Hurry up. It's my turn next. The bitches . . . the bitches. They killed Dieter. Go on . . . Can't you get it in?"

And the ring of soldiers closed in on the women in their midst, the tired dejected women, the beaten women who would pay the age-old price of defeat.

"Nitchevo," a sulky Ukrainian girl mouthed. "Nitchevo."

But as a hand seized her, Katrina Semyonovna saw an incredulous light come suddenly into Vyora Pekare's eyes.

"Rudi!" she gasped. "Rudi . . ."

But her voice was drowned in the hungry mutter of the men as they seized their prey, as their hands grappled and fumbled fiercely, dragging at tunics, ripping at the rough fabric of the uniform trousers.

Then abruptly there was silence. Silence and a barked order.

"Mount up! I said mount up!"

"That's just what we're doing, Captain Küster," called the inevitable wag.

"Get aboard your vehicles," came the cold repetition of

the order. "If they're sending out their women to fight, the road to Misgorod is open . . . Or would you sooner wait around and let the Division HQ pick all the good billets? Mount up, I say!"

The prisoners were bundled roughly towards some rear echelon trucks, some stripped of their tunics, some with their trousers so torn that legs and backsides gleamed palely through them. They were thrown into a truck with no more ceremony than if they had been sacks of coal. The tailboard was slammed up and clamped in place. And again they were moving towards Misgorod.

Katrina found herself lying beside Vyora.

"You know him?" she demanded. "You know that German officer?"

"I know him," said Vyora numbly. "I know him."

Vyora Pekare's memory moved back through time, back through time and place, away from Russia completely, back to Berlin, back to the Germany that had seen nearly all her childhood, back to the days when there had been no war.

CHAPTER 9

"Vyora!" Herr Doktor Pekare's voice was stern as he heard the flat door close stealthily.

"Yes, Papa."

She came in slowly, a slim, fair-haired girl with a defenceless fragility about her mouth and eyes that always brought a little catch to the Doktor's heart. She was so exactly like her mother of that age that sometimes it seemed to him she was her mother re-born. Her mother, poor Natasha. She should have lived to see herself re-born, to relive again her own youth through her daughter. And maybe indeed somewhere she was doing just that.

Berlin might be a long way from Moscow – but what was distance to a spirit? He tried to put the thought of poor, dead Natasha lying now in some mass grave without even a board over her head to say who she was, from his mind.

Moscow was another life, another age. All that was behind them now, forgotten. He had never wanted to go back.

Probably it would be death for him to try it. The memory of the Comintern was longer than the sufferings of Job. Somewhere there would be a list and he, like all the fleeing Mensheviks, would be on it. Red Russia had no use for White Russians. He would be as guilty in their eyes as any of the great boyars, though he had never so much as owned a serf or ground down a widow or an orphan.

There, as here, he had been a doctor. And if he had dabbled in politics it had been in the mildest way possible. But certainly he could not go back, not while the Georgian, Joseph Vissarionovich, sat on the Red throne of all the Russians.

And why go back, when all was said? This was a better land here though he had had his doubts in the first decade of his arrival when the Communists seemed on the brink of taking over. But there was no danger of that now, not with Herr Hitler in power and a marvellous prosperity restored to the land.

There was, it was true, the matter of the Jews. But then everywhere in all times there was the matter of the Jews. In Russia there had been the ghettoes and the occasional pogroms. Broadly, he was inclined to blame the Jews. There might be cultured and artistic people amongst them, but everyone knew what money-grubbers they were. Had Hitler himself not declared and proved that international Jewry was implicated in plot after plot to bring down the Third Reich? It was little wonder that he took his own steps to curb the power of the Jews, little wonder indeed. And how many of the Red leaders were Jews? Too many for coincidence.

Certainly there were disturbing rumours about the treatment of some of the Jews here in Germany. But then . . . he who listened to rumours would get a sore ear as the old saying had it.

"It is late, Vyora," he said now as his daughter walked slowly across the room towards him. "It is late, my dear. A young girl should not be out so late unchaperoned."

Vyora laughed merrily.

"Oh, Papa! Such ideas you have. This is the twentieth

century in which we live, not the nineteenth . . . Or is your watch a little slow, eh?"

Affectionately she rubbed her hand across the egg-shaped dome of his head where the hair had drifted back until, as she used to say, he was forehead all over.

She sat down at his knees, legs sprawling coltishly on the grey, thick-piled carpet.

"Besides," she said a little dreamily, "this was . . . studies."

"So late the university is open?"

He had thick eyebrows and they jerked up quizzically.

"Not a class, papa. An exploration. He is such a clever man . . ."

The Doktor frowned at the curiously dreamy expression that had come into her eyes.

"Who is this clever man? Who is this fount of all the knowledges?"

He tried to be lightly jocular but he was concerned. Vyora was so young, so sweetly simple. She could be so easily deceived, though her scholastic rating was so high.

"Professor Razin, Papa. I have told you of him. The new professor."

"The Russian?"

"Oh, Papa. You must not speak as if he is some red-haired ogre."

"He is from Moscow."

"And yourself, Papa? Are you not from Moscow? And I?"

"That is different . . . This exchanging of Professors I do not approve. How Herr Hitler permits I do not understand."

"Papa. We are at peace. The land of socialism and the land of national socialism."

"You do not know these Bolsheviki. You have not fled them. Or rather, you have, but not knowing. Everything left behind . . . everything."

"That was a lifetime ago, Papa . . ."

Prudently she fell silent then. And more prudently said nothing of the long, eager talks with Professor Andrei Razin.

"Well – what did you do then? Where did you go?"

"Pictures, Papa. We went to look at pictures . . . In the new gallery on the Friedrichstrasse."

"The Friedrichstrasse! A gallery there!"

"Papa! You get ancient again, dear Papa. Why not a gallery in the Friedrichstrasse? There are people there as well as anywhere else."

And indeed there were people and enough in that gaudy thoroughfare. Cafes and cheap dance halls, amusement arcades and brash, meretricious jewellers' where all that glistered was not gold.

"The Professor says it is very appropriate to have an art gallery in the Friedrichstrasse. Artists are alive. Their work is alive. It is not for embalming in some ancient, out-of-the-way castle or museum. Art belongs to the people and the people must have it where they can see it."

"Hmph! And in Moscow? What about the arts in Moscow?"

"Oh, the Professor does not speak of the things in Moscow," the girl lied easily. "We talk of Germany. Of what is here. The Professor is not a Party member you know, Papa."

Which may or may not have been true so far as she was concerned. At least her words helped to ease a little the anxieties in the doctor's mind.

And after all . . . a Professor. What danger was there from a professor? In his mind was a picture of the professors he had known, grave, solid citizens to whom any man could entrust a daughter without a moment's worry.

No doubt it would be all right.

In his own flat Professor Razin was undergoing an interrogation as searching as that which the girl had suffered.

"Andraievitch," said the little man who ran the Party in Berlin. "There are complaints. It seems that your task does not proceed with sufficient speed."

Andrei Razin ran his fingers through his thick hair and smiled with a lightness he did not feel.

"Since I alone know what progress has been made and at what speed, it would seem that I alone can be the judge, comrade."

"Tsst! You were sent here, to exchange with a German professor, with the particular purpose of persuading students of Russian origin and special merits in certain categories to return to the homeland. How many students have so returned?"

"It is not simple. There must be discretion. The ideas must be implanted with care. There is, I would point out, the Gestapo. They have agents everywhere. If I arouse suspicion, speak too openly – my mission is abated at once."

"There is also the NKVD," said the other flatly, making no overt threat but implying what they both knew to be the case; that there were certain close relatives of the Professor who might well have a spell in the Lyubyanka if certain words were said.

"Oh yes . . . there is always the NKVD," Razin agreed wearily. "There is always a sledgehammer to crack a nut . . . But what happens to the kernel of the nut?"

The man from the Party drew out a little sheet of paper from his pocket.

"There are some names. What progress have you made with . . . say, Vyora Pekare . . . and with the German, Rudolph Küster? Here we have excellent material. Officer material, perhaps. We will expect to read of some progress in your next report . . . Comrade Professor."

"Sieg Heil! . . . Sieg Heil! . . . Sieg Heil! . . . "

The thundering cries, the stamping feet in the great Sportspalast worked their accustomed magic. The hypnotic cries of the leader dinned in a hundred thousand ears.

"Ein Reich . . . Ein Volk . . . Ein Führer . . . "

High on the banking Vyora Pekare and Rudolph Küster hugged a secret delight. Their hands were interlocked and they "Sieg Heiled" with the best. But they knew the truth. They were going through the motions but they were not involved. They were the true Socialists, the heirs apparent of Karl Marx lying in his mean London graveyard.

"Germany stands at the crossroads of history," blasted the great, frenetic, impersonal voice of the amplifiers. "The New Order of the National Socialist Party . . . "

Rudolph Küster's mouth was at the girl's ear, hot breath

stirring up something that had nothing whatever to do with National Socialism or any other kind of Socialism."

"Like a frog," he said hoarsely. "Isn't he like a great fat frog, maybe the one in the saying. Blowing himself up. But it is the people who decide. Eventually it is the people who decide."

His hand fell on her thigh and lay there, edging up slowly and it seemed without conscious volition from the general region of her knee to the most intimate part of her person – but all this of course outside her garments. For this was a public meeting. And even if they had come between themselves to mock there were conventions to observe.

The whole structure of the National Socialist Party that the little Austrian bohemian with the square moustache had created was essentially middle class. It was not anything of the Junkers, it owed nothing to aristocracy. It was a middle class revolution. And that was the secret of its success, as Rudolph explained later, as the Professor had explained.

"Germany is a country of the middle classes. Even the workers aspire to be middle class. And the middle classes aspire no higher. They do not wish to be the arbiters of destiny, the pattern-makers of society. They are content to remain in the station to which they have been called. Good food, good beer, a snug house, a steady income. They want no more.

"Hitler may seem to be offering them dreams of glory but when we examine Mein Kampf we find that though there is to be glory for Germany, for the individual there is only security . . . security sprung from glory but essentially security. It is for this reason there can be no real revolution in Germany. Revolution means ultimate security for a nation but in the meantime disturbance and uncertainty. The German race cannot accept uncertainty."

"And yet Germany has been the source of the greatest revolutionary philosophers," Rudolph told him.

"Marx. Engels. Yes, of course. But their fervour did not rise here. It rose in the slums of England which are so much worse than anything in this land. And the Communist Manifesto was not a product of German philosophy at all, whatever the nationality of its progenitors. Further, though

Marx and Engels were originators, it was a philosophy purely that they produced. They backed it with no action. Now, in Russia , . . "

And the cultured, careful arguments of Professor Razin would continue.

Vyora let the meaningless tide of the Führer's speech pour over her, forgot the other arguments of Rudolph and the Professor and abandoned herself to the melting sweetness of the caresses.

And indeed those caresses could have been carried to any extent despite the crowds about them. No one was paying them any attention at all. All eyes were on the gesticulating figure on the platform, on the little corporal who led a nation, on the apotheosis of the middle classes.

Then the hectoring, inflammatory speech was over in another storm of "Sieg Heils." And the speakers began to boom out the brassy music of the Party.

"Die Fahne hoch, die Reihen dicht geschlosen,

"Sa marschiert mit ruhig festem Schritt . . . "

Bellowing faces all about them. A great panoply of sound that carried all over Berlin. And the young couple holding hands at the rear of the great hall, holding hands and hearing nothing but the beat of their own hearts.

It was as they made their way home that they saw the Jew being attacked.

He was an old man, orthodox from his beard and his dark hat and his curling ringlets. And the attackers were young men, three of them, light-hearted young men whose voices were loud with the echo of beer.

They pushed the Jew between them, from one to another, laughing raucously as he grew ever more terrified. One snatched his hat and then there was a merry game for a moment of tossing the hat from one to another. But the sport was poor enough. The old man simply stood there, making no effort to retrieve his head covering.

Head bowed, passive, in the ancient cowed posture of his race, he awaited what would come next.

Vyora felt a terrible sadness in her heart. If she had been a man, she thought, she would have run forward, challenged the young thugs. But Rudolph did not stir. When she glanced at him she saw his face set into fierce, cold lines.

"Can't we . . . do something?"

"Nothing," he answered harshly. "If we help the old man we condemn ourselves. Our work will be compromised. You know that."

Then the three youths tired of their sport. They pulled the old man's beard and one of them kicked him heartily in the rear. Then, laughing, they passed along the street.

And the Jew picked up his hat from the gutter and walked on as if nothing strange had happened. For him, perhaps, it was not strange, only too familiar an incident.

"Our work?" Vyora echoed. "What work?"

"For Socialism."

Rudolph took her arm. "Come to my room. I must speak to you . . . "

"Papa . . . "

"Your father knows you were at the Sportspalast. He knows how late the community singing goes on sometimes. Come to my room."

CHAPTER 10

The room was a grey, spartan place in a grey, spartan block with concrete stairs and concrete corridors. The furnishings were a single bed, a table and chair, a cupboard and a washbasin. There were also bookshelves, well-filled shelves. More books were stacked on the floor, philosophy, dialectics, history, economics.

"Plain living and high thinking," Rudolph Küster grinned.

From the cupboard he brought out a bottle of white wine and poured two glasses. Looking round the bare room Vyora felt ashamed of the middle class comfort of her own home in Dahlem. This was how she too should live, how every true socialist should live until equality was restored in the world.

"That Jew," Rudolph said abruptly. "About that Jew . . . "

Rudi was handsome, she thought. She had never realized

before how handsome he was with his hair as blond as her own and his strong nose and chin. Strength, she thought; he radiated strength and purpose. Purpose blazed in his blue, slightly deep-set eyes. He was so different from Papa, kindly, bumbling, frightened Papa. Uninvited she sat down on the narrow bed.

"I was ashamed to leave the Jew," he said, eyes abstracted. "To leave him to those brutes. I wanted to rush in, to pound them with my fists."

"I know."

She had drawn her long, slim legs up onto the bed and sat now with her knees high. Her chin rested on her hands which lay on her kneecaps and her skirt fell back so that he could look straight at her thighs, at the pale skin above the stockings, at the frill on the hem of her scanty knickers.

Not quite consciously she was following the dictates of her body, carrying out the old, original purpose of the female, to attract.

"If I'd gone for them, you know what would have happened. There would have been a fight. The police would have come. We would all have been arrested. Those thugs – they would have been freed at once. The Jew would have been charged with causing a disturbance to the peace. He might have gone to prison. And I would have been investigated. So would you. Now, at this time above all, I cannot be investigated."

He sat down beside her and his hand fell on her knee.

"I'm going to tell you something – something that could certainly put me behind bars."

For a long moment he turned to look at her.

"I love you, Vyora. That's why I'm telling you this. To show how much I love you . . ."

She felt his hand move up slowly under her skirt, up past the smooth fabric of her stocking and onto the smoother silk of her skin. She said nothing at all, not even looking at him, feeling that the magic of the moment that was throbbing through her would be shattered and dispelled if she spoke. This was not the first time he had touched her but it was the first time that it had had this ultimate meaning. Before, as in the Sportspalast, there had been others near. Or there had been others coming. The caresses had never gone farther than this.

His hand had gone as far as it could now and lay warm and dominating on her body, glowing through the cambric of her knickers and stirring fresh glows of warm desire.

"I'm joining the Party," he said abruptly. "The Party."

And both knew which Party he meant. It was not the Nazi Party. She caught her breath but still said nothing.

And now his fingers were working their way up and under the elastic, against the hair and the sensitive erogenous skin.

"It's no use talking any more. It's time to act – act. People like you and I, we can't act alone. It's no use sitting around, going to meetings, saying how terrible everything is. We've got to act . . . and the Party is the only way."

His fingers were kneading at her gently, bringing new paroxysms of delight at every movement. And if this seemed the strangest love-making of which she had ever heard, the thought took no conscious shape. Nor indeed was there any thought at all in her mind now. She was all body, all throbbing, excited body.

"They might send me to Spain," he breathed and now gently he was pivoting her on her buttocks, easing her down onto her back. I've done my junior training. I'd be a useful soldier."

He smiled as she lifted her bottom and began herself to pull off the frail knickers, sliding them down her legs and dropping them to the floor. His hand lifted her dress higher and slid up and down her belly in a long, gentle, endless caress.

"It would be appropriate somehow," he smiled as he slid down beside her, "to use Hitler's training to beat Hitler's army."

And now his body was heavy on hers and all the fruition of the strange mating neared its climax.

"Maybe," he said, "Maybe you'll join too . . . "

She gave a little sharp cry of mingled ecstasy and pain. And, for a little at least, he stopped talking.

Afterwards he said: "I didn't know you were a virgin. I didn't expect it. I . . . should I say I'm sorry?"

She smiled up at him sleepily, sated: "It would be

bourgeois at the least... And of course I'll join the Party."

It was only later, hurrying home, that she realized how late it was. Alibis began to form in her mind, but none of them were needed.

Herr Doktor Pekare was in no state to consider the hour. He was slumped in his deep leather upholstered armchair by the electric fire. He scarcely looked up as Vyora entered.

"I was at the Sportspalast, Papa, to hear the Führer. Did you listen to the broadcast?"

It was no excuse at all, she knew. But she prattled on brightly about the meeting, about Hitler's stirring address, how many songs they had sung and the parade of the Hitler Jugend. And all the time he sat slumped, not seeming to hear.

"Papa! Are you not well? Will I call Doktor Schultz?"

Anxiously she looked down at him. And to her dismay she heard him suddenly laugh harshly.

"A doctor! There is only one who could help me – the one who brought me into the world. He could help me if his work had failed, if I had been born dead . . ."

"Papa! What is it?"

Had he somehow divined what had happened in Rudolph's room? Was this what had upset him? But surely not. For that he would have been angry and reproachful. He would not have been lost in this complete despair.

Now his head rose and in his eyes as he stared at her there was an infinite tragedy.

"There was a phone call when you were out," he said quietly. "A man. He knows what I thought was surely hidden, forgotten and lost in the ruins of the past."

"Papa?"

She sat in a high-backed chair in front of him.

"Tell me, Papa. Please. I beg . . . What did he say, this man?"

What could Papa have to hide, kind, bumbling, gentle Papa? Surely there could be nothing.

"He said only two words," her father answered. "Two words. But it was as much as a book."

"Two words? What two words?"

"He said 'Josip Bronstein.' And then he laughed."

"Josip Bronstein? But . . . I don't understand, Papa. Why should a man's name . . . Who was Josip Bronstein?"

Bleakly he stared at her and now she saw that there were veritable tears trickling down his cheeks.

"Josip Bronstein was your grandfather, your mother's father. He was a fine man, very clever, very kind, very rich then."

His hand, trembling, reached out to her.

"He was also a Jew," he said.

Jewish blood. Vyora marvelled at the thought when at last she had gone to bed. She was a quarter Jewish. And to have any taint at all of the forbidden blood in the Third Reich was almost as bad as to be full-blooded. If they had known at the Sportspalast that a Jew was amongst them they might have turned on her and literally rent her limb from limb. Those youths teasing the old man, they would have thought nothing of stripping her.

They would not have raped her, of course. Oh no – the pure Nordic blood did not so demean itself. But certainly they might have stripped her, abused her and humiliated her. This had happened to other girls. She remembered how Judith Gruhnbaum had been treated, Judith who had been at school with her and had been stripped, shaven and daubed with paint by her own classmates. She remembered her own horror and indignation then. Now she wondered exactly what had caused it. Had it after all not been a pure and selfless indignation? Had it perhaps been a matter of blood calling to blood?

Then imperceptibly her mind drifted into the memory of Rudi's caresses. She began to re-live the moments on the bed until she stiffened with a new thought. What would Rudi say if he knew? How would he feel? How would his political convictions match up with his racial pride? Just how deep did that racial pride go?

Certainly he had longed to go to the aid of the old Jew. But helping him, and coupling with a girl who might have been his grand-daughter was another matter. Consciously he would never be anti-Semitic. But he had absorbed the same teaching, the same training, the same indoctrination as herself. Would he flinch from her if she told him the truth? Would his eyes turn cold and hard and his body withdraw from hers?

Angrily she reproached herself for doubting him. But the doubts remained.

And then she reproached herself still more for being concerned solely with her own problems. What of Papa? What a terrible blow this must be to him! All those years of service, of kindly, patient attendance to the sick. And now suddenly some evil man had his secret – a secret which he had not even thought of, perhaps.

Suddenly, someone had it in his power to destroy Papa ... and herself.

Who? Who could have learned the secret? And how? And what would they do with it? Would blackmail be the next step? Money? Was that what the voice on the phone was after? Papa was not rich. But he was not poor either. He could pay a blackmailer. He could be sucked dry.

And for her, she thought. It would be for her.

Papa was really in no danger. He had no Jewish blood. The taint was all on her side. Papa would be paying to protect her, suffering to protect her. Oh, Papa . . .

She rose quietly from her bed. She must speak to him now, tell him that she needed no protection, that he must guard himself.

In the living room the smell of schnapps hung heavy on the air.

Poor papa. Who could blame a man for drinking on a night like this? The shock of that phone call.

His bedroom door was a little open and when she peered in she saw him lying fully clothed on the bed.

The schnapps bottle was empty on the table beside him and here the smell of alcohol was even stronger. And yet, in the moonlight that struck down through the uncurtained window, his eyes were open. She moved slowly towards the bed, a terrible pity in her for the lost, withdrawn expression on his face. He seemed a thousand miles, a thousand years away as she halted at the bedside.

"Papa," Vyora said softly.

He moved very slowly, eyes turning and then his head to look at her in the moonlight.

"Natasha," he marvelled as his hand reached out to take her wrist in his grasp. "Natasha . . . Oh, Natasha . . ."

Suddenly he was sobbing and at the same time drawing her closer, pulling her down on the bed.

"Natasha!" he cried aloud.

She felt his head on her breast, hot, quivering in a passion of memory. She knew it was no use at all to speak now.

"So the Küster boy has been called up in the German Army? He is not the only one on your list . . . though indeed he was a very promising candidate. A pity. Our man in the drafting office unfortunately has been replaced. Permanently."

Razin hated the permanent smugness on the little secretary's face. He hated the suggestion of the whipcrack that lurked behind every word he said. Briefly, he hated the little man and what he stood for, the mass, grey anonymous power that stood behind him.

"We now require more progress. There are two young men – sons of Russians – and a girl on the list. Vyora Pekare will be your first assignment."

The Professor looked at him coldly.

"Assignment? I do not take assignments."

"Now you do. And the girl is the first. It will not be difficult."

It was easy, surprisingly easy. Rudolph's sudden departure had left a vacuum in Vyora's life. Razin did not so much step in to fill it; he was drawn in with the irresistible force of a whirlpool.

From the stiff, professional chats he moved smoothly to the status of confidante. It had happened so easily, so smoothly, with so little effort by himself that he scarcely reproached himself when he brought her to his bed.

Once there was a phone call from the secretary.

"There must be discretion. It is causing comment. A professor and a student . . ."

"Perhaps the comrade secretary would like to take my place?"

Razin laughed as he put the phone down. It was a petty victory. Yet after all it was a victory over the grey, faceless ones.

Such victories were rare. And they were possible only here when the threat of another and possibly greater tyranny kept the secretaries in some degree at least of subjection.

His wooing and his subtle suggestions continued. He could, he felt now, have actually told the girl to go to Moscow. She would have done this for him. But he wanted it all to come from her side. It would.

He knew now that the secretary had learned of that grandmother. He knew that the girl knew, for she had come only a little time after Küster had been called up to tell him and beg his advice. Deliberately he had given her no advice. Let her decide for herself. Then there would be no reproaches in his own memory. And yet at the same time he knew he was not leaving the girl to decide. It had all been decided far away. Each of them was only a puppet.

The knowledge of her quarter of Jewish blood would be the deciding factor. He could guess what storms of indecision were surging in her mind.

One day they walked down Unter Den Linden, close together but not hand in hand since there were other students who would certainly have noticed the occurrence.

Her face was strained suddenly as they stood on the pavement which was speckled here and there with the tiny flowers of the lime trees, of the lindens on the main avenue, drifted here by the casual wind.

Momentarily the sun disappeared behind a drifting cloud fragment.

"I'm going away. I . . . I can't stay any longer."

There were tears on the face she turned to him. "I'm going to Moscow," she said abruptly.

He wished, as they stepped into the sunlight again, that his life had taken another course – any other course.

CHAPTER 11

In those first weeks, in Moscow, Vyora thought she had never been so happy. Afterwards she was to remember wryly that intense, ingenuous happiness. Four other students arrived in Moscow about the same time. One was Hindu, a small fragile man with a remote smile and a passionate interest in learning everything by heart, even the signs in the shop windows, the prices. He could quote whole pages of the Communist Manifesto verbatim and if the right chord was struck would reel off imposing and appalling statistics of British brutality in nineteenth century India.

Afterwards she could never remember his name. He did not himself use it much but was fond of quoting from the words of Subhas Chandra Bose who was later to lead an Indian Freedom Army under the Japanese in Burma. Often she wondered what had happened to him when he returned to India – if indeed he returned.

He was such a gentle, ineffectual little man to be trained as the spearhead of a rising against British Imperialism. He could not even mend a fuse or change a light bulb in their quarters in the student's hostel. He reminded her of a dark, cloth doll she had once owned. He reminded her also of her father.

Oddly, she did not think often of her father once she was actually in Russia. Deliberately, perhaps, she had created a block in her memory, a block that started on the night he had been drunk, the night he had called her Natasha and thought she was Natasha.

Also in the group there was an Irish girl, a dark-haired, fiery-eyed girl sent there by some proscribed Irish left-wing organization, but who seemed less interested in Communism than in the downfall of the English. She was greatly given to drink and reeled often into their quarters with eyes glazed and a hundred songs on her lips.

She was, she revealed once, a priest's daughter.

"And it gives me a special sort of a standing, don't you

see? Like it's all right for the rest of you to be atheists but I'm a Catholic atheist, don't you see?"

She was very shrewd though in her sobriety and warned Vyora especially against a third student, Joseph Mpunga, from the British colony of Kenya.

"That fellah's no more a Communist than me backside. It's girls he's after, white girls. Sure those darkies is mad for it. I've seen them in Dublin meself. You watch him, acushla, a blink of your eye with that boy and he'll be up you like a shot. I mean it, mind."

It was hard to believe it. Mpunga was a tall, quiet-spoken Kikuyu with a gift for languages. He seemed as well educated as any of the others . . . and even more deeply indoctrinated with Communist beliefs.

In their open sessions when they met with other students and each told of life in their own land, that is of the grosser aspects of capitalist exploitation, it was Mpunga who gained the greatest attention.

"Even the Czars," he said, "abolished the knout. You here, living under the happy dictatorship of the proletariat, you are not having the experience that we dark people know. How many of you, not one here who are all so young, have seen their mother writhe and twist under the lash of a white man's sjambok . . . Sjambok? You ask me what is this? I will tell you. It is a whip. It is a long whip made from the raw hides of rhinoceros, dried in the sun. That is what is sjambok. This I have seen used to whip my mother . . ."

The Hindu nudged Vyora. "This thing. I think it is not so. In India today there is no whipping. I think maybe this black fellow is not always telling the truth."

Truth or not, he became a star pupil and very soon he left the students' hostel where the others lived. He became a lecturer, travelling across the country. He left their ken completely. But not before his visit to Vyora's room.

Silence had settled over the hostel, the long, dialectical discussions over for one night. Vyora lay sleepily thinking of what she had learned, what she had contributed, glad now that she had come to Russia, not even regretting leaving poor Papa behind.

She sensed rather than heard her door opening.

"Is that you, Eileen?"

The Irish girl came quite often to her room to unburden whatever lay on her heart from the day. There was no answer and Vyora could hear gentle breathing from the doorway.

There was a bedside lamp on the plain deal table. But it did not work. Quite a lot of things did not work in Moscow, she had learned. It was only to be expected. When a new state was rising, a new way of life, every tiny detail could not be expected to be perfect. Later it would be different. Everyone knew that. The Party would triumph over all the petty details.

The sound of the breathing grew closer and the darkness took a little shape, a darker darkness. When her hand went out it met flesh.

"Who is it?"

A bare, dark body in her room. Her hand wavered in the darkness. A man's body . . .

There was a soft laugh in the darkness.

"This is really a man, eh? Such a man you have not touched before."

"Joseph Mpunga! What do you want? Get out of here!"

He laughed again, so close now that she could see him in the faint light from the window, so close that she could smell him, the feral odour of roused male flesh. His own hand clasped on her wrist, making her hand hold to him.

"What do I want? What a silly question. What does any man want? And you cannot deny I am a man."

She felt panic in her heart and tried to wriggle back across the bed. But her wrist was still held. Now his other hand was on her head, running fingers lightly through her fair hair.

"Maybe you don't think I am a man. Maybe because I have a dark skin and you have a light one you think there is some difference between us. But I am a man – and you are a woman."

For an instant his hand stroked down across her breasts, swept up again to grip her neck and jerk her towards him. His lips met hers in a fierce, hungry kiss.

And then distantly down the corridor they both heard the approaching tittup of a woman's heels. The Irish girl, singing discordantly and yet softly some ancient rebel song, was coming back, a little drunk as usual.

"I'm going," hissed Mpunga, "but I'll be back some time."

He melted away, a deeper shadow in the night. The Irish girl swayed into the doorway, fumbling for the light-switch and finding it.

"They hung my grand-da' in Kilmainham gaol," she declared. "And what d'ye think o' that?"

She staggered away to her own room and Vyora leaped from her bed to close the door and bolt it. It was not comradely to bolt the door. It implied a lack of trust. But she bolted it just the same.

And as she lay afterwards on her bed she thought of that strange invasion. For the first time since she had arrived in Moscow she felt a little afraid. There was no one to help her but the Commissars and their underlings. And this was not a matter for officialdom. After all, she thought, the African might have supposed she had given him some encouragement. Maybe she had smiled at him or he thought she had smiled.

Rudolph . . . Professor Razin . . . and almost a black man. Oh, how shocked Papa would have been!

Then the memory of Papa came close to the danger-line and her memory froze solid.

The fourth foreign student was a fellow-German, the one Vyora should have had the closest ties with. But she was a Schwabian, speaking a thick dialect that Vyora could scarcely understand. And she was interested in nothing but herself and her own discovery of dialectical materialism. Afterwards Vyora could remember nothing about her but her staring eyes behind thick, bi-focal lenses, eyes like peeled gooseberries. Staring eyes and a thick, clumsy, peasant body.

And after all, what did it matter about the other students. They were only incidental to her own presence here. To her witness of the triumph of the proletariat.

At first in her free time she went starry-eyed about Moscow, seeing what she knew she would see, the triumph of the only true democracy.

Five times she queued to walk past Lenin's tomb in the Red Square. Countless times she stared at the onion domes of the Kremlin and pondered on what great plans for the salvation of humanity must be going on there. She thought of Stalin, pacing his room thoughtfully, pipe fuming, thoughts burgeoning in his head for the great strides onward. And she compared him with Adolf Hitler, whom she had now come to call derisively Schicklegruber, whose only thought was the glory of the German people.

Ein Reich . . . Ein Volk . . . Ein Führer, she would think satirically. But here it is all of suffering humanity we think of.

The women were the only subject to disturb her, the fat blousy Russian women. Especially the women who swept the streets and laboured on the building sites. There was equality. This was true. Women were the equal of men. This was also true. What a man could do, a woman could do. Yet still it disturbed her to see these sleazy, raucous women with their wide-headed, long-handled brooms sweeping away the litter of the day in the fine streets of the new Moscow. Or carrying bricks to the men on the building sites. Or mixing mortar.

Certainly if the revolution was to succeed every atom of power must be mobilised, man-power, woman-power, children-power if need be. Yet it still seemed . . . not right.

She stifled the disloyal thoughts. Because German hausfraus did not labour on building sites or at the cross-roads with their brushes it did not mean that they should not.

More disillusionizing was the inefficiency. The Party was all, just as at home. She had to pull herself up on this thought. This *was* home. Here she had been born. Once she went, secretly, to see the very house. It had in fact been pulled down but at least she could gaze at the site and the new district office built on it and feel herself a part of the city. But certainly there was a lot of inefficiency, a lot of delay. Tours would be arranged that never took place because someone had failed to stamp the passes or fill them in correctly or perhaps failed to realize that passes were necessary.

Frighteningly, it was very, very like the Third Reich. Except that it was less efficient.

But then, here everything had had to be created from nothing, from scratch. It was little wonder that everything did not always go exactly as planned.

She wrote often to Papa, bright, cheerful letters about her day's doing. She would have written to Rudolph also but to do this might be to condemn him. Letters from Russia to a soldier of the Reich!

The first letter would have brought the Gestapo on him. Yet she could think of him. And at night, before dropping off to sleep she thought of him often. Of his eager, lively face, of his fierce condemnation of Hitler and his works. Of the night when he had taken her to his room.

Oddly, she scarcely thought of Razin at all, though it had been the Professor who had sent her here. Even as he had caressed her there had been something shadowy and remote about Razin, something to be admired and venerated even. But something just a little abstract.

Certainly he had made a tender lover. But there was a gulf of years between them – and experience. When he spoke soft words of love they were like a poetry lesson. Even in his arms she had thought of him as the Professor, not as Andrei.

When she tried to think of him it was the image of Rudi that came always into her mind, so strangely since when he had been called up she had hardly thought of him at all. But then, Razin had swiftly filled the gap and stilled the pain of that parting.

Where was Rudi now? What was he doing? She smiled to herself. Little did the Army know what it was doing when it took Rudolph Küster into its ranks. He would be doing the work of the Party even there, softening the morale of his army comrades, bringing more and more men to the Socialist cause. But if only he could have come with her here to Moscow. Together they could really have progressed.

The notice on the hostel board was quite short though the list of names beneath it was long.

"The Department for Student Affairs and the Byurobin is happy to accept the noble offer of the foreign students to take their full part in the life of the Soviet by volunteering to join in the harvest activities, and the undernoted students are hereby allocated to the subjoined Sovkhoz agricultural projects . . ."

The Irish girl was angry as usual.

"What the hell's this? I didn't volunteer for no farm work. I didn't leave Dublin to come and hoke potatoes for anyone."

"Your name's there. You must have volunteered," Vyora pointed out. "Maybe you had too much vodka at the time."

"Minsk!" Eileen snapped. "You think I wouldn't have remembered saying I'd go to a place with a name like that?"

Her eyes sharpened.

"Anyway, I see you've volunteered too."

"Me?"

"You're down for a place called Misgorod. I hope it keeps nice for you."

There were protests, of course. Nearly everyone protested. And of course the protests were quite useless. Beaming secretaries agreed that there had perhaps been a – mistake.

"Perhaps some other group of foreign students has volunteered for harvest work. No doubt there has been some secretarial error in the Ministry. But the orders are there. The transportation documents are all made out. Later, no doubt, all will be made clear. Meanwhile it would be a pity not to see at Government expense more of the beautiful homeland, of the great Communist experiment . . ."

And so on.

For those who pressed their protests too hard the smiles were a little less wide: "But, Comrade, if you had known the State needed extra hands, surely you would have volunteered? Well then. It is as if you had volunteered."

In any case they went, scattered off across the U.S.S.R., to Minsk and Ufa, Polotsk and Chkalov, all across the broad face of Russia. Hardly any two of them went to the same place and afterwards when she had grown more accustomed to the devious methods of the Communist bureaucracy, Vyora wondered about this. It seemed to her then that there had been some deliberate attempt to split up the students, to scatter them away from each other. Had there been a suspicion of counter-revolutionary activities? A suspicion would have been enough, the shadow of a suspicion.

And had they not been foreign, potential nuclei of future Communist groups in their own lands, perhaps they would not merely have been separated.

Yet it could have been simply some administrative whim also, a vague convulsion of the vast, impersonal brain that ran the country in its haphazard way.

At the time, at any rate, Vyora had no strong feelings about the change.

"It will be pleasant, Papa," she wrote. "To see more of the country and learn more of its people."

CHAPTER 12

It was pleasant enough travelling south across the broad, rolling countryside, even though she was travelling "hard." In a classless society there could be no first class or second class on the trains. There was "soft" and "hard." And "hard" was just that, wooden benches in the compartment, cold water in the washbasin and for a toilet only a hole in the floor over which, she realized at last, she must crouch like an animal to relieve herself.

There was of course no dining car. But at every station there was a horde of sellers of tea and sweetmeats and fruit, all crowding the platforms, selling as furiously as any huckster in any capitalist land.

It may have been on these stations with their interminable delays while the very drivers seemed to enquire the way, that Vyora first began to doubt the pabulums with which she had been fed. For surely in a Socialist state there should be no hucksters, no need for hucksters, no need for men and women to cry so anxiously their wares of cakes or cucumbers or salted herrings. Yet indeed her doubts could have been retrospective. She could have remembered afterwards these scenes on the platforms.

For, as she knew when she grew wise in the ways of the

country, wise in the ways of her own mind's working, she had been a triumph of naivete in those days.

Misgorod was an old town, lying in a curve of the Don, a decaying town whose original purpose had been a fortified centre against the Turkish pirates and raiders who struck up the Don in their long, red galleys from the Sea of Azov.

When the Turkish threat died it became a market town and an administrative centre. Good land lay about it. Then came the railway. But somehow it seemed never to have progressed into the twentieth century.

From a distance it looked enchanting, here and there an onion dome over an Orthodox church, there a minaret to commemorate the Moslem invaders from Turkey.

But when she left the station Vyora's first impression was of the smell. Misgorod did not seem to have any drains. And in fact Misgorod had few drains.

There were, it was true, plans for drains at Party headquarters. Unfortunately the plans had been drawn up in Moscow by a civil engineer who had never actually visited the town and did not know that much of it lay below the level of the Don, the waters of the river held back by a high, thick levee constructed in Romanov times.

Drains laid according to the plans would in fact have flooded the town rather than clearing it of its sewage. Thus sewage in the main was disposed of in the old traditional way, by men in carts who discharged their collections into the river below the town. When they were drunk they sometimes discharged above the town and since Misgorod drew its drinking water from the great river, typhoid was almost endemic in the place.

But of this, of course, Vyora knew nothing then. She knew only that the smell of sewage was strong and that the dusty roads were unsurfaced.

She knew also that the train was four hours late and that there was no one to meet her. Helplessly she stood on the platform, looking round her. All her belongings were in a suitcase at her feet. Gradually the platform emptied and the train puffed slowly out of the station on its way to Rostov. What on earth did she do now?

A railway official, an old man with a short grey beard,

had been regarding her for some minutes, leaning against a wall and idly rolling a cigarette of the black mahorka. Now he strolled over casually, scratching an armpit.

"Comrade, it is not permitted to loiter on the platform."

"Comrade, I am not loitering. I am waiting."

"Loitering, waiting. It is not permitted."

"But I was to be met."

"Evidently not today."

She felt humiliated, neglected. Her travel orders had stated specifically that she would be met at the station by a representative from the Protva Kolkhoz.

"From Moscow, eh? It is a long way. We do not see many foreigners here. How is it in Moscow?"

Foreigners! He regarded Muscovites as foreigners. The thought struck her sharply as a small, bright-faced man stepped briskly into the station, bearing an air of authority with him. The old man shuffled off, stubbing his cigarette.

"Comrade Pekare? Zhrastvuyte! I am Ivan Gnotke."

He was just about as tall as herself, stockily built, with high cheekbones and dark sloes of eyes that twinkled at her merrily.

"From the Protva Kolkhoz?"

For a moment his eyes shadowed a little.

"Niet. I am from the rayon."

From area administrative headquarters.

"You are to come with me."

"But . . . but I was told to await someone from the kolkhoz."

"Kolkhoz . . . Sovkhoz. You would have to wait a long time I fear. Now if you will follow me, Comrade, I have a car."

It was an old car of American make but it started at the first touch of the button and its engine sounded healthy enough as he drove through the dusty, untidy wandering streets. Peasants who looked like bundles of rags in their loose clothes shambled in the middle of the roadway, giving way only reluctantly. Occasionally a pig could be seen rooting in the garbage of a side-street.

With a flourish Gnotke drew up outside a recently painted but ancient building over which a flag fluttered listlessly.

"This is where you'll work. Now, comrade . . . mozhno!"

She followed him inside, past one teeming office after another. Queues of men and women sat or stood in the corridors, seeking passes, permits, certificates – or perhaps just passing the time of day. Some of them looked as if they had sat there since the Revolution.

Gnotke ignored them all as he led the way down a dusty corridor to an office at the end. The office was a surprise. In contrast to the others, with their crowded desks, untidy files, harassed or didactic clerks, this office was empty save for a single desk, a large filing cabinet, two seats and a large coathanger made from a solid upright with bulls' horns mounted into it to take the garments.

There was no doubt, Vyora thought, that Gnotke must be an important man to have such a big office entirely to himself. Perhaps even he was the administrative head of the rayon. In Germany he would have had an even bigger office and more grand. Just the same, by local standards such as she had seen this was in itself very big and grand. Briskly he slipped behind his seat, motioned her to the other one and took a slip of paper from his desk drawer.

"Vyora Pekare. Born Moscow in 1918. Mother dead. Father Menshevik voluntary exile now resident in Berlin, practising medicine. Resident in Berlin until age of 18 when became volunteer student to Union of Soviet Socialist Republics. Formerly close friend of Rudolph Küster, 21, student and Party member now serving in German Army on Polish frontier. Also close friend of Professor Andrei Razin, formerly in Berlin, now recalled to service with the Red Army. Academic rating good . . . "

The reading went on for some time. Not only her own but her father's and his parents' histories were recorded in detail in the file. There were also photographs.

"What an elegant bottom you have, comrade," said Gnotke.

He pushed a print across the desk and Vyora's face flamed red. The picture showed herself – and Razin. She could not have been more naked but he still wore his socks. That was a detail she had not remembered, the socks.

She could not meet Gnotke's eyes as she held the picture.

Her fingers twitched as if she was about to tear the print and he leaned across the desk to snatch it from her.

"State property," he chided. "It is an offence to deface or otherwise damage state property. Besides, this is only a print – and shouldn't even be here. The negative exists still in Moscow. Also, I may say I take some pleasure from this picture. I would not care to lose it . . . It has indeed made me look forward to your arrival."

Her face was still burning. "It's shameful . . . shameful. People spying on me . . ."

"I doubt if it was as bad as that. Perhaps Razin arranged the camera himself. On external duty one learns many skills."

Gnotke smiled. "No doubt you wonder why I show you this file. It is not usual. Personal files are rarely if ever shown to their subjects. And in fact I should not have this file. Personal files are not sent to the provinces, either. However, as you see, I have the file. It was enclosed with your normal documentation addressed to the Sovkhoz.

"Quite plainly, a confidential clerk in the Department for Student Affairs has inadvertently enclosed the file together with your other documents. A bad slip-up on his part. Very bad. No doubt this will present problems for him – or her – at some later date. Meanwhile I hold the file. It remains locked in my desk to which I alone hold the keys. Do not fear. No one else shall see it."

Gnotke sat back in his chair, eyeing her with frank appraisal.

"You have a great deal to learn about our land," he said. "A very great deal. I will instruct you . . . But wait. I am inhospitable. You are certainly hungry. And thirsty."

He rose and almost skipped to the filing cabinet. From it he brought out a small tray with salted herrings, black bread and unsalted butter set neatly in dishes. Also he brought out a litre bottle of vodka and two glasses.

"Not elegant," he said, "but sustaining."

And Vyora realized immediately how very hungry she was. The black bread was strong-flavoured, sour with the smell of yeast, and the herrings were so salty she could hardly swallow them. But she still ate hungrily.

"I expect," Gnotke smiled – not himself eating save for a nibble at a fragment of herring – "in fact, I'm sure you're wondering why you're here in my office instead of at the farm."

He smiled blandly, showing perfect, rather large white teeth.

"The fact is – there is no kolkhoz at the moment."

"But they sent me . . . Moscow . . . "

"Without being in any way critical," he answered, "there are times when Moscow does not know everything. Or rather, when information is not sufficiently disseminated. Officials in ministries in Moscow are dependent on the little bits of paper they pass round. If the right bits fail to circulate then there comes a hiatus of information. Action is taken which should not be taken and would not be taken if the information was disseminated correctly."

She continued to eat while she listened.

"Collectivisation in this province was initiated under the surveillance of my predecessor, an inelastic man with a too-rigid regard for the Ukases of the Kremlin.

"Now this is excellent farming land as you may have observed. Historically it was a region of kulaks, small farmers and a few petty landlords. I am told it was well farmed, though not so well farmed, of course, as it would have been under collectivisation.

"Therefore, the kolkhoz was set up here to instruct the kulaks in the ways of collectivisation, to convince them of its benefits. They were a backward-looking people, reluctant to adopt new ways. But with the assistance of the OGPU and the NKVD, my predecessor succeeded in carrying through the programme."

His voice was quite even and Vyora could not tell if he intended to be satirical or not. There had been rumours in Moscow, rumours which all good Communists discounted, of a wholesale persecution of the kulaks, of the starving, burning and other elimination of countless millions of farmers and peasants who were too slow to adopt the methods of the new regime.

"Unfortunately, as I say, my predecessor adhered too slavishly to the edicts of Moscow. This had always been an area where rye was grown and wheat and barley. Moscow's view was that maize was the crop most to be desired. Maize was sown – and failed. The following year cotton was the most desired crop. It too was tried – and failed . . . "

"For three years the kolkhoz failed even to approach its norm and my predecessor was removed for re-education."

She shivered faintly. Re-education usually meant the Lyubyanka – or Siberia.

"I do not propose to be re-educated myself," Gnotke went on, smoothly. "And I was able to have my appointment here delayed beyond the time when I could have any responsibility for this year's harvest . . . Go to the window."

She obeyed. They were on the outskirts of the town, almost on the bank of the Don. Some little distance away she could see long lines of what looked like barracks. These, she guessed correctly, were the buildings of the kolkhoz. Beyond, countless green square miles spread out until in the distance they merged with the trees and the low, smooth hills.

"Is that the kolkhoz? Those buildings? The fields look green enough. Surely there'll be a crop this year."

"Weeds and coarse grass," Gnotke answered bitterly. "That's all. They haven't even been ploughed. There was no one here to order the ploughing. And no machinery. The machinery is now here and I propose to use it to save what I can from this year."

"But if no crops have been planted – "

"Grass and weeds. They're still crops, if they can be used. With them I'm going to make silage."

"Silage?"

"It's a new – or at any rate fairly new method used in the decadent West. With grass in the old days we made hay. Now we make silage. We make a great pit and as we cut the grass we moisten it with diluted molasses and when the pit is full we cover it with earth again. The molasses causes the grass to ferment and the fermentation causes a form of preservation. It is like sauerkraut with which you will be familiar. That is, fermented cabbage. A favoured dish in Germany I am told."

Vyora's brows wrinkled in a little bewilderment.

"But still I do not understand. This . . . silage. What do you do with it?"

"Use it for fodder."

"But for what animals? When I came in the train I saw only a few animals in the field, a few milking cows. That was all. Where will you get your livestock?"

"Good. You are observant. You have a practical mind. I thought I would not be mistaken. Yes. There are few enough cattle. But there is not a village in Russia that does not have its pigs. Within a few versts of Misgorod there must be thousands, the property of kulaks and peasants. They will be collectivised. The silage will feed them over the winter and their offspring. And by the spring, though we will not have achieved our norm on crops, we will be a thousandfold over it on meat production. Moscow will not be displeased."

He rose briskly.

"Now you will learn why I came to the station to greet you – or one of the reasons. You may leave your case here. We will be returning."

CHAPTER 13

The kolkhoz had not been long in existence yet already it looked like a derelict ruin. There were long barrack blocks with dormitories for the workers, communal dining rooms, kitchens and recreation rooms. There were also store rooms, repair shops and a big, covered vehicle park.

Within the vehicle park were serried rows of tractors and farm implements of every kind. All looked almost new, unused. Some were still in crates.

Vyora marvelled at this richness of modernity among the crumbling buildings and the cracked concrete roads. Millions of roubles worth of equipment was stored here – and yet she had seen only one or two sloppy-looking kolkhozniks about the place. Puzzled, she turned to Gnotke.

"All this equipment," the zavedivayushi smiled. "You wonder why it is not in use. That is one reason why you are here."

He slapped the solid radiator of a tractor.

"Made in Germany. That is why."

She looked as puzzled as ever.

"Buying commission go from Moscow to the West, to buy what we cannot or do not make. You say what about Magnetogorsk and the great tractor assembly line there? Why go to Germany? Why go to the decadent, capitalist West? The fact is that Magnetogorsk is not enough. We do not have the production capacity – and even that is being gradually turned to arms, to tanks. So our buying commissions go out. To Germany for instance. They buy this capitalist machinery against barter deals of oil or grain or perhaps the Tsar's jewels. How does one know? They get it. And excellent machinery it is – if we could only use it. If."

He smiled sourly.

"Only one thing stops us. We have the machinery. We have in the district sufficient trained drivers. We even have the makers' instruction books on the use and the maintenance of the machines. Unfortunately there is just one flaw. The instruction books are written in the German language. And Moscow has omitted to supply us with a translation."

He spat on the floor of the vast shed.

"Oh yes. They know. Translations are being prepared. And no doubt in the fullness of time stoutly bound manuals will be despatched. No doubt there will even be membership of the Soviet Academy for certain cultured professors. But by that time these machines will be rusted solid...

"So now do you understand why I wanted you? You were like a gift from what our superstitious ancestors were inclined to call God. Brought up in Germany! Speaking the language like a native! Oh, I trembled indeed in case some other bungling fool behind a desk sent you to some other kolkhoz. Over there in that chest are all the manuals and handbooks. You can start right away."

"But – but I don't know anything about technicalities! I've never done anything like this kind of work before."

"You're going to start now, just the same, my dear Comrade Pekare."

He stumped over to a big, heavy-timbered crate and lifted the lid. He handed her the top manual.

"Translate," he ordered.

And falteringly she began to turn into her clumsy Russian the even clumsier technicalities of the manual-writers.

Gnotke stopped her after the first page.

"Good. It will not be literature but it will do. What a fortunate thing that the German language is so very rational and precise, that it manufactures its portmanteau words so that even a child can break them down to their meaning. Good. Put it down now. You will really start work tomorrow. You will have two typists to help and one typewriter . . . There will be one typist to write and the other to mend the machine as it breaks down."

He bounced over to the nearest machine and began to compare her words with what he found there.

"Splendid. Yes. We will certainly succeed in spite of them all."

Suddenly he turned to her.

"You think I am a strange and dreadful man," he accused. "A cynic, an enemy of the Party. Of the Revolution even. I will tell you . . . you're completely wrong."

Sincerity blazed from his eyes suddenly. "I am a good Communist, a dedicated one. I believe in the Party and the cause with my mind and not only my emotions. I believe in the cause a good deal more than I believe in the actual Party though. And I will tell you why. The cause, Communism, is a matter of reason, of logical, sensible reason. It provides the best way of life for the greatest number of people . . . Or at any rate, it will.

"But the Party, unfortunately, is not a matter of logic or reason. The Party is a matter of people, fallible – very fallible – people. Some of them are incredibly stupid, some are corrupt, some are merely vain and ignorant. Many of them hold high positions for no better reason than that they were heroes of the Revolution, because they led a charge against the barricades or made rousing speeches – or were just friends of those that did. Nonetheless even they are for the most part imbued with the spirit of the cause. The only trouble is their frailty.

"The Party is incompetent. Joseph Vissarionovitch himself is probably incompetent. Certainly he acts on the wrong advice too often.

"Nonetheless the Party is the instrument of the cause. Stalin will die some day. The incompetents will be weeded out. And in the meanwhile the cause must go on. Russia must be preserved and nurtured. Despite all its follies the country must be saved. I am one of those who will save it. And you will help me."

She stared at him, wide-eyed, marvelling. Of his sincerity she had no doubt. But his sanity was another matter. Already she knew that criticism of the regime was a dangerous game. Those critics that did exist took care to mask their views and express them only to the most trusted friends. The memory of the great purges were still fresh. And even the most trusted friends could be traitors.

Yet he had spoken to her openly and bluntly. Why?

"You're thinking," he divined her thoughts, "that I've said enough to be sent to the salt mines already. You are right. The Party invites self-criticism. It makes quite an orgy of it. Criticism of itself it does not invite – or permit.

"You are wondering also how I have dared to say such words to you, a stranger, one who might even be sent by the NKVD to test me out. Now I will tell you.

"You are too young to be from the NKVD, too soft, too pliant. Secondly, I need someone to talk to, someone I can unleash my ideas on. A man has to talk sometimes or explode. And you I can trust."

He smiled, a faintly mocking smile.

"There are two classes of people one can trust. Those who love one. That is, those who genuinely love one and are not merely tied by economic bonds or sentimental memories. The second category is the people who are in one's power. You, Vyora Pekare, are in my power.

"That is not simply because of my own position. It is because of what I know. I have read your file. I can destroy you. There is, for instance, your father. A letter from me about that Jewish connection . . . "

"I doubt if the Gestapo would be interested. You forget the Jewish strain is on my side of the family."

"True, but I bet you'd rather not take any chances. But

that will never be necessary. You have not the stuff of traitors in you. You are a book, my dear Vyora, a book which has not been written. On the title page a few words have been scribbled loosely by other men. But the book is still to be written and I will be the one to write it, to bring you into real life out of that fragile innocence which still pervades you. There is a negative quantity about you still. I will turn it into the positive."

He took her arm and they began to walk towards the back of the shed, through the tall, monstrous ranks of the machines.

"There is another matter," he said, his voice growing ever more gentle. "Your photograph in the file attracted me strangely. It was not for nothing that I said you had a pretty bottom."

By now they were almost at the rear wall, far beyond the danger of interruption from outside.

Vyora's heart was beating wildly. Though his hand was gentle on her arm it was firm. She felt it could tighten on the instant if she tried to escape.

"I am a man," he went on, voice thickening a little. "And men have needs. This is conceded even by the Party, which has re-legalised the holy institution of matrimony – though you must not think I am going to marry you.

"As you can imagine, in my position I have no difficulty in satisfying those needs. But unfortunately the women of this region do not please me. Frankly, they are dirty. They rarely wash and they stink in bed like a fishing boat. Also they tend to grow moustaches at a very young age – and some of them even have lice. It is not cultured to have lice.

"No. I do not care for the women of this region as bedmates. Their legs are too short and their shoulders too broad and I do not like dirty people."

And indeed, she thought, he was almost aggressively clean himself, almost Germanic in the gleam of his skin.

"There are aparatchiks, of course, Party women who come from Moscow from time to time. Mostly they are quite clean. But hard, Vyora, very hard, their bodies used by a hundred men, their tongues like little vipers and their hearts rotten."

He had by now taken off his coat and stood in his shirt sleeves.

"I don't think you'll be hard, Vyora Pekare," he said softly. "Start to take your clothes off, please. Not too quickly. I take a great pleasure in watching a pretty girl undress, a girl who will be soft and clean and trustworthy."

The pupils of her eyes had enlarged in the shadowed light and there was no will in her at all to resist. There was a sort of vacuum within her as if all the torrents of words he had poured on her had numbed her somehow.

She fumbled off her coat and lay it on the wing of a tractor. And as she undid her blouse she thought incongruously that she must look a mess. Her hair had not been done, not even combed properly, since she entered the train in Moscow. She had no make-up on.

"Such lovely breasts," he murmured. "Let me look at them a little before you take the rest off. Ah yes, the photograph did not lie. Such lovely, full yet small breasts and what a glow of health about them, what a rich pinkness to the nipples. I felt sure you had never been pregnant . . . Oh. You did not know? Pregnancy darkens the aureoles about the nipples . . ."

She did not feel even the slightest bit afraid now as the warm treacle of his voice poured over her and his eyes took in every curve and line of her.

"Now the skirt, I think. Yes . . . now the skirt. No. Not yet the knickers. There is something especially appealing about you now . . . Did you know that in this district half the women do not even own knickers or wear them perhaps only for their own funerals? This is a badge of poverty, of course. There are more important things than knickers. There is food, for instance. None the less it is the badge of poverty – and not here alone. In France, for example, I call to your expression the very phrase sans-culotte, the implication of the heart and soul of the glorious French Revolution. Now you may walk about in them a little . . . just gently back and forward."

He chuckled happily, deeply in his throat.

"A very sweet sight. Oh, but you are supremely nubile. You are a splendid sight. So well shaped, so natural. But then, I am told that there are in Germany holiday centres where men and women appear naked together to enjoy the sun. Perhaps some day . . . Now the knickers if you please."

Already he had taken off the remainder of his own clothes though she was not conscious of him doing so. It was as if he had become a presence rather than someone who was present; as if he was no more than a mirror reflecting her body. She felt no shame at all, no embarrassment, pulling off the last fragile garment though indeed she did turn away from him a little to do this.

"I was right," he chortled in delight. "Everything answers the advance description. Oh, how very, very splendid. Just walk up and down a little more and then . . . "

The entrance to the shed seemed very far away. The light coming through it made the tractors and the reapers and the ploughs and the harrows like strange, black outlines of unworldly worshippers at some esoteric ceremony.

"You can come over here now," he ordered softly. "We must not waste too much time. There is still work to be done back at the office."

With an eagerness that surprised herself she darted to his side, felt his small, square hands slide swiftly across the glossy silk of her body.

And in the back of her mind came the thought that in the romances it was never like this. Was she always to have such strange lovers?

CHAPTER 14

Yet, in Misgorod, strange lover or not, Vyora Pekare was happy, happier than she had ever been. For the first time in her life she was really needed, not needed as Papa had needed her as a reminder of her mother, but for herself, for what she could do, what she was.

And Gnotke knew that he had picked well, that the inspiration which had come on him when he first saw her file had not betrayed him.

The instruction manuals which she translated had the tractors in operation that summer. As Gnotke had planned, the grass, the weeds, everything that was green, was harvested and ensiled.

The collectivisation of the districts' pigs began. Groups of kolkhozniki scoured the country like locusts. Some were city youths and girls from Stalingrad, Rostov or Kharkov, rounded up and despatched to the kolkhoz much in the way that they themselves were to round up the animals.

They had about as much feeling as the beasts. They were children of the revolution and to them peasants and kulaks were traitors to the State, the hiding of their beasts an offence against the State. Even the older kolkhozniki, those who had themselves been peasants or kulaks – took a grim satisfaction in plundering their brethren. Each of them had lost his little piece of land, his one or two cows, his pigs and his chickens. Why should anyone else go free.

And indeed it was the older ones who were of most use in the campaign. For in the villages, when the approach of the lorries from the kolkhoz was seen, every animal and fowl was hidden save perhaps for an occasional scrawny pig left rooting in the streets as a sort of scapegoat.

The city people would have had little idea where to search. But the old kulaks, they knew. They knew where they themselves would have hidden their animals. And those were the places they searched.

Though a peasant might have hidden his pigs in the root cellar below his house and stamped the earth floor flat again until no trace showed, a peasant searcher would know there should be a cellar. And he would find it.

The pigs would be dragged out squealing to the lorries – but squealing no louder than the women who lamented the loss of their animals more than their men when the Red Army was on its recruiting drive. Men could be got and children too. But where would they ever get another pig?

Vyora went with Gnotke on only one such foraging expedition.

In a village they had succeeded in garnering only two lean sows.

"There should be more," Gnotke insisted. "Look. The

streets are clean. The people are quite fat. There must be more."

They were condemned by their prosperity. And there were, of course, other pigs.

They were hidden below the church, the gaudy, ramshackle little Orthodox church with its black-hatted, long-bearded priest protesting and weeping real tears as the kolkhozniki looted the wealth of the village from behind an altar that hinged back to reveal a tunnel beneath. There were twenty-five pigs in that tunnel, good animals, young and with fat already on their flanks.

A People's Court, a Narsud, was convened at once, Gnotke presiding. The proceedings were swift, the evidence brief, the sentence sure.

The little church was burning when they left the village with the pigs, and the priest was hanging above his own door.

"The priests are always the centre of reaction and counter-revolutionary habit," Gnotke said as he drove back to Misgorod. "It's the same wherever you go in the Soviet Union. And because the State still allows them to exist, to practise their superstitions, they presume. If I were a Christian I think I would say that that was no church. The animals had already desecrated it."

Vyora still felt a shuddering horror in her mind at the scene. The cold violence, the fear and tears of the old priest, the sullen, stricken apathy of the villagers that almost lacked the fire of hate, these memories stayed with her for a long time.

"He was an enemy of the people," Gnotke soothed her. "Did you not see how well-fed he was, too? And his good clothes. Yet this is a religion of poverty!"

He spat from the open window.

"I hate priests. If the Revolution ever fails it will be partly because of priests."

He fumbled in his pocket.

"Light me a cigarette."

Gnotke did not smoke mahorka. His were always "tailor-made" and they came from Moscow in boxes of five hundred, slightly scented and cardboard tipped. They were virtually his only luxury.

Vyora lit his cigarette as she had been bid. For herself she did not and would not smoke. Not from principle but simply because the habit had never caught her. Papa had rarely smoked and then only cigars which grateful patients gave him.

"I killed my first priest when I was nine," Gnotke remarked casually, puffing out a great streamer of smoke.

"Nine!"

"I was an orphan. And before the Revolution I was in a church orphanage. It was said to be kept by charitable subscriptions. We saw little charity. It was little better than the Lyubyanka, I fancy."

He sketched in a picture of an iron discipline, of skimpy rations. Of icy quarters, of beatings for petty sins and interminable religious ceremonies.

"They taught us to read and write and I suppose that was good. But nothing else was."

"So you killed a priest – but why?"

"He was a man of middle age, fatter than that one back there. I suppose some of the priests were all right . . . but this one made our lives a misery. He had fingers like lardy sausages. And habits with young boys."

"Habits?"

"He was a pervert, of course. He would send for them . . . the pretty ones you understand. It was hot in his room with a great ceramic stove always blazing. Some of the boys even liked to go there because for a little they were heated up in their poor clothes. Sometimes he would beat them and sometimes not."

"Could you not have complained?"

"We wouldn't have been believed. Anyway, one day he sent for me and when I hid, two of the older boys found me out in the potato cellar and dragged me to him. There was, of course, a reward.

"We were left alone. He picked up his birch and told me to strip. I refused. He rushed at me. And I snatched up a paper knife from his desk and stuck it straight into his fat, piggish neck. He died very quickly and as he died I urinated on him. Then I escaped out of his window and into the street."

He swung from the Misgorod road towards the river.

"We will see if there is any caviare at the fisherman's co-operative," he said.

And a little later they pulled up at the low, small huts on the banks of the Don where a score of families of fishermen made their living from the great sturgeon that nosed their way up the river with their vacuum cleaner mouths dredging the bottom, heading for their spawning grounds in the upper reaches.

Only one fish had been taken in the twenty-four hours before, a lank, slimy monster seven or eight feet long with its skin covered in horny warts, that was hung from a sort of gallows outside one of the huts. A woman was slitting down the belly as Vyora and Gnotke strolled up and her face beamed as her blade exposed the bulging roe sac of a female fish.

"They separate out the actual roe from the membranes and other tissues. Then it's salted and sometimes smoked. You've tasted it?"

"Oh, yes. I didn't like it very much though . . . "

"You'll like this. It's better fresh."

In fact Vyora thought it was worse as a man came up with a dirty saucer of the grey globules, sprinkled with coarse salt, and a battered spoon. But Gnotke plainly enjoyed it, finishing Vyora's also when she dallied. To Vyora's surprise he paid for what they had had and flushed a little at her expression.

"You've seen me take stuff from peasants. Now you wonder . . . ah? For these people I feel a little sympathy. Their trade is dying every year. Pollution is killing the fish. Down-river there are ever more nets. In a year or two maybe no sturgeon will come this far at all."

"Are there no other fish?"

"Perch . . . some carp . . . Oh yes. There are other fish. But Misgorod is too small a market. And the cost of salt or ice to keep common fish until they could reach market is too great. Sturgeon is the only fish they can get a return on. It keeps well and it needs little salt. They are a dying race."

He laughed harshly. "Ask her what sturgeon tastes like."

Vyora obeyed and saw a look of astonishment on the fishwife's face.

"Eat it!" she cried. "Eat it!"

"Maybe no living soul in this village has eaten sturgeon. They can't afford to. It would be like eating gold dust. Come on. We've work in the office waiting for us."

Gnotke's programme worked well. The collectivised pigs throve on the silage. They were housed in the kolkhoz buildings that had been intended for men. The kolkhozniki had to make do with what was left.

By the spring the kolkhoz president that Gnotke had appointed could report the availability of several thousand tons of pork. Moscow was pleased. And as a sign of its pleasure it acceded to Gnotke's suggestion to grow the traditional crops in the area.

The tractors began to plough up the vast fields. Rye and barley and wheat were sown.

Misgorod began to come to life. Gnotke established a street cleaning service, imprisoned two of the lavatory men for depositing their loads upstream of the town, even paid compensation to some of the kulaks for their pigs.

There was a feeling almost of hope in the countryside – or if not of hope at least that there was a hope of hope. Even the world news seemed better to those who read "Pravda" or "Izvestia."

Had the Hozyain and Hitler not signed a pact of non-aggression? Peace and a good harvest coming. Surely August 1939 was the start of the good times the Hozyain had promised.

Even when Hitler marched his troops into Poland on the first of September of the same year no one really worried. The Poles had always been a turbulent threat on the Soviet borders. Now Hitler would remove that threat. And naturally Joseph Vissarionovitch Stalin also arranged that seventeen days later Mother Russia should begin to take her share of the spoils. There would be plenty of the good fat Polish geese on the Russian tables this winter!

Only the attack on Finland was disturbing. Not in itself perhaps, for to students of international politics it was plain that the Soviet must act against a neighbour whose Fascist regime was a plain threat to her own integrity.

What was disturbing was the Red Army should not have engulfed the whole little country in a matter of days, wiped out its puny army and imposed its will on the little group of imperialist lackeys.

Instead Ivan lay bunched in death by the shores and on the ice of Lake Ladoga, dying gloriously it is true but dying just the same. There were no decadent Tsarist officers to blame this time. It was disturbing. But no doubt the fierce weather was mainly to blame. And if the good times were coming . . .

This was the period when the hard core of disillusion further solidified in Vyora Pekare.

With Gnotke she was making an inspection of a lower part of the town when they heard a disturbance.

Fleeing round a corner came an elderly man, blows raining on him from a host of youths and men. Stones were thrown at him and when he fell at last the crowd gathered to kick him.

Vyora waited expectantly for Gnotke to act. She had seen him twice quell a food riot with far more people involved, hardly raising his voice.

But now he did not interfere.

"They'll kill him, Ivanovitch!" she cried.

He turned, puzzled, to look at her.

"But he's only a Jew," he said – and turned away.

Then it was Berlin again in her mind and Rudolph Küster. And the memory of that fragment of Jewish blood in her own veins.

And it was all the same as it had ever been, would ever be.

Colonel Andrienko of the Red Army had always had a way with women, right from his boyhood in the early Soviet free love period. It was, he told himself, because he liked women. That is, apart from bedding them he liked to watch them, listen to them, talk to them.

Not that he respected them as thinking, rational creatures. There was in their make-up far too much of emotion for them to gain his whole-hearted intellectual appreciation, even the clever ones. In fact, clever women were to him a sort of *lusus naturea*, a freak. And when he met a clever woman he tended to treat her rather as an honorary man without the gentleness that went with his usual manner to the sex.

When he came to Misgorod it did not look to him to be the ideal leave station, for he still had some pieces of shrapnel in his shoulder from the Finnish campaign. But then at least there seemed to be plenty of women – and some attractive ones, too.

Vyora he first met in Gnotke's office where he had gone to register his arrival. Gnotke himself was absent, called to Moscow for a conference. And Vyora had to fill in his form, stamp it, record the details.

And Vyora was a little flustered then, the responsibility lying heavily on her shoulders. Gnotke did in fact have a deputy but he had no intention at all of letting him sit in the seat for even a few days. He preferred that Vyora should keep the reins even if she could not handle them. Whatever muddle she created could be sorted out when he returned.

Now Vyora was acutely conscious of the colonel's presence in the office, could feel the electric flow of his personality as he stood beside her. Her pen blotted twice.

"Excuse me, comrade," said the colonel politely and took the pen from her hand. He crumpled the form she had spoiled and in his own hand filled in the columns.

She turned a little indignantly and found his eyes laughing down at her. She smiled a little tremulously.

"We're not used to senior officers here," she said.

"Oh, we're not all so bad. We hardly ever eat pretty young ladies."

As he gave her back the pen his hand touched hers, firmly and deliberately. He saw her eyes cloud in confusion for a moment and smiled again. This one he would have, he thought.

"It is not a busy day, I think, in your office, eh, comrade?"

"Why . . . no," she agreed.

"Then it is an excellent day for an official to take an officer and show him the sights of the town, eh? Come, comrade, rank has its advantages too."

And as easily as this he drew her from behind the desk and out into the street.

A little later, after an inspection of the Don's brown

waters and a brief look at the kolkhoz, they were seated in Misgorod's best restaurant, which was not very good at that, drinking white Caucasian wine and talking as animatedly as if they had known each other for years.

Andrienko exerted every ounce of his kindly, powerful personality to captivate the girl. In contrast with Gnotke's brisk, efficient materialism, he was a revelation. It was a long time since Vyora had laughed so much or felt so relaxed.

The seduction was almost too simple. He asked her to direct him to his hotel and once there to his room.

And in the room he simply laid his hands gently on her shoulder and looked into her eyes.

"I think you would like me to make love to you, eh? It would be a pleasure."

Her eyes were very wide and her teeth glinted through parted lips as his hands stroked down from her shoulders to her breasts and then quite slowly began to unfasten the buttons of her dress.

"You have a very beautiful figure," he told her gravely as he led her to the bed. "It is a privilege to see it."

Now there was even more confusion in Vyora's mind for partly at least she had been thinking of Gnotke, thinking – in the beginning – that she would punish Gnotke by accepting the colonel, punish him for the Jew and his own unemotional approach.

But now as the expert hands caressed her there was no thought of Gnotke at all in her mind. She was not punishing anyone. She was enjoying herself.

In the days of Gnotke's absence, Andrienko learned all there was to know of Vyora Pekare, of her past and her present and her future. He grew genuinely fond of her, almost paternally fond of her for all their long languorous hours either in his room or out in the open, in the trees beyond the town.

This was the way a girl should be, he thought, simple, kindly, willing – and a little stupid.

Not, he thought, as they lay naked in the sun well down the river, like that fearsome writing woman he had also met in Vyora's office where she was stirring up trouble about some communication with Moscow.

Katrina Semyonovna, he thought. He could not imagine making love to her. He had read some of her books and despised them for their patently tendentious Party line. And the woman herself – he knew the type, the self-centred, self-seeking, ever-pushing type.

There was nothing of the soft woman about that one. She was as hard as nails and bedding her would be like a curious form of homosexuality, a man in a woman's shape.

He plucked gently at Vyora's nipple, feeling it rise in answer to the caress and knowing that in a moment her hand would steal to him.

Suddenly she laughed.

The bracelets he had bought from the old Jewish jeweller, the simple silver chains with plaques attached, had interlocked and for a moment they were tied to each other.

"You're handcuffed to me," she chuckled softly. "You won't find me so easy to get rid of as your other women."

He kissed her on the lips and the chin and the neck, working slowly down her body.

"I don't know that I want to get rid of you," he answered easily. "I think I might just keep you. Would you like that?"

She raised herself on an elbow and looked at him seriously.

"Marry me? Is that what you mean, Vanya?"

"Maybe."

Now he began to make a small chain of flowers and threw it over her head.

"I might mean that indeed."

And why not, he wondered. It was a long time since he had met a woman who pleased him so well. Why not marry, start the long process of family rearing, domestication. It would be pleasant to leave the barrack life at last. For the years were moving on swiftly and how soon would it be too late?

As they walked back to the town later they saw Katrina Semyonovna, perched on a log by the river, brooding like some bird of ill omen.

Had she been watching, Andrienko wondered. It would not surprise him. There were women like that – and men too. Maybe, he thought with an inner chuckle, he would find himself in one of her books.

He said no more about marriage then – or ever.

A telegram from Moscow was waiting for him, recalling him that day to duty.

Vyora did not weep when he left and he marked her up with another credit.

"I'll be back," he said on the platform. "In a little, I'll be back."

But of course he did not come back and he did not write and when Gnotke came back to Misgorod Vyora Pekare had only the silver bracelet engraved with the word Pamyat – Memory – as a reminder of what had been. She did not repine the incident and sometimes during Gnotke's brisk, selfish love-making she would remember the Colonel's gentle hands and grave eyes. It had been too much to hope for that he would come back, she thought. And at least those few days had been worth it, well worth it.

Usually she kept the bracelet in her drawer but sometimes she would wear it. Gnotke was quite incurious and never once asked where she had got it or why she wore it.

"I suppose," she thought sometimes, "I'm a bit of a tart really, lying with one man and thinking of another."

The thought pleased her rather than otherwise.

For a dull little girl, she decided, she had done quite well. Rudi, the Professor, Gnotke . . . and the Colonel. And yet sometimes they were all mingled in her mind so that she had to open her eyes and assure herself that the demanding body with her was Gnotke's, not Rudi's, not the Colonel's.

They were good memories, most of them, memories to cling to when despair was close.

Memories for a prisoner to keep alive.

CHAPTER 15

There are two refuges from strain – laughter and tears. For men, laughter is the usual escape. To laugh at danger is to reduce it just a little, or, at any rate, apparently to reduce it.

When death can be made a joke it can not then be so very terrible.

Soldiers do laugh on the battlefield. There is an ultimate truth in the joke of the wounded man who answered, when asked if his wounds hurt: "Only when I laugh."

For a woman tears are the more usual answer to the same problem. Tears do not in fact make danger seem less to the mind. Tears are in themselves a self-consuming agony which drown out all else. A person weeping or a person laughing feels less than a person in a normal state of mind.

Not that any of the girls of the Zhenski Battalion being bundled from the truck in the shattered street in Misgorod could be said to be in a normal state of mind. There was fear in all of them, fear of what was to come, what was most certainly to come. And most of them were weeping, withdrawn into a numb, semi-consciousness.

They did not see the few shattered bodies in the street, the broken houses, the smoke of the brief battle that the Panzers of the Waffen SS had won almost before it had begun. Only a scattered rearguard had remained in the town to fight them, a few ragged, starving privates of the penal battalion who had stayed because in the brief time between their NKVD warders leaving them and the Germans coming they had the freedom of the town.

They had gorged themselves on the stores in the food shops, drunk wildly of raw vodka, paraded roguishly in women's dresses or played wild games with cheeses as footballs down the streets. Their shrunken stomachs threw up the food as soon as it was down but they gorged again, determined that though they were to die, at least they would die with their bellies full.

Now their bodies lay here and there on the pavement. One had even contrived to drape itself over a projecting sign. Perhaps it had been blasted there by a shell. Or perhaps the man had climbed up there in a drunken spree – and had died there as the bullets careened down the street.

But even in a macabre way he was not really funny, not funny enough to explain Vyora's laughter, helpless, near-hysterical laughter.

Only Katrina Semyonovna neither laughed nor wept.

Unflinchingly, she recognized what lay ahead. Unflinchingly, soberly, she was ready to meet it. In her body she would atone for the past, atone for Sasha, atone for her own blindness. Grimly, silently, she would suffer. They could do to her whatever they liked. Nothing could be base enough, painful enough.

And Vyora's laughter was a jarring note in her resolve.

"Don't despair," she tried to comfort the slim, blonde girl. "Maybe . . . maybe this friend, this Rudi Küster, maybe he'll remember. Maybe he'll help you."

"But it's so funny, don't you see. It's funny. Back here. This very building. It's as if everything was going round and round on the same path, happening again and again."

"What do you mean?"

They were being bundled off the street now by their guards, bustled in through a doorway by hands that stole familiarly and lewdly across their half-naked bodies, hands like the hands of peasant women at market assessing the flesh on a living chicken.

"This office, I told you. I told you everything while we were waiting there."

And indeed they had been two hours or three in the truck, enough for a life's story to be told, enough for a history of the world it had seemed as they shared confidences in a darkness that grew increasingly noxious from the needs of nature denied and made more imperative by fear, and refusing to be denied.

They heard the driver cry his wrath as the door closed: "For God's sake I'd sooner carry cattle. Look at it. Look at the filth. They're beasts. Only beasts. Make them clean it out themselves."

Then the door was shut and the dusty passage was as it had always been save that now there were no waiting queues, no packed offices. Only the applications and the forms and the rubber stamps on their drying ink pads were the same.

"This was Gnotke's office," Vyora wheezed. "Where he brought me the first day I arrived in Misgorod. Don't you think that's funny then? Don't you think that's really a cream of a joke? And to find Rudi here, to be Rudi's prisoner – well, that just makes it perfect. Oh, perfect. Can't you see it? Oh, wouldn't it make a wonderful story for you, comrade author?"

And her laughter rang again down the corridor.

This had been her own dominion once, Vyora thought through giggles as she looked round the office. Through that door was Gnotke's office. No, not Gnotke's, the Comrade Major's office . . . No. No. The Comrade Major had used it only for two hours. No more, no less. Two hours she had said and one hundred and twenty minutes later the sorting through the file cards had been finished and the lists had been typed out. The very lists that had brought these others here.

"I'll tell you something else very funny, comrade author," Vyora said. "You shouldn't be here at all. It was a mistake."

The other girls were sobbing softly, seated on the floor, heads on their knees. Even Anna Turuchin was sobbing, very young now, the sergeant's insignia on her sleeve a mockery.

"A mistake?"

"Your code. The code on your card. I misread it. You were marked down as an Osaviakhim member. Or, I thought you were. It looked as if there was an 'O' on your card. But afterwards, when I was putting the cards back, I saw it wasn't an 'O'. It was only a blot, a smudge . . . But I couldn't tell Major Kroup. I didn't dare. I was afraid of her. I was afraid to say I'd made a mistake."

In the next room someone was saying: "Dump all the papers in that box. The S.D. will maybe make something of them. Pull the table out more. Into the centre of the room."

Furniture squealed and protested. Booted feet clumped.

"You should never have been in the Zhenski Battalion at all. But I made a mistake."

"There have been a lot of mistakes in Russia," Katrina answered. "A very great number. It seems to me now that the whole Revolution is compounded of mistakes."

For a moment Vyora's laughter stopped.

"I thought so too," she said. "I thought so when I saw them kicking the Jew. All Gnotke said was 'It's only a Jew.' I thought if he could say that and believe that then somewhere everything had gone wrong."

She laughed softly.

"But really it's rather funny. You can't deny that. Next door is my Rudi and my Rudi is a Communist and he will be scheming now how he is to save us."

Katrina shook her head sadly.

"Don't hope," she said. "It's better not to hope. I think that was what kept them alive in Vorkuta, not hoping, not daring to hope. Just surviving."

She felt she had learned a whole world of knowledge in her roadside talk with Ilya Rokossov.

"You'll see," Vyora insisted. "I know the Germans. They're not like the Russians. I lived in Germany. I know them. And Rudi . . . he's gentle."

She laughed again.

"You'll see. He'll do something terribly clever and we'll all be free. You'll see. What a joke on Hitler to have Rudi leading one of his spearheads."

It was a long time since Katrina Semyonovna had done anything impulsive. Now she put an arm around the girl's shoulder, still quaking with her laughter. She felt an infinite sad wisdom within her, as if now she stood a little outside the world and could divine all that was going to happen, all that would ever happen.

"You mustn't mind too much," she said. "Whatever happens you mustn't mind. That's salvation."

The door to the other office opened. A vast figure loomed there, outlined against the greater light in the other room so he seemed larger than life. And indeed Corporal Henschke was larger than life, larger than normal life.

He crooked a huge finger.

"Come through," he said in almost unintelligible Russian. But the gesture was unmistakeable.

The little, sad column, the twelve girls rose from where they had squatted on the floor and followed him through to the other office, to Gnotke's office. He did not look back to ensure that they obeyed him. He had crooked his finger, beckoned. He knew they would follow.

And in the other room it was Corporal Henschke who took the girls' gaze as they lined at his gesture against the wall, Henschke and not his officer.

Ernst Henschke was almost a caricature of a caricature of a Hun. Six feet six in height, huge-shouldered and small-headed, he had a face like a baboon, even to the enlarged canines that could always be seen since his mouth was never quite closed since as well he had adenoids. Between his eyebrows and the close-cropped fuzz of hair on his pear-shaped head there was, it seemed, only a scant inch of forehead. He looked more animal than man and from the cuffs of his tunic little tufts of hair burst out over his wrists as if beneath the clothes he was pelted like a bear.

And yet, if he was an animal, he was an animal under command.

Under the command of Herr Hauptman Rudolph Küster.

It was Rudi all right. Vyora had no doubt of that. She tried to catch his eye, to make him see the pure, hilarious unreason of this strange encounter, this improbable reunion. But steadfastly he failed to catch her eye. But then of course he would not want to do so in public. In public they must be strangers. Later they would talk and discuss what had happened and marvel at the strangeness of the world. It was funny. It was incredibly funny.

And he had changed hardly at all. He was the same Rudi who had first felt up her legs, the same Rudi who had been so serious about the business of politics even as he had taken her. She would have known him anywhere. Even in the dark, she thought, she would have known him.

But of course he had to keep up this front. He had to remember that whatever he was inside on the surface he wore the uniform of a Captain of the Waffen SS. She wondered if he still had that little boy habit of mashing up his strawberries in the cream, making a pink, gruesome mixture of the dish. She was sure he did. Men never changed.

Now he was addressing them, still seated with legs crossed on the chair that had been Gnotke's, the chair that Gnotke had boasted was the one comfortable seat in Misgorod.

"You are prisoners," Küster said in harsh but exact Russian. "Shortly I will question you. You will tell me what you know about your own troop dispositions. You will tell me of future plans. You will tell me what mines or booby traps have been set in this town, contrary to the rules of the Geneva Convention of 1906.

"I am an officer of the German Army. I am at present in command of the town of Misgorod. I am entitled by international law to ask you these questions."

Vyora Pekare chuckled softly to herself. He could ask what questions he liked. They could not tell him. No one there knew the answers. They knew nothing.

Küster's gaze swept them bleakly.

"Where is Corps Headquarters? Where is Division Headquarters? Where are Army Headquarters? Who is in command of the area? What are the plans for countering our advance?"

No one answered. No one could answer.

"Very well. You refuse to answer. I will make an example of one of you."

His gaze swept along the line of tattered girls and women, lingering on each for a moment before it passed on. Vyora saw his gaze on her and she smiled at him, a swift secret smile to show that she knew and understood that he must for the time being pretend he did not know her.

"That one, Corporal Henschke."

"Jawohl, Herr Hauptman!"

The corporal answered in a thick South German accent and stepped towards Anna Turuchin.

"No."

Katrina Semyonovna had stepped forward boldly, eyes unafraid.

"Take me. She is only a child."

Henschke's hand spread across her face and pushed. She slammed back against the wall, crumpled slowly to the floor, mouth open, almost unconscious.

"The sergeant." Küster's calm voice insisted. "The sergeant, Henschke. One starts with the senior ranks."

Anna Turuchin's blue eyes were staring, her round, chubby face rigid in a sort of catalepsy. She had been so proud of her promotion. And now it was her doom. But perhaps anyway she would have been selected.

She was the youngest there. And in her peasant way one

of the prettiest. She would have been the one to be picked all right.

Her teeth had clamped into a rigid lock that brought out little ridges of muscles along her jawbones. But she did not move as Henschke beckoned. He reached out an abnormally long arm and jerked her forward, his hands enormous paws on her slim wrists.

"Has anyone anything to say?"

Küster's voice was cold and impersonal as he scanned them all again. There was no answer. There could be no answer.

And in the mind of Vyora Pekare the first doubt came. How far would Rudolph carry the masquerade?

"Strip her, Henschke," Küster said coldly. "The top first."

The girl shuddered as the huge hands ran up the buttons of her tunic and jerked it off. Underneath she wore, like all of them, a coarse vest. This Henschke did not even try to pull off. His great paws simply ripped.

Anna's plump, perky breasts jerked upward as their confinement ended. Küster surveyed her coldly for long moments, no spark of emotion in his eyes.

"She is well equipped for the feeding of young," he said at last.

And again his gaze swept the other women, unemotionally, coldly, questioningly.

"Has no one anything to say to save the sergeant from further inconvenience? So be it. Carry on, Henschke."

The corporal's big mouth had a hungry smile as he gripped the waistband of Anna Turuchin's trousers and ripped the garment in two. Beneath were a pair of old, stained cotton drawers. Henschke's hands demolished them in an instant.

The girl had begun to weep at last, face dissolving into blotchiness with her tears. Deliberately the corporal spun her round slowly, as if inviting them all to gaze on the body that was being prepared for the sacrifice.

His hands closed across her breasts for an instant, nipping them, then plunged down the smooth, round belly to the scarcely grown forest of her pubic hair.

"I can't offer to stop the corporal when he starts," Küster

observed. "If anyone has information to give – give it now."

Katrina Semyonovna shook her dazed head and tried to throw herself forward.

"Take . . . take me," she begged. "Free the girl. Please . . . "

She fumbled at her buttons.

"Spare her. Spare her."

Henschke stared for a moment at her small, stringy breasts, at her skinny belly. And terribly, derisively, he began to laugh. This time he did not even throw her back against the wall. He simply turned his heaving, laughing back on her.

"Now, Herr Hauptman?" he asked.

"Now, Henschke. You may begin."

From all the women there was a low, concerted groan, a strange mingling of terror and something else as the giant corporal slipped off his trousers and revealed himself in all his swollen, distorted vastness. Nothing at all was normal about Corporal Henschke.

Now, with no effort at all apparent on his face, he lifted the sergeant, Anna Turuchin, and laid her on the table, buttocks on the edge, legs dangling, sprawling.

His hands pressed down, holding her effortlessly and his vast body moved in as she began at last to scream.

CHAPTER 16

"He should have taken me! He should have taken me," Katrina Semyonovna was sobbing on the floor. "It's my fault. It's all my fault."

Black jackboots halted just in front of her face.

"Your time will come," Küster said quietly. "For all of you, it will come. Have no doubts of that. You have failed to co-operate. You must take the consequences."

And without another look at any of them he stalked from the room, followed by the corporal.

Incredulously Vyora stared at the closed door. He hadn't known her. Rudi had forgotten her. Vyora Pekare was laughing no longer.

In a corner the other women were gathered round Anna

Turuchin, comforting her, soothing her – and strangely excited by what they had seen happen to her.

A woman dabbed at the girl's thighs. Another tried to slip her torn clothes on again.

"But what a man. What a man," a coarse voice mused. "And I don't mean the officer."

Now, because another had suffered, they had forgotten their weeping for a little, forgotten also the hauptman's promise. There were hungry troops beyond that door, and all of them must go the same way as their sergeant.

On hands and knees Katrina Semyonovna crawled to Anna's feet.

"Forgive me!" she cried. "Forgive me . . ."

Wildly she kissed the sergeant's feet, wildly and fervently. And for the first time her own tears began to flow. As the others stopped their weeping she began.

"Gentry," scowled the woman who had admired the corporal. "They're always the same – gentry. The Moscow ones. The fancy women . . . Oh, get out of it, you dirty cat."

And viciously she tugged back on Katrina's hair, tugged her head back and slapped her viciously across the mouth.

"You wanted it," she sneered. "You wanted it and you'll get it all right, fine lady. Now get off and eat your own sick somewhere else."

"You don't understand. It's my fault . . . my fault . . . "

Tears blurred Katrina's vision so that she could not see the wild faces glaring down on her, the hands that slapped and pinched and dragged her about the room in a furious explosion of irrational resentment.

A strange, warm glow began inside her, a glow that started nowhere in particular but began to centre in her loins as, like a pack of wolves attacking the sick member, the other women hurled ever more violent abuse at her, heavier blows.

"Here!" cried the coarse one. "We'll show her what we really think of her fancy ways. Hold her now . . . "

And as the wet warmth sprayed across her body in the final gesture of ignominy Katrina Semyonovna's body twisted in its own inner warmth of ecstasy.

"My fault . . . My fault . . . " she cried happily with the

tears running down her cheeks to mingle with the other wetness. "I have to be punished. I have to suffer."

Vyora Pekare had crouched in a corner all this while. She was in one corner and Anna lay in the other, limp, legs crossed laxly, breath hoarse and patchy. And the other nine women, like viragoes from a nightmare, fought each other to pour fresh humiliation on Katrina Semyonovna.

Vyora's eyes were wide but she was seeing nothing, nothing at all. Her mind was an almost blank. It had not happened. It could not have happened. Anna had not been raped before her eyes. The women were not abusing Katrina's body. Rudi had not denied her. Maybe even she had never come to Russia. Maybe in a minute she would awake and Papa would be calling her, chiding her gently, telling her she was late for school.

Again the outer door opened and a thin, small Rhinelander gazed in at the women. His nose wrinkled in disgust.

"What a lot of dirty beasts," he muttered in German.

"Who made them beasts?" Vyora retorted instinctively in the same tongue.

The soldier smiled thinly.

"Ah. Speak German, do you? Then you'll be the one. On your feet now. On your feet."

Vyora pulled herself slowly erect and hope irrationally came back to her. Rudi had recognised her after all.

She felt a glorious surge of warmth to her heart. Of course it was natural that he should have denied her before those others. Now that she thought of it, it was very natural. He would not dare reveal his secret, their secret, in public. In this world there were too many spies about.

"Come on then."

The soldier propelled her out through the door, a hand caressing her left buttock familiarly through the rent in her trouser seat. But she forgave him that. He was taking her to Rudi.

In the corridor there were twenty or thirty men waiting.

"Rest of you can go in now – if you want. Though speaking for myself I'd as soon hang it out the window. Talk about dirt. I've seen less shit in a pigsty."

"This one don't look too bad."

A hand reached for Vyora. The Rhinelander struck it down.

"This one's reserved for the captain. So keep your dirty paws to yourself. There's plenty in there for the rest of you – if you take your turn. But I'd put a hose on them first myself if I was that way inclined which I'm not, being happily married, thank goodness."

"Never mind. Next battle we'll capture some nice little boys for you . . ."

"You're another . . ."

The Rhinelander pushed her through the corridor of hungry men and behind her Vyora heard the first screams from the women. They were not very loud screams, she thought.

And again the laughter was bubbling up within her, the laughter at the divine humour of it all. It was naughty of poor Rudi to have made Anna suffer like that. But this was war and people suffered in war. Anna had been a little sacrifice made so that she and Rudi could be safe.

Up the stairs she knew so well, the dusty uncarpeted stairs that led to Gnotke's quarters, to her quarters, no . . . to Rudi's quarters.

And soon there would never have been a war and she would never have gone to Moscow. Soon it would be all right again.

The soldier knocked on the door she knew so well.

"I've got the girl here, Herr Hauptman. Will I bring her in?"

He pushed the thin deal planks of the door and thrust Vyora ahead of him. His fingers gave a valedictory tweak to her left buttock and for an instant she almost loved him because he had brought her to Rudi.

Captain Rudolph Küster was seated again in the chair that had been Gnotke's not a comfortable one this, but as Gnotke had often pointed out, a man did not often sit in a chair in his bedroom.

"Rudi!"

She heard the door close behind her as she ran towards him, arms outstretched.

But Rudolph Küster did not respond. He gazed at her coldly and before her arms reached him his gaze switched to behind her back. Before she had touched him she had halted, turning.

And before she saw the other she knew they were not alone.

Looming where he stood behind the door, the giant corporal's face twisted into its slow, hungry animal smile.

"Well, Corporal Henschke, are you fit again?"

"Jawohl, Herr Hauptman. Quite fit."

Not believing this was happening, Vyora Pekare felt the great, ape-like hands close on her arms. She was helpless in their hold, utterly helpless. And Rudi was gazing at her as if she were a stranger, as if he had never seen her before.

"Very well, corporal. Take her now."

CHAPTER 17

Life is like an onion. Skin after skin of illusion imposed on the inner, radical core. And progress through life means the removal of these skins, the shedding of illusion after illusion until the final core is reached.

Vyora Pekare had shed a multitude of skins since first she left Berlin. She had lost the illusion of the efficiency inherent in the Soviet system. Gnotke had taught her that, though the ideals might be perfect, the system had to be fought and manipulated if the ultimate aims were to be achieved. Yet Gnotke had ripped away another illusion when he said, "It's only a Jew." In the last weeks illusions had been ripped away with bewildering rapidity.

Yet at the core of her being had been one certainty. Rudolph Küster loved her. And she loved him.

And now this same Rudi was giving her to this man-ape.

Would there be anything left at all when this final onion skin was ripped away? More than the physical threat she dreaded now the utter void that must open in her heart.

But she made no resistance when Henschke's paws fumbled her tunic buttons open, when his great fingers dug into what was left of her trousers and pulled them apart.

She stood there, searching inside herself for what lay within the last layer. In a way she was not there at all, not standing naked in front of the purely animal gaze of the gigantic corporal and the abstract eyes of Rudolph Küster.

The paws strayed up and down her body and she did not feel them. She felt only the last iciness in herself, the ultimate loneliness. Now she believed at last that nobody cared. Now it did not matter at all what happened to her, for if anything is to matter someone must care. She did not even care herself.

But Rudi, she thought, oh, what have they done to Rudi.

The corporal thrust her forward suddenly across the high, old-fashioned bed.

Her eyes were on Rudi's even as she felt the heat of the corporal behind her, the hot flesh seeking her out.

What had they done to Rudi?

And suddenly Rudi was jerking from his seat, speaking in his clipped officer's voice.

"That's enough, Henschke! That's enough!"

"But sir . . . I haven't . . . "

"I said that's enough. Get out! Damn you, get out!"

There was a tiny fleck of spittle on Rudi's lips. Behind her, Vyora felt the clumsy withdrawal of the corporal to the door.

"Will there be anything more, sir?" He sounded very stiff. He was puzzled. She gave an inner giggle. It was no time for a giggle, but relief and danger bring the same reaction. Puzzled and stiff . . .

And again the door closed behind her.

Now at last the mask was off and Hauptman Rudolph Küster was Rudi again.

"I couldn't go through with it."

Wonderingly she saw tears had begun to run down his cheeks, a terrible fountain of tears, a lifetime of tears coming all at once.

"Rudi," she begged. "Rudi . . . don't . . . don't cry. It's all right . . . "

And he was in her arms now. She was seated on the bed, naked but not at all embarrassed, not surprised, not anything but the old dark comforter of man. His head was in her lap and her fingers were running gently through his hair as they had done in the old, old days. She stooped so that she could kiss his forehead.

"There, there," she cooed. "There, there . . ."

She could feel the heat of his tears on her thighs, trickling down into a mounting pool that gathered there while her legs were closed but which would spill as soon as she moved.

And still he sobbed.

"I couldn't . . . Not you, Vyora. I tried. I tried. But – not you. My God, not you, too."

And as his shoulders heaved and his head buried itself in her body she felt her own tears begin.

What had they done to Rudi? What had they done?

At last the passion of his inner sorrow began to die. At last he lifted his head from the smooth, soft skin of her thighs, and not rising, gazed into her eyes.

"I never thought it would be like this when we met again. But . . . who could have known."

She kissed him again, between the eyes, her nipples brushing across the backs of his hands as she stooped. But the contact raised no faint spark of desire in him. And slowly, painfully he straightened.

"Liebchen," he said softly. "You have forgiven me without knowing why I did what I did. Now you must know. You must know and then perhaps forgive."

While she watched and waited, not disturbed now but with a sudden maturity in her that had never been there before, he fumbled with the lower tunic buttons and then the fastenings of his trousers. With a despairing gesture he threw the garment wide and stared wildly across her head.

"There," he muttered hoarsely. "That's it. That's Rudolph Küster, now. That's what they've done to me. That's our fine, bloody war."

And for a moment she gazed into a crater of scar tissue, into the riven flesh between his thighs.

"A shell splinter," he said. "A shell splinter . . . when we were throwing the English out of France. And Rudi Küster is no more a man. He even has to piss like a woman sitting down."

Suddenly his face was convulsed with tears again and he buried his face between her breasts, sobbing uncontrollably.

"Oh, Vyora . . . Vyora . . . "

Gently she led him back to the bed and they lay there locked together in a long, terrible paroxysm of grief and despair. They kissed and their tears mingled and their bodies clung together convulsively in a sorrow that burned and cleansed them both.

"A Nazi! Me a Nazi! You can't imagine it. You can't . . . I can't. I'm the Rudi you knew. I'm the one who wanted everything for the people, justice, truth, freedom. That man's still here inside me. But he's not a Communist any more . . ."

"Nor I . . . Nor I . . . Oh, Rudi . . . " She nuzzled against his cheek, body writhing vainly against his in an utter futility.

"It started when they called me up," he remembered. "I went into the army with the same beliefs I had when I left you. But . . . God, how do you explain . . . "

There had been the comradeship of the army, the all-enveloping comradeship. At first he had tried to be an outsider, to despise their murderous games. But he had a natural ability at everything military. Without even trying he became a corporal – then a sergeant.

Still despising Hitler, still hating Nazism, he had crept a rung or two up the ladder.

Then had come war. The platoon commander had been knocked out in Poland. The platoon was in a bad position.

"I had to take command. I had to. I couldn't let them all get killed. These were my friends, my comrades."

He had saved the platoon – and had been rewarded by a field commission.

"That hooked me, I suppose. Me, an officer! Well, you know what my father was. A slater in a village outside Berlin. He loved it. 'My son, the Herr Leutnant'. And I loved it too. I'd been hooked . . . Not to Hitler, not to Nazism. To the Army. I was in it and of it now. I saw myself as a general eventually. A general! Decorations all over me. Taking the march past. What a lot of bloody crap! But that was me. Poor Rudi was a long way buried. It was Herr Leutnant Rudolph Küster."

He twisted away from her a little.

"I used to think of you a lot, how you'd look at me when I came back an officer, how I'd explain it all to you and show you where we'd gone wrong. But you didn't write . . . "

"Letters from Russia – what would they have done to you?"

"So that was it? I thought you'd found someone else. When I had leave I used to prowl round all our old haunts. I used to have some flashy tart with me all the time, and I hoped I'd see you and you'd see me and then I'd ignore you, cut you dead as the English say. That was the sort of mind I'd picked up. But of course you'd gone as I found out at last. You'd gone – and that was that."

His face grew more sombre.

"I didn't have all that much time anyway. It was France next on the bill of fare for the Berchtesgaden menu. And the SS had their eye on me by now. I got a troop of tanks in their Panzer division."

He shook his head sadly.

"No one who hasn't conquered a country can know how we felt, steaming on across kilometre after kilometre with no resistance to speak of. Through one village after another, towns, cities. Victory upon victory upon victory.

"And those French girls . . . I had three in my tank in one day. Three. I despise the French men. But the women, they were lovely. And they loved it. They weren't playing. We gave them something they had lacked for a long time. Don't let anyone tell you about the French as marvellous lovers."

A hoarse sob burst from him then.

"Lovers! I should talk about lovers now."

Shuddering he buried his face in her breasts again.

"It was outside Calais. Those bloody English. They were beaten but they hadn't the decency to admit it like the French. And so bloody silly . . . Sitting on top of the tank like the monarch of all I surveyed. Whizz-bang! And some bloody Englishman had fired off a twenty-five pounder and

Leutnant Rudolph Küster had his knackers sliced off as sweetly as if a surgeon had done the job. I thought of killing myself, you know."

"Of course, liebling, of course."

"Then there was hospital. Then they said I was fit for service . . . with jokes you understand, medical jokes about the kind of service I was fit for . . . And then this Russia thing."

He sank back on the bed away from her. His eyes plumbed into a hidden vastness beyond the boards of the ceiling.

"I've done terrible things, Vyora," he mouthed softly. "You've seen . . . But today was nothing. Nothing. My God, Vyora, when I think of the things I've done or I've ordered done . . . It was because of *that*."

He sighed painfully.

"I'd lost it. A woman couldn't know what that means to a man. I'd lost it and . . . all I could do was make it seem not to matter.

"Henschke . . . I used Henschke. He's only an animal in the shape of a man. I used him. I made him take women in front of me. I made him do it so I could despise the act as I despised him. That poor girl downstairs . . . dozens like her. Henschke . . . he's insatiable. Like a stud bull. If it's there he'll have it. And because he's a moron, because I despise him, I thought I could come to despise what I had lost. I thought so."

His face was twisted in a terrible anguish when he turned to her again.

"You've been in my mind always, Vyora. The knowledge that I could never have you again . . . Always there, nagging, nagging. A woman can't know. When I saw you I thought – Oh, I can't tell you what I thought. I recognized you the first moment I saw you among the prisoners. I . . . hated you then. You brought it back too clearly. The memories! Then I thought . . . Henschke . . . Henschke . . . brutalizing you, making you an animal too. That would have freed me."

Suddenly he kissed her, their lips meeting in a long, hot yet passionless pressure. He broke reluctantly away.

"But I couldn't go through with it."

"You couldn't go through with it."

With his head on her breast they fell together into a gentle, utterly relaxed sleep.

CHAPTER 18

Henschke made good coffee. He brought in a pot of it when Rudi called him, steaming, fragrant, real coffee, not ersatz. And with it there were crisp biscuits. The orderly's huge hands that had so recently been clawing the clothes from helpless women were now finicking, delicate as they handled the tray with its Dresden china.

"That'll be all, Henschke."

Rudolph smiled at the girl, clad again in her rags of clothes.

"Dresden china. Funny for an officer in war, eh? For a Panzer? An SS man. My mother made me take the cups on my last leave. To remind me of home."

His face slipped into sombre lines as they sipped. In the streets outside there was the clatter of machinery as more tanks moved in.

"Brigade headquarters at last, I expect. I wonder how long they'll let me keep this place. There's a pig of a staff who thinks that fighting units were made only to annoy him. He'll try to clear us out all right – tomorrow or the next day."

He laughed boyishly and abruptly.

"He's played that one on us pretty often, pushed us out of the best buildings to make room for the general – not a bad stick himself – and especially his own little staff. But we've been one up on him last two times. I've got a sergeant, Schmidt, a real devil, Hanoverian. There's nothing he wouldn't do for a laugh.

"Now when Brigade evicts us we leave a few presents behind . . . a dead dog under the floorboards maybe. One place actually had a flush lavatory still working. We fixed half a pound or so of calcium carbide – you know the stuff, they use it for making gas for lighting; I used to have a cycle lamp once that worked on it – we fixed this carbide under the seat; Sergeant Schmidt did, that is. It was fixed so that when anyone sat on that seat down went the carbide into the water.

"And you know what happens when carbide and water come together. Practically an explosion. Whoof!

"We knew of course that the major would be first to use the seat – one of his funny little habits. Always squatting, that one. And he did . . . and whoof! Up he went! They tell me it was quite a sight as he came charging out of the room with his trousers down and the fear of God in his eyes. And to make it even better that carbide gas stinks like nobody's business; garlic, that's what it's like. The major was rotten with the stuff. The general wouldn't have him in his company for a week afterwards."

He laughed again at the memory.

"Well, you see – we don't spend all our time raping women and killing commissars."

His lips twitched and for a moment the laughter seemed ready to turn to tears.

"Is it true – about the killings?" Vyora asked and saw him stiffen.

"So the word has spread . . . It's true. But it wasn't our chaps."

He looked at her earnestly, beseeching her belief.

"We're soldiers. We're fighting men. I'll grant we're rough with women. But Ivan's no angel when it comes to that. I'll tell you – wherever we've gone it's been the same. The red carpet. Welcome. They don't love Communism here in its homeland. We were deliverers . . . deliverers. My God, I've seen old Ukrainian women hugging our boys with the tears of joy streaming down their cheeks."

"Then . . . who?"

"The S.D. The Sicherheitsdienst. The terror boys. The boys in the nice caps and the clean uniforms who come along when all the fighting's over.

"Racial purity. Rosenberg's doctrines. Russians are sub-human. But if only they'd take their chances. This war would be over now if it wasn't for the SD – over and with the Russian people on our side. Instead, the resistance is stiffening all the time. We'll win, of course. There's nothing surer than that. But it'll cost us a lot of good men. And afterwards there will always be trouble, local risings, an everlasting hatred. Some of the men coming back from leave say that now some of the rear areas which were quite friendly before are turning on us. Ambushes. Knives in the back. Drunken soldiers tipped in the river. All that sort of thing . . . And it could have been so different."

Despondently he swore. Then slowly he rose and went to the window, frowning.

"I'm wondering what to do about you."

She showed her surprise.

"I can't take you with me. We're probably pressing on in a day or two."

He turned and held her arms, gazing down into her face.

"I couldn't get away with it, Vyora. Not in action. Especially a Russian girl. My own men would be all right. They'd think it was a hell of a joke. Probably they wouldn't even use it as a lever to make me let them bring their own women. They might though, and it would be bad for discipline, impossible. And of course the word would get out. It'd be the chopper for poor Rudi and prison camp for you – if not worse. Division is setting up travelling brothels now. They're looking for stock."

"You could leave me here. Come back . . . on leave."

He laughed harshly.

"When we've taken Stalingrad we might get leave. Not before. As for staying here . . . The SD will be moving in in a day or two, when it's safe and clean for them. No. You can't stay here. There's only one answer. You'll have to go back to your own people."

An icy desolation fell on the girl as she gazed at him through stricken eyes.

"Go back? But . . . "

She fell silent. It was useless to argue. The logic of his words was unassailable. She could not stay in Misgorod. She could not go with Rudi. What else could she do but go back.

"It won't be too hard to arrange. There are bound to be plenty of your people round here. At least not far away.

And our own positions haven't been consolidated. It won't be hard."

"Back to the Zhenski Battalion." Her lips twitched in a bitter smile. "Next time we meet – maybe I'll kill you."

"You didn't last time," he smiled, trying to keep his voice light. "Women shots! I'll be safe enough."

He went to the door.

"Wait there a minute. I'll be back."

When he returned he carried a German greatcoat and a field service cap.

"Put these on; to get you out of the place. The prettiest little SS man we ever had."

Without difficulty they left the building by a side door. Vyora had a feeling of guilt as she left. She was escaping. But what of the other women?

And yet what could she do about them? Steal Rudi's gun, hold up all the men? Fight the German army? And after all – maybe the women were better where they were. Maybe, even, some would not want to leave.

In her brief hours in the barrack room she had heard them talking with bravado of men, lusting for them as if they were themselves the predatory species. Not all, of course. Not all. Not that little, young sergeant for one, playing at soldiers with naive delight – until the present reality stifled her laughter and her eagerness. For some of the prisoners then this would be more of a pleasure than a purgatory – and for that weird writing woman especially, for Katrina Semyonovna, who seemed now to writhe under the burden of some special guilt that only the humiliation of her own body could expiate.

No. There was nothing she could do, nothing at all. She could only be glad that she herself was free, alive and had once again met Rudi.

Küster's car, not a staff car but a small, open communications vehicle well adapted for cross-country work, had no windscreen or side screens and as it jerked into life the chill of the night struck on her still bare thighs, funnelling up the skirts of the greatcoat.

No one had stopped them or even glanced twice at the officer and the soldier at his side.

No one stopped them as they drove out of Misgorod, through the waving fields of rye.

"The harvest's late here," Rudi remarked.

Their talk had become distant, almost formal.

"The reaping was to have started this week. In this area it is always late. It is a short harvest. But the crops would have been good this year. Gnotke would have been proud."

Once a small convoy, some scout cars, a few trucks, two petrol tankers, passed them, heading for Misgorod. But there was no other traffic on this route.

"Winter comes soon, I suppose. It will be a severe winter here?"

"Very hard. The Don freezes solid. Last year there was skating on the ice. There was a dance for some inspectors from Moscow. On the ice. They roasted an ox on the ice and it did not melt. The Narkom thought it was very gay."

Like two strangers, she thought, like two stiff, cold strangers in the icy little car, churning across the rutted road.

"There is a side road up here. I'm going to turn up it. Last intelligence reports showed that your people were in force about three miles up the road."

"Will you attack them?"

"I don't think so. The mystique of the blitzkrieg is to strike on and on, ever deeper into the heartland. If there are enemy on the flanks they are left. Later one can turn to take them in the rear.

"On, is the policy, on, on, on at all costs. I think perhaps it is not so sound a policy here as it was in Europe. There we did not have so far to go. Take the capitals and the countries crumble round them. Here . . . the distances are so long."

He swung from the main road, such as it was, onto what was no more than a track. The car had to slow to a crawl because now it was dusk, late dusk, almost night.

What had been ruts on the main road were now deep channels, channels that were the exact width apart of the wheels of a country cart. The channels had been worn by countless generations of lumbering carts with squeaky axles, swaying along behind jaded old horses or mules who needed no guidance from the sleeping carters behind them.

Now the trees were ahead, a black belt of pine and larch. The car slowed almost to a stop.

"Better take off that greatcoat, Vyora. And the hat. There could be some of your friends about from here on."

She threw off her disguise and the car chugged another half mile into the forest before it halted.

"Rudi . . . Rudi . . . why not . . . come with me? You've been in the Party. They'd accept you. You'd – "

His voice was suddenly harsh again, the voice of the man who had set Henschke on her.

"No!"

And then, as if ashamed of himself, he patted her knee gently.

"Those are my comrades back there. We've fought together. We have ties that are nothing to do with politics or race. And what can your side offer? I've seen it, remember. We've been the welcome conquerors. We're . . ."

His voice broke.

"And I . . . You know what it's cost me. You know. Is that to go for nothing? Did I sacrifice my manhood for nothing? I've got to stay the course. I've got to justify that sacrifice. I've got to go on. After what I've sacrificed for it, National Socialism must win."

There was a desperate passion in his voice as he turned to her, holding her close for the last time.

"You and I, Vyora, we are caught up in something greater than ourselves. You – maybe you could edge out of it. You are a Russian but no longer a Communist. You believe in the freedom of all people. And so do I. But you have not lost a part of yourself for what you have been driven to fight for. You are not a sterile husk. You need no justification. I do. I've got to go on. Germany must win this war. I can't let my personal sacrifice be for nothing . . . nothing . . ."

And those were the last words of Rudolph Küster to Vyora Pekare.

For out of the trees there erupted violently what seemed a whole stampede of horses and of riders.

The lambskin caps, the black moustaches, the little,

virile horses all proclaimed the Cossacks. So did the sabres that proclaimed their trade.

In fact there were five Cossacks and that was enough. One swung down from his saddle to snatch Vyora from her seat. And two more had hold of Rudolph Küster before his hand could even reach the butt of his Luger. He was jerked from the car as swiftly as Vyora had been.

The girl felt herself swung aloft while the man who had gripped her shouted in the Cossack dialect: "Look. A Red Army girl . . . and see what the swine has done to her."

Her skin shone palely through the great rents of her trousers and when her tunic fell open it showed the bruising of Henschke's fingers.

"No!" she called. "No. That wasn't how it was. No. It wasn't him."

But her German-accented Russian made no sense to them. The leader of the group, moustaches iron grey and turned up proudly at the end, nodded to the youngest Cossack.

"Grigori . . . it is your turn, I think."

In the same moment he jerked Rudolph Küster's arm up fiercely behind his back. The German was forced forward from the waist in a travesty of a formal bow.

Grigori's sabre swung up and back, poised for a moment like a golf stroke – and came down with all the weight of his back and loins behind the blow.

Vyora screamed, a long thin scream as she saw Rudi's head jump from his shoulders and blood spurt up in a brief fountain from the raw flesh that had been his neck. Then the leader thrust the body away from him, letting it fall twitching to the ground.

The smell of pine needles was strong in the night air and Vyora screamed no more as she was hoisted to the pillion of the man who had taken her from the car.

CHAPTER 19

If Rudolph Küster had been there he would have rejoiced greatly at the scene in brigade headquarters next morning.

Wedelmann, the brigade major, was on the carpet.

"So," said the brigade commander with ominous calmness. "There is no bridge at Misgorod, no bridge across the Don."

Major Wedelmann gazed across his superior's head at an indeterminate point on the wall opposite.

"No, sir."

"And yet you informed me there was such a bridge."

"Yes, sir. The maps . . . "

"The Russian maps, Wedelmann?"

"Yes, sir."

"And you paid some heed to the Russian maps? Great God, Wedelmann, how many enemy maps have you seen? How many were accurate? Don't you know that when they make a map they don't only put in what's actually there. They put in what's supposed to be there, what's down on the plan, what the Party says ought to be there. (And the Russians weren't the only ones who did that, he thought. They weren't the only ones ruled by a Party. He was not of course a Party member himself. Otherwise he might have been commanding something more than a brigade). What steps did you take to confirm the truth of the maps?"

"Aerial reconnaissance by Storch, sir. Their photographs seemed to indicate a bridge – though not in the exact position indicated on the maps."

"Seemed to indicate? And what exactly does that mean?"

"Sir, there was a line across the river."

Wedelmann gulped. "On examination it transpires that it is some form of fish trap, sir, obsolete and ruined."

"A fish trap. My bridge is a fish trap! You understand that this means the advance is held up until Division gets enough pontoons up to make a bridge?"

"Yes, sir."

The general pursed his lips.

"Wedelmann, you are less alert than you were. Perhaps you have been on staff work too long. Perhaps a spell of regimental duties might be of benefit. It might perhaps teach you some of the realities of life."

"Never mind what Moscow says," growled General Budin, pulling as ever at the lobe of his right ear. "What are the realities of the situation? The realities, Vassily, the realities."

Corps headquarters were in a village school, a simple, two-roomed building, six miles to the north of Misgorod. That was one reality. Another was the map on the schoolroom wall. But whether the positions marked on it were realities or not was another matter.

The general continued to pull at his ear in the gesture that made him known to his troops, with some affection, as Long-Lug.

He was of the old school, Grigori Budin, a sergeant in the Tsarist cavalry who had plotted with the first leaders of the Revolution, been commissioned by them and in the turbulent years of 1917–1920 had been especially useful in sifting out Tsarist officers who could be persuaded into the Red Army.

"We need their experience," he had dinned into fellow-revolutionaries. "We need their knowledge. Pay them well enough and they'll be as loyal to us as they were to the Tsar."

He had grinned then with peasant slyness. "We won't need them for long anyway. They'll train up officers of the Revolution. And when we have enough of them . . ."

They applauded. And indeed the Tsarist officers gave good service to the state and Party that most of them hated. And, in due course, were liquidated in one way or another. Even Tukhachevsky, a staff captain under the Tsar and the virtual creator of the Red Army was to die in Stalin's purge of the generals in 1937.

And the army came into the hands of the old Tsarist NCO's. Of Semyon Timoshenko, of Voroshilov, of Budin's own old cavalry comrade Budyenny. The veterans of the civil war, the men who had driven Denikin's White army into the ground. But how many of them would survive this war?

For there was no doubt, Budin thought, the army had been caught with its trousers down. Or, he corrected himself, the intelligence sections. No one had believed that Hitler would attack. Even that grim old man back there in

Moscow had not expected the surprise attack that burst across the Polish plains.

And yet there should have been more stiffening in the Red Army. It should not have crumbled so fast. Privately, though this he would never have said aloud, he blamed the commissars. An army should be run as a war machine, not a political machine.

It was all very well to have commissars whipping up the men's enthusiasm, making them more devoted to the Party. But when they interfered with strategic decisions, even with battlefield tactics, there was something wrong, something very far wrong.

And when they could actually have formation commanders deposed in the very midst of a battle . . .

Altogether too many orders of a special sort had come from the Defence Committee in Moscow. The formula was always the same.

"General X has been found guilty of treason. He has been immediately degraded and removed from his post . . . Citizen X is condemned to death for treason. The sentence will be read to the accused and carried out by the officer so detailed by the Special Commission of the 'Y' Bureau . . . "

Treason! Losing a battle . . . and losing because the commissars made it impossible to win. He was reminded of an incident in English history when an Admiral Byng was executed for failing to capture Majorca. It was an execution which had provoked from a French philosopher the remark: "The English execute their admirals to encourage the others."

But of course that was not the effect at all. The effect was that a general made very sure first and foremost that he took no action at all that the commissars did not approve. He became like one of Professor Pavlov's dogs, conditioned reflex responding to the repeated stimuli. He slowed down. And of course had one eye always on Moscow; more interested in Moscow's opinion of his action than in the battle itself. Initiative was stultified, progress ham-strung.

His chief of staff, Vassily Jakubovitsch, looked at him unhappily.

"Moscow says we must advance at once, cut off this

Waffen SS advance." He held up the signal flimsy. "Misgorod must be retaken. The Corps must advance."

"Corps! What Corps! If we have a division all told that's the limit. Corps! That's Moscow. The realities, Vassily. That's why I told you we must have regard to the realities. If we had a full corps to play with, artillery, tanks, then yes ... I would take Misgorod in the morning. In fact, we have a disjointed division made up of troops who have broken once and will break again if they do not have a rest. How many guns, Vassily? How many guns?"

"Two troops of seventy-fives ... two one-o-fives ... two guns, not two troops."

"And their ammunition state?"

"Perhaps seven rounds to each gun."

"Realities, Vassily. These are the realities."

He stumped across the knotted, unplaned floor to the map again and gazed at it for a long time.

"I wouldn't for anything have the German's logistics problems," he remarked. "They're stretching out and stretching out all the time . . . Any sign of their pontoons appearing?"

"Pontoons?"

"Well, how the devil do you think they're going to cross the Don?"

He chuckled softly.

"I wouldn't mind betting they expected to find a bridge here. It's on our maps, you know. And our few prisoners have all been using Russian maps. Yes, I think we can expect that they'll have come steaming into Misgorod expecting a fine modern bridge across the Don ... a bridge that is a little less than a twinkle in some planner's eye."

He began to stride up and down, pulling again at the lobe of his ear with a calloused finger and thumb.

"Very nice, really, very nice ... There are no intelligence reports of pontoons being roaded towards Misgorod?"

"Not yet, comrade general."

"There will be, Vassily . . . Is there any tea left in that samovar? Pour me some, like a good fellow."

He drank the tea in the Jewish manner, putting a lump

of hard sugar in his mouth, straining the tea from its glass across it as his tongue held it captive.

"They certainly have pontoons at Army level. If I remember their organization aright there are two bridge-building companies to the corps – one with portable girder bridges for narrow streams. And one has pontoons for rivers like the Don."

He began to chuckle as a plan formed in his mind.

"The pontoons are our answer, Vassily."

"An ambush on the road, comrade general? We could do that. A swift raid, demolitions . . . "

Long-Lug laughed aloud.

"You have no imagination, Vassily!"

He strode to the door and peered out into the night. He could smell cooking fires nearby, meat scorching, stolen meat without a doubt, but meat just the same. That was good. Meat-fed soldiers always fought better. And it was too long since there had been any meat. There had not even been herrings this past fortnight and salted herrings were poor enough fodder for a fighting man's belly.

Vaguely, sniffing at the night air, he wondered where the meat had come from. It had a sweetish flavour, horsemeat or pork. He hoped it was pork. He hoped so most devoutly. If it was horse it could mean that there was going to be more trouble with the Cossacks. They had a reasonable objection to their mounts being stolen and butchered to make an infantryman's supper.

As an old cavalryman he sympathised. Here membered far back in his youth when he and Budyenny had been on a small skirmish against the Turcomans. The troop had been cut off, without supplies. And they had had to eat one of the horses – Budin's own. It was the worst animal in the troop by that stage, badly gone in one hock and a little blind in one eye as well. It would have had to be put down anyway. Even so he could remember his own revulsion as the troop sat round the fire, toasting strips of the horse on their cleaning rods. His horse. He had hardly been able to stomach it at first. But men had to live. Yet it was strange the bond that grew between a man and his horse. And if the

Cossacks cut up rough there might be more than horsemeat grilling tonight.

He hoped it was a pig they had found, some scurvy moujik's hidden nest-egg.

He was going to be very dependent on the Cossacks for the next spell. They would be his ears and eyes since it seemed that Moscow was not going to send him any spotter planes – if in fact there were any to send. It was everything for Moscow now, the guns, the ammunition, the petrol, the tanks. Out here they must just fend for themselves. And this would have been all right too but for that damned radio bleating out its orders and its exhortations by the hour.

It was time, he thought, that something happened to the radio, something drastic.

He would have a word with Shiryaev about that, he thought. Good old Sergei Shiryaev, old comrade Shiryaev, who had never wanted to be anything more than a corporal and who had contrived always to lose his third stripe when it came. Who had failed his promotion exams so abysmally that not even his length of service, his loyalty or his bravery could force him into commissioned rank. Lucky old Shiraev who did not have the remnants of a corps to worry about but only his own flea-bitten, lousy, scarred old body. Yes, Shiryaev would be the one to organise some small but permanent accident to the radio and cut off finally the communicating link with Moscow.

Then he could get down to fighting his battle.

He stumped back into the schoolhouse as a panting figure came running through the trees.

Vassily took the runner's message, scanned it quickly.

"You were right about the pontoons, comrade general. They're coming now. A scout from Maximov's horse spotted them. They're about thirty versts down the road. We've plenty of time to destroy them . . . Mine the road, mortar them . . ."

"No, Vassily."

The runner had gone now and they were alone again in the command room.

"We will let them go through to Misgorod," said Budin.

He was tugging his ear more furiously than ever.

"It'll be very hard to destroy them actually in the town," his chief of staff objected.

"That's so. This we will not do."

"But . . . they'll be able to throw their bridge across."

"A reasonable deduction."

"The panzers will be able to cross the river."

"Unless they make a very bad job of the bridge. Yes."

Vassily's face showed the whole gamut of emotions. Had the Comrade General turned traitor? Had the scarred old hero of the Revolution now turned his coat? Was he going the way of General Vlasov who was now fighting on the German side along with his troops? Was this the ultimate end of all Budin's recent cynical criticism of Moscow's direction of the war effort? It was hard to believe.

Vassily Jakubovitsch was one of the new school of staff officers, trained in the Frunze Military Academy in Moscow, indoctrinated from childhood in Party discipline and military theory.

War, as taught in the academy and the staff college, had had a dialectical simplicity. You moved across the map or the sand table counters that represented divisions or battalions. You gave orders by radio. And miles away vast, neat groups of men and machines moved as you planned.

Reality had proved somewhat different and since coming onto Budin's staff he had formed a mounting admiration for this coarse, uneducated soldier who could ignore the messages of his underlings – and his masters – who could tell by some sixth sense what was actually happening on the field.

It had been a disastrous campaign so far. But Budin's corps had ridden it better than most. He had kept his corps in being. The links of command still stretched out from his own brain to the man with the gun in his hand.

He had never expected this sort of treason and his own mind went into a panic as he wondered what he should do. Dialectically he knew there was only one answer. He should shoot his superior and assume command.

Let the Panzers over the bridge! Unleash them on the trail to Stalingrad! What was he thinking of?

And as if he had divined his underling's thoughts, Budin was smiling at him.

"You think the old brain's cracked, eh? But not yet, Vassily, not yet."

He went to the map.

"It will take two days at least to get the bridge ready for use. I will let them cross – the armour and the soft vehicles. And then, Vassily, then I will break their bridge. Do you begin to understand me?"

He smiled wolfishly.

"On the far side of the river we will have the panzers. On this side only soft lines of communication troops. When the bridge is blown the tanks will not be able to return. Nor will they be able to go very far on the other side. Their own petrol tankers always travel in the second echelon – which we will chop off on this side of the river. That leaves them only with what they have in their fuel tanks. Or, in other words, with an operating radius of a hundred miles from the far side of the river – in the best conditions."

His cracked fingernail traced a circle on the map.

"They can't go beyond this circle. They can't come back to Misgorod. They're isolated. When their fuel's expended we can mop them up at our leisure – or rather, Army can."

"Comrade general . . ." Vassily's face showed some alarm as he himself strode to the map and tapped a point with his finger. "Army main fuel dump is here – only thirty-five miles from the river. If they reach it . . ."

"It won't matter," Budin grinned savagely. "We backward, subhuman Russkis have not yet attained the heights of Western technology. Our petrol is not so refined as theirs – good enough for our own clumsy engines. But its octane rating is too low for the German tanks. They're tuned to use something approaching aircraft quality fuel."

He grinned again, this time at the respect, if not downright awe, in his chief of staff's eyes. He could see what Vassily was thinking: Old Long-Lug had thought of everything.

"You have it then? A simple little plan. Detach the hard troops from the soft – then mop up Misgorod. That won't be hard. This is a flanking movement and I don't think German HQ will be sending much in the way of reinforcements in this direction. The Waffen SS will have orders to push on as fast as possible and link with the main attack beyond the Don.

"The theory of the blitzkrieg is excellent you know – if you can reach the enemy's seat of government in time and destroy all organized resistance. It worked very well in Europe. But Russia is not Europe, whatever the maps may say. They taught you history, no doubt, military history? You will remember Ludendorf's theory of internal lines? The blitzkrieg flies in the face of that! Just as Napoleon did before Ludendorf had even formulated his theory. Indeed I should imagine that Napoleon is the best justification of Ludendorf, his inspiration, I wouldn't wonder.

"The faster and farther you push on, the more supplies you have to bring up. The more supplies you bring up the more troops you need to convey and guard them. Extend too far – and chop! If you leave an army in being behind you, you can be starved out of existence at any moment."

He smiled and pulled again at his ear.

"And we've got another general on our side that the Germans don't seem to have taken into account."

"A general?"

"The one Napoleon forgot too. The one that drove him back from Moscow . . . General Winter. It's going to be an early winter, Vassily, an early winter. And we'll be spending it in Misgorod while the Germans are dug in in wretched holes and trenches . . . or plodding on to Stalingrad. They won't go so fast, Vassily, in the mud. They'll use a lot more fuel travelling in low gears."

He shook his head at the folly of the German High Command and fell to a prolonged pulling of his earlobe.

"Now," he said briskly. "A signal to Moscow. Inform them that having regrouped my corps I am about to mount an offensive against the hated Fascist invaders of the Fatherland, or whatever today's phrase is. Then, call in all commanders down to brigade level – or perhaps make that battalion."

His chief of staff looked bewildered.

"Why, we're going to make an attack, Vassily, an attack. You don't suppose I'd send false information to Moscow, do you? But this is going to be a very carefully controlled attack, one that mustn't succeed – until the bridge is blown. A little light skirmishing round the outskirts – and no bombardments, please. We'll be wanting that town in a week or two. Don't let's knock it about."

A sudden thought struck him.

"That woman that's been plaguing me, the NKVD one."

"Major Kroup?"

"That's the one . . . always wanting to get her precious Zhenski Battalion back into the fight. Get her to the meeting too. I think we could give her some little job that wouldn't involve too much fighting – and would keep her quiet for a while. Yes, have her come too."

He snorted angrily.

"Women fighting! A damned silly idea. They're just not intended for it. Damned silly. But then maybe I'm an old die-hard, eh? An old fogey. Well, get on with it, Vassily. Message off to Moscow . . . conference in one hour from now. Meanwhile I'll take a look round the troops, see what sort of heart they're in."

And find old Shiryaev, he thought fondly. A yarn with old Shiryaev and a hint about the radio. And at least Moscow would be off his back. He could fight in peace.

CHAPTER 20

It was like walking out of one nightmare into another. The world was nothing now but series after series of nightmares for Vyora Pekare as she clung to the Cossack's belt and jogged numbly through the trees.

Rudi, she thought, poor Rudi.

And she had not even had time to scream, she thought. She had not been able to scream a warning. She was quite unconscious that she had in fact screamed. It seemed to her that she had been paralysed from the instant that she had been snatched from the car. That though her mind sought to scream her tongue had remained still.

In fact, though she might have called out some explanation to the Cossacks the whole operation had been carried out with such slick speed that her words would scarcely have had time to reach the men's ears before that swift sabre blow had been struck.

Rudi, she thought, I let you down.

And yet, the thought began to creep in on her, for Rudi maybe, this had not been a let-down. He would be tortured no more at least, the torment of his mind was over. After all, he had found a peace.

She was not conscious that she had been sobbing until the Cossack to whose belt she clung half-turned in the saddle.

"It's all right, little one," he comforted. "You're free now, back with your own people. That Fascist monster can't touch you any more."

Ahead the leader called for more speed: "The others won't be far behind that one. They tortured the girl to make her give them directions. They're bound to be just behind. Lucky for us the others got held up somehow."

He laughed harshly: "Wonder what they'll make of their headless boy when they find him . . . But isn't it a shame we haven't more men. We could have done a nice little ambush back there."

Vyora could have told them then, explained that she was not a tortured victim leading the enemy to her own troops. She could have told them what really happened, the true meaning of what they had done.

But she held her peace. The Cossacks had acted in the light of the facts as they saw them. And in that light they had been right. To tell the truth would help no one, she thought. To tell the truth would only hurt them, lay a burden of guilt upon them that they did not really deserve. She kept silent. And very soon regretted it.

"Comrade Pekare, you are being obstructive," said the man with the NKVD badges, a lieutenant. Behind him the commissar glared at her. It was at the commissar that Vyora kept glancing. He was a tall, thin man wearing glasses. He had a very long nose, hooked at the end. And at the tip a little blob of moisture kept forming, dangling until it seemed it would surely drip – and then being sucked back with the next breath. Vyora could not take her eyes from that drip, waiting for the moment when finally it would become detached.

"You claim that you were captured in an attack by the Zhenski Battalion on the position of the German tanks. That thereafter you and some dozen other prisoners were taken into Misgorod by the Germans when they captured it – and then that you alone were actually taken out into the country to be freed by a German officer. Does that sound like a convincing story? Does it sound like a German action? Can you really expect us to believe it?"

Vyora was seated in a chair in front of the desk where the NKVD man sat. She felt as if she was sprawled out everywhere. She could not forget the state of her clothes.

"Stand up!" barked the NKVD man abruptly.

Vyora shambled to her feet.

"Brace yourself up! You're a soldier of the Red Army. Act like one. Sit down. Stand up . . . sit down . . ."

Numbly she obeyed the orders which went on and on. Up and down, about turn, left turn, sit down . . . who told you to sit down . . . stand up . . .

"Now, Comrade Pekare, perhaps we can have the truth. Perhaps we will get at what you gave the Germans in return for your release. What secrets did you tell them? How many of our positions did you give away?"

Vyora's eyes grew wide. And within she wanted to laugh. But no laugh would come up through the numbed tissues of her body. What did she give away? What could she give away? What did she know? How could a recruit of only a few hours' training give anything away?

The drip on the commissar's nose grew so long that this time surely it must break away to a brief, vertical life of its own. But no. The nose wrinkled in a sniff and the drip vanished again. The commissar's gaze never left her eyes and in a way she felt more afraid of him than the young, hard-faced lieutenant who shouted and blustered but seemed a creature from another world.

There was something in the commissar's eyes that reminded her of someone else. She could not place the memory for a little. Then the lieutenant strode round his desk and gripped the tattered collar of her tunic. He shook her fiercely, hard face thrusting into hers so closely that she could smell the onions of his last meal.

"You silly little girl," he hissed. "Don't you know what we do to traitors, to men and women who give information to the enemy, who betray their Fatherland? We execute them. Your guilt is plain and all you can do is tell us all you know. Tell us what you told the Germans. Tell us what you know about their positions. This might earn you some clemency."

Vyora tried frantically to think, to remember something – to say anything. She would have invented German positions then if she could have found words, anything so long as she was free of this terror.

"We don't shoot traitors you know," the lieutenant said softly. "We hang them. Think of that, Pekare. Think of that ... And we don't have all the facilities of a prison here. If we hang anyone we just put a rope round their neck and haul them up to the nearest branch. Think of that . . . the rope biting into your neck, choking, strangling . . . feeling everything."

Vyora's eyes were glazed in horror. And yet it was not so much the lieutenant's voice that made her bones seem to melt. It was the commissar's eyes.

And now she knew the memory she had tried to recall. She knew whose eyes the commissar's reminded her of.

There was the same cold light in them she had seen in Rudi's when Anna Turuchin was being raped. The cold light of abstract pleasure, the pleasure in another's pain. With Rudi, when he had explained, it was almost natural. But... what was wrong with the commissar?

Fear, the great analgesic, had her in its grip and no matter what was threatened, what was actually done to her it would have been the same. She could say nothing. She could only stand there, seeing the commissar's eyes, seeing Rudi's eyes. Helpless.

Then the door opened and a greater fear walked in.

Major Kroup's square, bulky body filled the doorway.

"What's going on here? What are you doing with one of my girls?"

The lieutenant did not look round.

"Get out," he said coldly. "Don't interfere with the NKVD."

Kroup said nothing at all. Her big tombstone of a face simply set into hard, chiselled lines. And when he did not hear the door close the lieutenant's head swung slowly round. Then his own fear was quite comical. He snapped to attention, dashed off a salute.

"My apologies, Comrade Major, I did not know."

"You know now," she said drily.

"This girl was a prisoner of the Germans. Plainly she is a spy. Instructions are quite definite that personnel who escape or who claim to have escaped from German custody are to be treated with extreme care. They are to be examined and their stories tested. Order of September 14, paragraph seven."

"I read my orders."

Kroup's gaze showed no friendliness as she gazed at Vyora.

"You can go," she said flatly. "You too . . ."

The drip detached itself from the commissar's nose at long last.

"You have no right . . ."

Kroup's fingers fluttered on her purple-epauletted collar, on her badges of rank, the NKVD insignia. She said nothing more but jerked her head towards the door. The commissar's nose bit down towards his chin . . . And he headed for the door. But he halted there.

"That girl must be interrogated. Properly investigated."

"I have been interrogation officer in the Lyubyanka. Perhaps, comrade, I will see you there some time."

Her lip twitched in what might have been disdain or even perhaps a laugh as the two men vanished outside.

"Swine," she said dispassionately. "Toadying swine. But then all men are swine . . . Now, Pekare, what's been happening to you?"

Thankfully, Vyora told her story, knowing that now at last she was being believed.

Kroup stood beside her, a warm, sympathetic hand on her shoulder. Now Vyora found she did not flinch at the touch. Instead she seemed to draw strength from it.

The NKVD major asked few questions.

"Right. You've had a rough time, Pekare," was her main comment. "But not so rough, maybe, as the others? Do you think they're still in the same place? But how could you know that? No. Of course you couldn't. No. Well – better get back to the battalion."

"The . . . battalion?"

"Where else? You surely didn't think that because one battle went off badly the Zhenski Battalion would simply cease to be? Come along."

The lieutenant was skulking outside.

"Comrade Major, about the prisoner . . ."

"What prisoner? Do you mean Private Pekare of the First Zhenski Battalion? Comrade Lieutenant, I wonder how long it is since you finished your training – or if you finished it."

She strode off then with Vyora at her side, leaving the shaken interrogator behind her. Of the commissar there was no sign at all.

The commissar was in fact trying vainly to establish contact with Moscow. A fault seemed to have developed in Corps HQ's radio transmitter.

"Not so comfortable as the kolkhoz, eh? Still, it's a roof over our head," said Natalya Kroup as they entered the farmhouse.

It was a poor enough place, a long building which had housed under the same roof the living quarters of the farmer's family and the farmer's animals.

Only an open palisade separated the animals' room from the kitchen. Over the pot-bellied iron stove there was a broad sleeping ledge or shelf on which the whole family must have bedded.

There was no family here now. They had fled before the Zhenski Battalion moved in. They had fled hurriedly, too, that was plain. They had even left some of their food behind, a side of bacon dangling from the rafters. The salt in which it had been pickled was glittering on its surface like a frost. They had left some of their bedding, crude sacks filled with maize husks.

And though they had taken their animals, the smell of

their manure filled the whole building; rich, ammoniacal, comforting in a way.

A single oil lamp dangled from a string to the rafters and at first Vyora thought that the place was empty.

Then, from the bedding above the stove, a dark face bobbed up, glittering eyes fixed on Vyora.

"Tsiganka, it is your night for sentry duty," the major grunted as she led Vyora in. "I want you to check all the posts."

The half-gipsy slipped down lithely from her place.

"I kept you some borsch. Good borsch. Beetroot, not cabbage. It is hot on the stove."

"Good," nodded Kroup indifferently. "Now check the sentries. If anyone sleeps – report it."

Irina Tsiganka glared at Vyora with undisguised hate. But she said nothing. Tidying her uniform she made for the door where a rifle leaned against the wall. She gathered it up in passing, paused for a last backward glance and then slid silently out into the night.

"She does not like me," Vyora commented with a quavering laugh.

"She does not like anyone," Kroup answered. "If you were her, you would not either . . . Now take some soup. You look cold."

They sat close together on a rough bench by the stove and finished the soup. The borsch had some slices of sausage in it as well as the vegetables and Vyora found a curious languor creeping over her as she finished the meal.

"That uniform won't do you much longer," the major said suddenly. "In fact it won't do you at all. Better get rid of it. I'll find you something else for the morning."

Her own hands helped Vyora to doff the rags of the clothes that she wore. And as she stood close to her Vyora could hear her breathing. It came quickly, catching in her throat as she saw the uniform fall away.

"You'll get cold. Take my tunic."

The major, without her tunic, without her badges of rank and the awful power of the NKVD had a curiously amorphous shape. Great breasts sagged downward, like pillows, her belly was another pillow.

And now as she pulled off her uniform trousers her thighs were like pillows too.

A great mass of pillows, a vast mountain of undulating, soft flesh.

"I think you must be tired," she commanded. "Let me help you up to bed."

And her hand closed on the girl's thigh, lifting her and yet holding her.

Instead of hoisting her to the bed, the major was clasping Vyora to her, holding her tighter and tighter, nuzzling her huge shaggy head into the cleft between the girl's breasts while her fingers thrust at Vyora, thrust and probed.

Vyora Pekare felt a little apart, a little elevated from the actual sphere of existence. She felt as she had felt with Rudi, a terrible pity as she was lifted to the sleeping shelf and the urgent, demanding, undulant body of Major Natalya Kroup fell onto the noisy bedsack beside her.

CHAPTER 21

"Twelve. Twelve Red Army women, Comrade General. You can't ignore them. You can't forget them. You can't leave them prisoners in Misgorod."

"Naturally not," General Budin answered. "I'll have them rescued at once. I'll send in a division. Which one would you recommend?"

Yet, though he taunted the NKVD major, General Budin felt a rare sympathy for her. After all, he thought, she was human. She had feelings. Or was it merely hurt vanity that something of hers was not entirely perfect?

"It is not a matter for jest, Comrade General."

"Am I jesting, Comrade Major? Would I dare to jest with the NKVD?"

Kroup could see a smouldering light of satisfaction in Budin's eyes. She knew that he was thinking of the weakness of her own position. Here she did not have a company of well-trained, well-fed, well-equipped NKVD men to enforce her authority. In this corps there were only a score of police. They could not overawe anyone.

And the general was beyond being overawed by anything except absolute force. He had lost contact with Moscow. His force had been shattered and cut to a third of its size. He was short of ammunition, food and transport. Unless he could produce something very startling out of his fur hat, black karakal she noted, he was in any case due for liquidation. He was a dead man – and dead men fear nothing.

Her shrewd eyes saw the signs she had seen often in the Lyubyanka, the beginning of utter indifference. When a prisoner became like that there was nothing more to be done with him. Torture would have no more effect. Threats and bullying were like rain off an oiled roof. Persuasion was as useless.

When the stage of final indifference set in there was only one thing to do with a prisoner – shoot him.

Budin had not reached that state yet – and he was not a prisoner either. But in the next day or two unless his spirit received something to revive it, he would crack. He would become a living hulk and incapable of command.

And yet there was still that mordant light in his eyes, as if he had something up his sleeve.

Now suddenly he smiled.

"Comrade Major, I cannot commit my whole forces for the rescue of your women. It would not be reasonable. They are expendable, just as we all are expendable. Nonetheless, I do not like to think of Russian women in German hands. Therefore, if you are yourself able to mount an operation to free them I hereby authorise it. And I will be prepared to myself mount some small action at a different part of the German perimeter to draw their fire and divert attention from your activities. Does that suit you?"

She looked at him suspiciously. Was he trying to let her overreach herself? Was there a trap here? But she could see none. Abruptly she nodded.

"Thank you, Comrade General. I will notify you of my plans."

And suddenly she smiled.

Budin blinked. It was the first time he had ever seen Kroup smile. She had small, even, very white teeth and their display totally transformed her face. It did not make her beautiful. Only an act of God could do that. But it did at least make her look human.

"You should do that more often, Comrade Major."

"What's that?" she paused, turning as she headed for the door.

"Smile," he said.

She scowled furiously and strode on out of the door.

At 62nd Army headquarters Georgi Ivanovich Chuikov chewed on an unlit cigar and pored over his battle map. It was not good. It was not at all good. He had lost contact completely with one corps. Two more were so disorganized as to be useless. If the German Panzer attack which he knew about more as a rumour than as a fact developed its flanking move across the Don the Germans would be in Stalingrad before he was.

On the other hand they had old Budin to pass before they went any farther.

Budin, a sly old fox, a man who would keep his corps in being, keep it as a fighting formation as long as one platoon remained. If anyone could give the Germans a bloody nose Budin could.

And it worried him less that Budin was out of touch than it did Moscow. What right anyhow had Moscow to interfere with his subordinate units? This was his war and he was entitled to sole control. But Moscow liked to get its finger into every pie, to know every detail of what was happening on the ground. It was no way to run a war.

And as for Budin . . . he smiled to himself. That breakdown in communications had very much the appearance of a Budin touch.

He remembered when they were colonels together, when they were advancing swiftly against Denikin's White Russians. Corps had taken cold feet then; thought they were advancing into a trap. Runners – no radio then – had gone out with orders to halt the point battalion – Budin's.

By some mischance the runner was killed, it seemed, and the message did not get through, and Budin pressed on. And after all there was no trap. Budin's advance was the basis for a large victory for which corps, of course, took the credit.

He remembered that very well. He remembered also that later he had seen a man very like the runner who had been killed on Budin's own staff. What was his name, Shiryaev? An old soldier.

There would always be Shiryaevs for Budin, reasons why orders regrettably could not get through, why he had to operate on his own initiative.

He would be doing that now. If he had anything left at all he would be doing that now. And the Germans would be getting some very nasty surprises.

Were they through Misgorod yet? Crossing the Don?

Deliberately he blanked off the thought of the possible flanking move and concentrated on his main front. The problem was how to keep it as a front at all, how to let it fall back towards Stalingrad without a complete loss of cohesion.

No transport, he thought, little ammunition reserve – and no point in bringing up reserves to an army that was retreating.

He looked sourly at the morning's communique from Moscow. "Successful drive against the German invaders in the curve of the River Don..."

And how many curves had the Don? If anyone had been advancing there they had omitted to tell Army.

How long before it was the Volga in place of the Don?

For the Volga would be the last possible line to hold. Beyond the Volga there was no natural line for hundreds of miles to the east. There would be only the Urals to the north and east and the Caucasus to the south. A nucleus of an army could hold out in either. But it would be only a nucleus, only a sort of irregular guerrilla force whose discipline would break up swiftly and whose effectiveness would be minimal.

So it had to be the Volga. The 62nd Army had to hold the Volga line. And Stalingrad would be the fulcrum of that line. He hoped that the defensive work was well ahead in Stalingrad, perimeter trenches, emplacements, deep shelters.

The shelters would certainly be needed when the Junkers and the Heinkels and Stukas started to pound it into the ground. It was a pity for he was fond of Stalingrad. It had just started to grow into a modern city. And yet all that had to be destroyed, would be destroyed.

The only thing that would save Stalingrad would doom the Army of the East and that was its capture by the Germans.

If that damned Waffen SS column managed to outflank him, managed to break Budin and pass him, managed to reach the Volga before he had reformed on the river line . . .

"Here come the songsters, Comrade General."

The drone of aircraft engines grew louder.

Like great, red-nosed, web-footed birds of prey the formation of Stukas clawed across the western sky towards the village that was also a junction of two roads. Trucks and men clogged the highways, the men scattering as the dive bombers tipped over in the sky to come screaming down out of the sun. The hellish wail of the siren they carried beneath their wings was as terrifying as the eventual crash of the bombs, worse maybe because it lasted longer.

Chuikov picked up his map and reluctantly went down to the cellar. He did not particularly like taking cover, especially when his men had to suffer in the open. But he had to look after himself for the army's sake.

The bombs began to burst on the road and the screams of men and the wilder screams of wounded horses lent terror to the day.

CHAPTER 22

Number Three Company of the Zhenski Battalion was called the "strafniki". They were the convicts. Many of them had volunteered from the Misgorod prison. They included a few prostitutes, some petty thieves, some regulation-breakers and one or two semi-politicals.

But there were among them a few hard cases, older women who, even in a provincial town, had been able to find some scope for their anti-social instincts.

There was Maryusha, a big beetle-browed woman who had been a black marketeer; Yelena who had specialised in robbing drunk soldiers; Shura, a slim, lithe girl with a big nose who had been something of a cat burglar.

These were the women Major Kroup sought out after she had left the corps commander.

"You've been useless parasites all your life," she told them bluntly. "Now you can be of some use. Devise a way for me to get those other girls out of Misgorod."

They were practical women these. The impossibility of the task was obvious. Equally obvious was the impossibility of arguing with Natalya Kroup. Therefore a plan was devised, a plan based on such information as Vyora Pekare had been able to give and on the strafnikis' own intimate knowledge of their own town.

The line of the German outposts was the main point in that plan.

"If it goes past the sewage farm," glowered Maryusha sullenly, "there is nothing to be done. Only a barrage. An attack in force. But if they have not occupied the sewage farm . . ."

"There is no sewage farm in Misgorod," Kroup snorted. "Sewage was disposed of by manual means."

"Yes, Comrade Major," Maryusha nodded. "It is so. But under the last but one five-year-plan a sewage farm was built. Also, there were sewers laid below the streets of Misgorod. My own husband, a filthy, lazy swine of a man, helped to dig them."

Major Kroup's eyes narrowed hopefully.

"Sewers? The sewers were dug?"

"It was in the five-year plan, Comrade Major. Why should they not have been dug? It is true that because the town lies below the river level the sewers could not be used. But they were laid. The sewage farm was dug . . . One hears that the Comrade Commissar for Engineering Works was liquidated but the sewers were dug."

"And you sewer rats know how to use them."

Kroup swore a mighty oath of delight. This was more than she had dared to hope for.

The sewers for entry. The sewer rats to guide her . . .

The German outpost line was about a hundred metres beyond the sewage farm and the little column of women moved silently through the derelict tanks and buildings to the entrance to the main sewer.

Kroup led them, carrying an American Thompson sub-machine gun, product of the strange alliance between Soviet Russia and the Capitalist West. Three more of the women behind her carried the same. Of the rest, some bore rifles, some pistols. In forming the column, Kroup's main intention was to have behind her those who knew what they were handling.

This was not to be a pitched battle. With luck perhaps they would scarcely fire a shot. With luck . . .

Her nose wrinkled at the mouth of the sewer.

"You're sure this is out of use?"

Maryusha's lip twitched sardonically.

"Even rats have their requirements."

And indeed save for a certain amount of sewage that came from the basic dampness of a soil below river level the concrete piping, a metre in diameter, was dry enough.

The air was fetid, overhung with a fungoid flavour, as if they had all become mushrooms, part themselves of the earth about them. But it was breathable enough. And though once a woman squealed when a great rat ran between her legs, there was no evidence of any real rodent occupation of the pipes.

"There hasn't been the food for them yet," Maryusha commented wryly. "In Moscow they say the sewer rats are as big as dogs. But under the Soviet, everything is bigger."

"Have a care, Comrade," Kroup warned. "I tell you quietly, have a care. One has a memory."

"Of course, Comrade Major."

Natalya Kroup did not allow her mind to form the thought that lurked somewhere deep in her subconscious; that she was surrounded by strafniki, that these were the sort of people she had spent her life in punishing for their offences against the state. That they would have delighted in exposing her to death, pain or torture.

She suppressed the thought. These were Russian women, seeking to save other Russian women who were the victims of German brutality.

Yet she did feel a certain prickling in her spine when they were behind her.

Then their creeping journey through the sewer was over. Maryusha called for a halt.

"It is here."

"What is?"

"The air shaft."

Above them a vertical well led to the surface, an air vent that led to behind the rayon building. It was intended to relieve pressure on the sewer walls in the event of floods and also as an extra means of access for workmen. Iron rungs were set into the wall.

"Very well. Follow me."

Kroup reached up and drew her bulky body into the narrow shaft. Hips and shoulders fitted tightly into the channel and movement was an effort. From below she thought she heard someone mutter, "If old Fat Arse sticks, what do we do?" Regrettably she could not recognise the voice. Or hear the answer.

And grim-faced she continued to force her way upward until the cool, welcome freshness of the night air was in her face.

They were in a yard now behind the rayon building, the little group pulling themselves up and dropping to the ground as lightly as men.

They kept perfect silence, waiting for the major's orders. And Major Kroup too waited, waited for her breath to come back after the fearful exertion of that climb – waited for a sign in the night sky.

She was still breathing heavily when the sign came, three brilliant red flares to the north.

General Budin's promised diversionary action was about to begin.

A little artillery fire followed, very little, for ammunition was precious. Then some machine guns opened up, firing tracer mostly and explosive bullets. This was fire for show, not for effect.

And the effect was all that Kroup could have wished. The fire was answered on the sector under attack. And NCOs and messengers began to run clattering through the streets of Misgorod calling all off-duty men back to their units.

The Germans had thought they were going to have a nice little rest home in Misgorod. Now they would learn differently.

In the yard of the rayon building the women could hear the furious arguments within, snatches of words, phrases. For most of them the words were meaningless but Kroup knew German as part of her duties. She spoke also French and English.

"Where's my trousers? . . ."

"Just a minute . . . for God's sake one minute more . . ."

"But it was my turn next . . ."

"Go and jump on yourself . . ."

Cries of frustration, indignation, resentment . . . but eventual obedience. The call of nature was strong but that of duty stronger.

Within the building the sounds grew less.

"Now," said Major Natalya Kroup softly. "Now."

And the silent, avenging troop of women swept forward.

There was, of course, a sentry at the back. And of course like many headquarters sentries in a soft billet he was half-drunk, half-asleep.

With Major Kroup's big hands about his throat he was very quickly wholly dead.

"You," breathed Kroup and nudged a woman. "Put on his helmet. In this light you'll look like him if anyone comes, not that I think anyone will."

And she led the way in through the back door, into the building that had been headquarters for the civil administration such a little while before and was now a pleasure centre for the conquering Wehrmacht.

In fact Major Wedelmann had scheduled the building for brigade HQ but had been overruled by his general who preferred to have his being in inconspicuous residences. He had found he lived longer that way.

Now the reek of schnapps, vodka, wine and beer filled the lower floor which had been converted into a canteen, one room for privates, one for junior NCOs, one for senior

NCOs and warrant officers. Even in battle there must be a due regard for form.

The rooms were all deserted save for the senior NCOs' canteen in which a drunk Feltwebel snored stertorously and behind whose bar a startled barman looked up from his takings into the barrel of Major Kroup's machine gun.

He was a pale-faced man with sandy, close-cropped hair and his eyes showed utter astonishment as he saw the women of the Zhenski Battalion. His mouth worked but he could get no words out.

"You," growled Kroup. "How many men here? Sentries? At the front?"

"No . . . no sentries. Here is only . . ."

He nodded towards the sleeping Feltwebel.

"See the front door is bolted," Kroup ordered over her shoulder. From the man she demanded: "Other men? Upstairs?"

"Only . . . only women," gulped the barman. "Don't . . . don't shoot."

And Major Natalya Kroup did not in fact shoot for shots might draw unwelcome attention. Instead, with a sudden, almost casual movement, she jabbed forward with her submachine gun.

It seemed a simple little movement with no force behind it. But Kroup weighed fourteen stone. The gun weighed eight pounds. The concerted force concentrated on the tiny area of the gun's muzzle had the same terminal momentum as a bullet would have done – or a pole axe. The barrel actually sank half an inch into the man's forehead and he was certainly dead as he fell behind the bar, scattering his takings in a little shower of marks and pfennigs round him.

Behind Kroup, the Feltwebel grunted in his sleep, wriggled in his chair and smiled seraphically at some dream. Probably this was his last smile.

"Tie him and gag him," Kroup ordered and shouldered her way past the other women and up the stairs.

"Only women," the barman had said and for that alone he deserved his death in her mind. "Only women."

They would learn what "only women" could do.

CHAPTER 23

Major Kroup had, in the Lyubyanka, seen terrible things. She had herself done terrible things. She had done them for the most part unmoved because those she did them to were enemies of the state, deserving nothing better. She should have been hardened to any horror.

But the rooms above brought her to an abrupt irrational conclusion that there was no end to horror, no depth which could not be plumbed by the vileness which was man.

And if at that moment the whole of male humanity could have been presented to her in one person with its throat exposed to her knife she would not have hesitated. The knife would have cut.

There were three or four women in each room, all of them naked, all lying on the floor in supine, exhausted postures, legs splayed, arms sprawled, heads averted from the relentless glow of the bare light bulbs.

Some of them whimpered a little as they lay but most seemed as if they had withdrawn into some kind of apathy, into another world where their bodies were not present, where the savage lusts of men could not penetrate.

In Gnotke's room, Kroup found Anna Turuchin tied face down across the desk, unconscious. On the floor of the same room Katrina Semyonovna was writhing slowly, a terrible, pale smile on her face.

"More," she moaned. "I must suffer more . . ."

And in the same room a big-bosomed woman rose incredulously as she saw Kroup.

"You! They've saved us . . . They've taken Misgorod back?"

She was the first Kroup had seen who still seemed in full control of her senses.

"No. This is a rescue. Get dressed . . . Help the others."

She herself drew a knife and slashed the string holding the girl she had made a sergeant. She chafed her wrists and ankles.

"Hurry," she ordered.

The big woman was looking down at Katrina Semyonovna with a sneer.

"Help her? How? She's had twenty-five already and still she wants more!"

She spat her disgust and stalked from the room.

"I'll help the others but not her."

Now the rescuers were mustering the victims, helping them down the stairs, tenderly, horror and rage mingling in their hearts.

And yet in one or two there was a curious, perverted, submerged envy which they would never consciously have admitted.

Natalya Kroup made her way up the final flight of stairs. Up here, Vyora Pekare had said, was the quarters of the German captain, Küster. There could well be valuable information to be gleaned and although time was so precious – for already the distant sound of General Budin's feint was dying – she knew very well that to miss a chance like this would be criminal.

By now, she reckoned, Küster's absence had probably been noted – together with that of Pekare.

It was not hard to guess how this would be interpreted. There would be winks and nods in the German Command: "Our Rudi has gone out to disport himself . . ." Probably his body had not yet been found. His effects would not have been disturbed. There should be maps, battle plans.

She hurried into the room, carelessly almost.

And the whole rescue fell into jeopardy.

"That you, Herr Hauptman?"

A vast form rose from the floor. And only then did she remember what Vyora Pekare had said about the orderly.

Corporal Henschke had actually begun a sleepy salute before he realised that this was not his officer come back. It took his slow brain another two seconds to recognise that this was not even someone in German uniform.

And by then Corporal Henschke was staring dumbfounded into the muzzle of a Thompson sub-machine gun, made in the United States of America and held in the undoubted grip of a woman in Russian officer's uniform.

"If I shoot I'll cut you in half," Kroup rapped in German. "Don't make me shoot."

Ernst Henschke had always been slow-witted. But even he was not so slow that he could not recognise death when it stared him in the face at three feet range. He began to sweat.

He said nothing and did nothing but stood quite still with a bovine acceptance on his simian face. Only when Kroup began to riffle swiftly through Küster's papers did he protest.

"Here. That's the Captain's," he began.

The gun's muzzle jerked towards him and he fell silent.

"Go slowly down the stairs. Keep your hands on top of your head."

With Küster's map-case and papers under her left arm, Kroup drove the huge man down the stairs to the ground floor.

From the Senior NCOs' canteen the woman Maryusha was just coming out. There was blood on her hands and she tried to slip something into her pocket.

"What's that . . . what've you been doing?"

"Just . . . just a souvenir, Comrade Major."

Kroup strode into the room. The Feltwebel was still sprawled in the chair, still lashed to it. And there was a gag in his mouth. But he was no longer unconscious. He had, since Kroup last saw him, lost his trousers.

He had also lost part of himself and there was agony in his eyes and his twisting body.

For a moment Kroup pondered a reprimand. But she bit back the words.

For the Germans, returning to the canteen, this would be an even greater terror than discovering the loss of the women, the dead sentry and barman.

"Very good," she rapped. "But now we're going . . . And we won't need any more souvenirs. We're taking one with us."

She thrust the gun into Henschke's back.

"March," she ordered grimly. "Souvenir."

CHAPTER 24

"The realities, Vassily. What of the realities." General Grigori Budin plucked again at his right ear. "Now I will tell you the whole truth about women as soldiers, the realities.

"From the dawn of time it has been the man who was the fighter, always the man. And why? You know that perfectly well. Because men are stronger than women, more able to bear arms. It takes strength to wield a sabre, Vassily, more strength than a woman has. Consider the weight of a sabre. Consider the slenderness of a woman's wrist. How can she use a weapon like this."

He rolled a cigarette from loose mahorka in his pocket and a piece of the front page of a three-month-old "Pravda" commenting as he did: "You may have noted that 'Pravda' makes a better cigarette than 'Izvestia' – but on the other hand it is a worse toilet paper. All things have their particular uses."

His chief of staff snapped a heavy gun-metal German lighter into flame and stooped forward to light the ragged end of the cigarette. What, wondered Vassily Jakubovitsch, was going to be the underlying aim of this particular lecture? The old devil might seem to ramble at times but the chief of staff knew that old Long-Lug rarely talked without purpose.

"From the dawn of time," Budin mused, "war has been a matter of physical strength and therefore a matter for men. You will tell me, I do not doubt, about the Amazons, those fiery women who are supposed to have sheared off their left breasts so as to make their bodies more fit for the use of the bow and arrow. But who knows if there ever were Amazons . . . Ha! It surprises you that old Grigori knows of these ancient legends."

"The General's knowledge is always surprising me," Jakubovitsch smiled.

"Very well. The Amazons, I concede you. Such there may

have been. But one has heard too of cocks that laid eggs. Then you may mention that Frenchwoman who beat the English, what did they call her?"

"Joan of Arc, Comrade General."

"Arc signifying a bow, no doubt. Joan of the bow? The Amazons again. If I remember aright the English burned her alive. A severely practical race the English . . . Good at war also, subtle and very hard to beat – though I remember when we were chasing Denikin they sent troops against us. We chased them too . . . but didn't catch them. But they had a grasp of the realities, Vassily. They knew the cause was lost and very cleverly indeed they evaded any decisive action."

His cigarette began to disintegrate and he spat the remnants from his lips. Little sparks of glowing tobacco smouldered unheeded on the map on the table before him.

"This Joan of Arc – she is shown sometimes in pictures wearing a coat of full armour. She is supposed to have fought in this. Which is absurd. Eighty pounds, a suit of plate weighed. Could a woman use a sword carrying such a weight?"

"Major Kroup," murmured Vassily.

Budin laughed explosively.

"Good. Very good. Yes. She could wear one – and carry a sword in each hand too. But how many Natalya Kroups are there? And according to tradition at least this Joan woman was slender and perhaps beautiful."

"She was a peasant," Vassily pointed out. "Tradition is often at fault. Maybe she was one just like Kroup."

"Good! Good. You improve all the time, Vassily. Yes. A great peasant woman. But an exception, even as the Amazons were an exception. So what is the point of this rambling discourse? Eh? Answer me that."

Vassily Jakubovitsch's sensitive face thought it out. What was the old devil after? What was he trying to prove? That he had no use for the Zhenski Battalion?

"I think you are trying to devise a reason for not using Major Kroup's women."

"You think so, eh? But I haven't finished my discourse. Now hear me. From the dawn of time men were the warriors because to be a warrior needed strength. But now – how much strength does it take to pull a trigger? How much strength does it take to carry a Nagan pistol – and fire it? Or a Degtyaryov machine gun? Or a 4.5 mortar?"

He smiled satirically at his chief of staff and pulled more furiously than before at his ear.

"You're going to mention skill . . . well, how many women have been rifle champions of Russia? Quite a lot, eh? And those Osaviakhim women – many wonderful shots among them. You know that. Pistol or rifle or machine gun, there are women who can match men. Which is why we have such things as women's machine gun detachments, mortar troops . . . apart from aircraft pilots, train drivers and all the rest. These are the realities, Vassily, the realities. They can do these things."

"Then – you're going to use Major Kroup's battalion?"

"For cover fire, maybe. She's got machine-gunners, rifle shots, a few are qualified with the mortar. But for assault troops – no, when it comes to hand-to-hand combat man is still the warrior. For close quarters, the rifle butt and the bayonet and even the grenade, I cannot see women playing a useful part."

He began to roll another cigarette, this time carefully choosing a section of leader column from "Pravda".

"There is the matter of morale. In hand-to-hand fighting there are too many casualties. You can think what it would do to our men to see a company of women mowed down by a machine gun . . . Besides, they haven't the experience. These Waffen SS are all tough, trained soldiers. Probably the best fighting troops this war has produced. Even throwing in our own men against them they have the experience of battle, the advantage of weapons. The women would have no chance at all. On the other hand, when the Panzers move forward . . ."

An orderly came in with a steaming bowl of kasha for each of them.

"It is all there is," he apologized.

"I've fared worse," the general grunted indifferently.

From the breast pocket of his blouse he took out a spoon,

wiped it with his hanky and laughed at Vassily Jakubovitsch's expression.

"Not what they do in the messes, eh? But this is not an officers' mess now, Vassily. Take my tip. Always carry your own eating irons."

He began hungrily to sup the coarse porridge of millet which had been flavoured with a little molasses from the bottom of a keg used for cattle food.

"Not like the Krunze, eh?" Budin burped unaffectedly and began to roll another cigarette.

Two messengers came in with signals which he read swiftly.

"The first pontoon is in position," he observed. "They should have their bridge finished by the morning. By mid-afternoon the armour should be crossing. Tomorrow night we will take them."

He made some rough notes on the edge of his map.

"The best way will be to use the boats from the fishermen's village. In the dark they should be able to reach the pontoons in mid-river without being seen. We've still got enough engineers left to do the demolition, I think. For sure we won't be able to do enough damage with shell-fire. Arrange that, Vassily, will you? The engineers have enough explosive left. Tell them they can use it all."

Jakubovitsch rose from his half-eaten kasha but Budin motioned him back into his seat.

"Finish your food. You never know when you'll get another meal. Always eat when you can in war, Vassily. A full-fed man can exist for a week without another meal, if pushed. So when that is done you have a week ahead of you."

He pulled at his ear.

"This blowing of the pontoon would be a good little job for the woman major, if only it were engineers she had brought me. She has a good command of stealth that woman – but then, NKVD! I liked her little raid. I liked that very much. Especially the bringing back of the papers – and the prisoner."

He shook his head in mock sorrow: "For that prisoner I am sorry. Very sorry."

From the outskirts of the city they heard a sudden flurry of fire.

"The fourth battalion's harassing action," Jakubovitsch murmured.

"Quite. We mustn't let them think we've forgotten them. If we keep a light pressure up all day they may assume this is the most we intend."

Budin grimaced as they both heard the harsh, braying sound of a German six-barrelled mortar.

"Ishak," Budin breathed. "I didn't know they had one. Poor devils."

And he stopped thinking about the Zhenski Battalion's prisoner.

CHAPTER 25

For Corporal Ernst Henschke, sex had always been a problem, even from his very earliest days, even from school. Some glandular imbalance had made him grow to man's size before he had reached his teens and the same imbalance had started beard and moustache into growth, brought him to a swift puberty and tortured mind and body with forbidden longings.

In the little Black Forest village where he was reared, he was a freak, a man sitting in a child's little desk, in the wood-built school, knocking his knees at every move, spilling the ink with his great paws of hands and suffering endlessly from the taunts of his fellow-children.

The little girls especially used to tease him.

"Look at Ernst, all inky like Struwelpeter. Look at the great carthorse . . ."

He was like Gulliver being pricked daily by the multitudinous darts of the Lilliputians. He was a helpless giant, ringed around by a horde of malicious Little People.

Nor was their spite restricted to words. There were nips, trips, nasty little practical jokes, all the demonstrations that the pack makes against those who are different.

Endocrinology might have saved him but at that time the

functions of the ductless glands were only imperfectly understood. And in any case the Black Forest was not the place to find an expensive specialist.

Even if there had been, Ernst's father, Willi Henschke, was not the kind to have paid for one – even if he had the money. Willi Henschke, a widower since the birth of the boy, was in a perverted way proud of Ernst's size as a demonstration of his own virility and in a practical way pleased. The bigger the boy the more work he could do.

And there was plenty of work to do, the pigs to be fed or watched as they rootled through the forest for their food, the cow to be milked, timber to be sawn, trimmed and hauled. Ernst was as good as an extra man about the place – and an unpaid one.

If Willi had married again it might not have been so bad. There had been housekeepers from time to time but none had stayed long, for Willi had his problems too of a sexual character and no doubt it was from him that Ernst had inherited some at least of his nature.

At any rate the word very swiftly circulated that the isolated cottage by the Schwartz Stein was not a good place for a woman to be alone – even quite an old woman.

And this prejudice too was reflected in the children's attitude to Ernst.

"That monster," they would hear their elders murmur round the stove. "That beast from the Schwartz Stein."

And they would think of Ernst.

They would torment him the more.

The schoolmaster was a small, thin, puritanical Schwabian who neither liked the Forest nor its people. Almost incessantly he punished Ernst for his failure to do his homework, ignoring or not knowing the fact that at home he was kept busy for hours before and after school, that he had a four mile walk each way and that he was in any case not very intelligent.

Not that Ernst minded the beatings. He scarcely felt them for his work-calloused skin was almost impervious to pain. But he hated the mockery that followed, the pointing fingers and the dancing legs under their flirting skirts. Those dancing legs and what lay hidden under the skirts.

Sometimes the other boys would favour him in their sneering way with some of the rudimentary facts of life. Some of them had sisters and could describe in detail all the physical peculiarities of the female body. And indeed this accorded with what Ernst knew of animals. But could it in fact be so that there was only this tiny difference between girls and young pigs or calves?

Because of what went on in his body, the uncontrollable onsurge of premature maturity, he had an inordinate desire to know, to experience.

Inevitably the time came when he had to find out for himself. And instead of the tentative, secret explorations of childhood his learning was done almost publicly.

For the girls, undeveloped though they were, could sense the urges throbbing through him. And they took this as a new basis for torment.

They would deliberately flirt their skirts at him, half reveal themselves when they knew he was looking, plague him with a conscious, precocious coquetry.

And in a corner of the playground the day came when three or four of these little, flaxen-haired, angelic-looking girls teased him beyond the bounds of restraint.

"Look at me," one would cry and lift her skirt a little.

"No, look at me, Ernst," another broke in and teased a little further.

This was a torment even greater than their mocking and their scorn for his clumsiness.

And at last his patience broke as inevitably it was bound to. He grabbed at one of the girls, caught at her skirt and felt it tear in his mighty paw.

Now they all began to scream as the game turned into reality and his huge, child's hands dragged the girl's knickers off and granted him at last a sight of what had been denied him.

Certainly it would have gone further than that then for now he had been inflamed beyond the point of recall. His loins were a flaming fire and he could think of nothing, see nothing but the soft thighs that were now exposed.

But the schoolmaster had heard the screams and came

running out with his cane to lash about the boy's shoulders and head and face.

Ernst had been whipped off like a dog from a bitch on heat. He was, of course, expelled instantly from the school, sent home in ignominy.

But the fires burned in him still, fires that had to be quenched.

And when he came home to an empty house, his father being in the woods, it came to him that, after all, the boys had been right. There was no difference between the girls' apparatus and the animals'.

There were no girls here in the forest. But there was the brown cow in the shed beyond the cottage.

The forest was a lonely place and it was a strange life for Willi Henschke and his huge son. Yet, on the whole, it was a contented enough life for both of them. They spoke little, each doing their work, each bedding down when night came.

But by now Adolf Hitler was fully in power and all the children of his imagination had come into being.

So far as the Henschkes went, the first impact was the Wandervögel, the hostellers, tramping in their little groups down the paths of the Forest, camping or spending the night at the multitude of hostels that the Party had called into being.

In its way the Wandervögel was a fine idea; get the young out of the grime of the cities; let them tramp the country, see all the beauties of the Reich. Perhaps it was the most innocent of all Hitler's promotions.

But for Ernst Henschke is meant disaster.

There was a pool some few hundred yards from the cottage where a stream widened among rocks. It was a favoured bathing place for the Wandervögel for the sun struck down through an opening in the trees and there was a broad mossy bank for sun-bathing.

There was also a thicket beyond which would hide even such bulk as Ernst Henschke's and from that hiding place he used to watch the young travellers strip off and dive into the pool, their bodies displayed without shame, male and female mixing together with neither prudery nor prurience.

Ernst loved to lie in the thicket and watch the girls, drinking in the texture of their skins, the supple play of the muscles, the rich femininity of their bodies.

And though the sight used to stir up a vast frustration in him, yet when he heard the distant singing of a party he would drop whatever work he was doing and move stealthily to his hiding place.

There was, after all, some little difference between girls and animals, he had realised. He longed to go among these happy groups, to move among the girls and stroke and fondle the soft, brown smooth bodies.

But he knew very well what would happen. He knew and dreaded the sharp female tongues, the jibes that must surely come.

Therefore he stayed in his hiding place, watched, longed and kept silent.

Until the day when, with no warning sound of singing, he heard a splashing from the pool.

There had been otters in the stream and gamekeeping was part of the Henschkes' duties. Otter destroyed the trout and if there was an otter he should destroy it.

This time though it was not an otter. It was a girl, a slim, brown-haired, brown-skinned girl who was just drawing herself from the pool as he reached it. Drops of water hung on her skin like jewels and her hair, plastered down by the water, was more like the fur of an animal that has been swimming.

And perhaps because of this faint animal quality he was not afraid of her.

"Hello," she greeted him. "Do you live here? How lovely."

Unconcerned by her nudity she began to towel herself under his hungry gaze.

She was from Berlin, she said, a typist in a ministry, and her name was Ursula Neurath. She had come with a party who had gone off in the other direction to look at the ruins of a castle.

"Pooh to ruins!" she snorted, wrinkling a rather long nose. "I'd sooner swim and sunbathe. Ruins are always so dusty. I say, you're a big chap, aren't you?"

For the first time he felt a woman's eyes show admiration and he could find no words to answer her.

"You're shy," she laughed. "I do believe you're shy. Haven't you ever seen a woman before?"

Her eyes narrowed suddenly.

"Maybe you've never even had a woman," she breathed. "My . . ."

And as well as the building tension in his loins he felt now the terror of the sharp, malicious tongues of women. She was going to start the torment. She would mock him . . . mock him.

"Don't say that," he growled.

And his hand went out to cover her mouth. It was like a blanket over her face, hiding it.

"Don't say those things. Girls . . . girls . . ."

He hardly noticed the struggles of her slim body for the first touch of her skin had brought the fires of desire to flashpoint.

Now, without effort, he threw her to the ground, pinning her with his weight on her chest, keeping his hand over her mouth to stifle back her taunts as he fumbled with his own clothes.

There must be no taunts, he thought, no taunts. She mustn't mock him.

And silencing her was as important to him as the thrust of his body into hers in the wonderful warmth of this new sensation.

And at last he felt the tension leave him, the muscles begin to relax all over.

"You mustn't say things," he begged. "You see. I can do it."

There was no answer from the body beneath him as he rose a little.

"I don't like to be made little," he pleaded.

Still there was no answer. The girl lay quite still and the back of her head was turned to him.

Yet this was impossible. No one could turn their head quite round like that. No one could do it. No one alive could do it certainly, no one whose cervical vertebrae had not been completely dislocated.

She lay there on her back, her brown, beautiful young bosoms offering themselves to the sun. And yet her face was pressed into the damp moss of the bank.

A long shudder passed over Ernst Henschke as he rose and looked down incredulously at his hands and then at what they had done.

Standing in the sunlight in the glade by the pool he began to cry, a terrible, lost child's weeping which no one would ever comfort.

Willi Henschke did not worry overmuch about his son's disappearance, not even when eventually the police began to make enquiries about the missing girl.

He did feel a natural sense of aggrievement. He had after all lost a valuable source of labour. On the other hand it had come at a good time for he had made acceptable advances to a big peasant woman from the next valley who knew nothing of him – or did not care.

There would have been no room really in the cottage for two men. Yet he did marvel a little that Ernst had found a girl willing to take him, to run away with him.

And when, two years later, he found the carefully concealed body – hidden as only a forest boy could hide it – he did not connect this with Ernst's going. The body was reduced by then in any case to a virtual skeleton. He did not even report the discovery since the report would mean more police, more forms to fill in, more trouble.

And his new woman was trouble enough, the good God knew. The new woman and this huge child of hers that was further proof of his own vast virility.

By his father, Ernst was forgotten. Nor was the law seeking him.

Therefore he had few enough problems when he drifted from city to city. His size and strength guaranteed him work wherever he went – and made him soon a welcome member of the S.A., a good example of the physical benefits of National Socialism.

Then the war came and he lost his identity again in the Waffen SS, because Rudi Küster's orderly – and the implement of his self-hate.

By then he had had scores of women, for his size and the furious potency of his loins drew them to him like bees to honey. Yet always behind their willingness he suspected there might be the barbed tongues of his childhood. Within himself he was still afraid of them and he had yet to have a woman with the slightest degree of love.

To them, he was a challenge. To him, they were a tease, a torment, an endless source of both desire and fear.

The Hauptman had saved his life in France and to that extent he was in any case his slave. But even more he loved him for giving him women who would not talk back, who would not say the things he feared to hear, who would not jibe at his uncouth words, his huge body, his animalism.

He had experienced a new and wonderful relief with the women Captain Küster threw him. He even enjoyed the Hauptman's presence during the act, as if in some way Küster was protecting him from the women's tongues, from the things they would say, from the spite that would make him again a great, shambling child seated in a desk too small for him.

When he held a screaming victim down it was the little, flaxen-haired girls from the Schwarz Wald with the spiteful tongues who were the real bodies under him, the little girls who had taunted and tormented him and made him what he was.

And now at last he was the victim.

Heart's desire: an infinity of women, ready women, willing women, eager women.

One man and a hundred women.

And there could have been, should have been, joy enough for all. Save that it was not joy the women sought but revenge.

The Lilliputians were round the giant again. And now there was no doubt of their malice. Now all that the child had feared was coming to pass.

CHAPTER 26

Kroup had left Henschke to the other women, not because of any qualms in herself but lest her own presence might inhibit them. Probably she need not have worried.

The great, muscled body was pushed and pulled and dragged into the barn that was the women's quarters and the mighty arms, helpless now, lashed by the elbows to an upright that supported the roof.

The convict woman Maryusha had taken command of the celebrations. In the lamplight, her shaggy hair falling about her face she seemed like some virago from hell as she danced round the prisoner.

At the very back of the room Vyora Pekare watched with a curious pity. She should feel nothing for this brute but hatred and horror, she thought. Yet she could feel only pity. Whatever he had done he was going to atone now, more than atone.

She remembered once reading somewhere about some Red Indian tribe in America – the Apaches was it (it seemed important to her to remember the exact tribe) among whom it was the custom to give prisoners to the women to torture. The women, it seemed, were more cruel and ingenious at inflicting pain than were the men. At the time, it had not seemed possible to her. Women were the gentler sex, the soothers of pain and not the inflictors. Now she knew that it was true, all true.

"Get his clothes off," cried Maryusha. "Get the clothes off this big man who likes to take the young girls. Get his clothes off and we'll see what makes him so big and strong and brave."

It was Anna Turuchin now who first began to claw off the big man's tunic. Her little, chubby face was a cold mask of hate. She, at least, was feeling no pity, no forgiveness. As she clawed at the man she was remembering him – and all the others in the rayon building.

"You'll need to untie his arms," said the strafniki, Yelena, "Or we can't get it off."

"Don't be a bloody fool. Cut them off," Maryusha sneered. "He won't be needing them again."

And as the knives began to slash through the cloth, exposing the pale skin and the great muscles, Ernst Henschke began to sob. He cried like a child, with his mouth wide, bawling helplessly. Tears streamed down his bristly cheeks.

And the sight of his fear seemed only to stimulate his torturers.

"How do we start?" cried Maryusha.

"Knacker him," Yelena suggested. "You've got your souvenir but what about me."

Irina Tsiganka, eyes narrow like a cat's as she gazed at the huge, naked body, jostled her roughly.

"What a fool," she sniffed. "What a short-sighted fool. What sort of sport can we have with him then? Keep him whole I say. Keep him in one piece till we've all finished with him."

There was a dark, fierce glitter to her eyes now. She looked all gypsy. Perhaps she was seeing in Henschke the stepfather of so long ago. And there was an additional venom in her heart because Kroup had spurned her. It was Vyora Pekare too, that soft, silly little girl that the major preferred, who lay there helpless and naked.

Henschke's massive head rolled uncomprehendingly from side to side as he looked at one woman and then another seeking desperately for hope, for the faintest sign of pity in any face . . . and failing to find it.

Irina Tsiganka walked slowly round the man, eyeing the shaggy hair that covered his body, the massive muscles, the flaccid organs.

"He's not so cocky now," Maryusha tittered. "But we'll soon change that."

Behind the man Irina's knife ran suddenly up his spine, not the edge of the blade but the harmless back. But the feel of the cold steel was the same.

Henschke screamed aloud.

CHAPTER 27

Sergeant Shiryaev puffed cynically at his cigarette as he squatted comfortably in the darkness of what had been a pigsty and still stank like one.

It was nasty, he was thinking, very nasty. Old Grigori Budin would really need to pull something out of his knapsack this time if they were not to get the chopper good and proper. It gave a professional soldier a nasty feeling to be out in the open, encircled practically save for that narrow corridor to the north which was probably closed now anyway.

Open flanks were always a bad job as he remembered only too well. The only consolation was that the German flanks were open too.

From an ammunition pack he pulled out a crust of black bread and began to gnaw on it, still puffing occasionally at his cigarette.

A nasty old position it was – but Grigori Budin had been in worse and wriggled out. A good old fox was Grigori and it was the one comfort in the whole wrap-up that Grigori was in command and not one of these Party generals who didn't know their backside from a column in extended order.

The butt of his cigarette began to disintegrate and as it did the darkness grew still darker at the doorway. Instinctively his hand closed on the butt of the tommy gun he had stolen from a battalion commander. Decadent capitalists the Anglo-Americans might be, but they made a good gun and no mistake.

"Every pig to his own sty," murmured a familiar voice.

"Take a seat, Comrade General," the sergeant retorted. "The velvet one is the most elegant but the cotton-covered one has better springs."

"Spasibo."

The general seated himself beside the sergeant in the straw.

"Bloody staff officers," Budin murmured. "It's good to

get away from them for a little. They're in a real panic I can tell you."

"They've got something to panic about. No ammunition, no communications, flanks in the air and one of Hitler's crack divisions on their doorstep. If I was an officer I'd panic too. But then I'm only a dirty, thieving old sergeant."

"Your words – but true just the same."

Budin began to roll a cigarette, doing it by touch in the darkness.

"How do the men feel?" he asked. "Have they the shits bad?"

"I wouldn't like to change trousers with many of them. But it's no worse than usual. The last two days helped. A bit of peace. A bit of time to get themselves sorted out. Not being on the run for a little."

"Do they know how bad it is?"

"Do you?"

General Budin laughed at the sergeant's blunt question and he clapped him affectionately on the shoulder.

"Of course I don't. The Cossacks are my only contact with anyone outside the Germans in the town. And you know Cossacks. If they see a platoon they'll report a bloody division."

He puffed on the rank cigarette for a little.

"It's not quite as bad as it was. They're sending us something at last. A regiment plus an assault group. Also there's a convoy of ammunition and stores on the way. Plus some Katyushas."

"And I've got a pink ribbon round my penis . . . Don't give me that, Grigori. You've got no radio link, courtesy of good old Sergeant Shiryaev, so how do you know what's on the way."

There came an edge of anger into his voice.

"Look. If you want me to spread a happy word round the boys, well and good, I'll do that. But don't expect me to believe it too."

"What a fine, trusting old friend. Remind me to have you shot some time . . . No. It's true. Didn't you see the motor bike come in an hour back? Army have some fresh stuff in and very likely they're letting us have some."

"Look, pigs lived here before and you could tell them anything. But I'm not a pig no matter what I smell like. Where did army get anything from? There isn't anything for them to get. Everything's been committed long ago."

"You're a defeatist, a dirty, battered, reactionary old defeatist. But it's true all right. They've been training up three new army groups behind the Urals. They're raw, of course, probably gun-shy. But they're men. Look, you old sinner, here's the despatch."

Paper rustled in the darkness and the general's lighter snapped into flame.

"All right, Grigori. Put it away. I'll believe you . . . And that means, I suppose, we're going to have a push?"

"The weather forecast isn't good," Budin answered with seeming irrelevance. "Would you sooner winter out here, or in Misgorod?"

The sergeant lit another foul cigarette and his seamed face looked bitter in the faint light.

"And how much of Misgorod will be left by the time we take it. Katyushas! The country at least will be cleaner."

The big Russian mortars would not leave much of the city standing once they set to work.

"I don't think it'll be too tough," the general consoled his old friend. "Once the armour crosses the Don they'll only have line of communication troops in the town. They might have a couple of companies of fighting men but that'll be the limit. They're not reinforcing this thrust."

"So now you know how Fritz is planning his war as well," taunted the sergeant. "My, but we're very clever now."

"The women of the Zhenski Battalion brought me in the German plans," Budin countered. "This is only intended as a one division thrust. There's no arrangement for holding ground taken. They want to get Stalingrad as quickly as possible. They're consolidating only on the main front. They just don't have the troops for holding and the whole theory of the blitzkrieg is that it doesn't matter if you leave pockets of resistance behind you so long as you take your main objective."

"The women," mused the sergeant. "This is a hell of a war when women do the raiding. Maybe after all I do believe you. Do you want me to spread the glad tidings about the reinforcements?"

"It could help," Budin nodded in the darkness.

They both fell into a companionable silence, the general and the sergeant seated in the straw in a pig sty, drawing strength from each other and hope perhaps.

"You're right about the women, though," Budin said suddenly. "It's not the sort of war we knew. But that Kroup's a real fire-eater. I'd just hate to have her against me."

Abruptly through the night came the sound of a terrible scream. Even these hardened men shivered at it.

"The women," said Budin softly. "They took a German prisoner you know."

"Boge moy," breathed Shiryaev. "My God. What a way to go."

On the barrel at the back of the barn, seated beside Vyora Pekare, was Katrina Semyonovna. Her thin, intense features were set in a mask of concentration as she watched the torture of Henschke, and Vyora could not have told what emotions went on within her.

For herself she could feel nothing but pity for the terrified hulk of what had been a brutal rapist. Maybe it was because he was in some way a link with Rudi that she had this strange sympathy.

Or maybe it was simply that the man was so much an animal that it was impossible to look on him in any other light than as a bull in a Spanish ring.

Or perhaps even more as the picador's horse, suffering continual, uncomprehended attacks and wounds, being ripped open only to be stitched up again and sent back into the fray.

Surely there must be others who felt as she did, she thought, searching their faces. They were women as she was a woman. Surely they shared common feelings of humanity.

But if they did they did not show it.

Their faces showed a morbid gloating, a hatred, a glittering satisfaction at this vicarious revenge on all the men who had ever wronged them.

There was a dancer from the Bolshoi Ballet, Glasha, a slim, fragile-looking girl whose fragility was entirely imaginary. In fact her body was a trained mass of supple muscle even though it was more than a year since she had danced. She had been dismissed from the company for her refusal to join a privately arranged nude show that the director wanted to give to certain high Party officials.

Now, as the woman's hands fluttered and tweaked and teased over the prisoner's body, it was not Henschke she was seeing but the director himself. Through her narrowed eyelids she was rejoicing in his humiliation, seeing him as she had so often longed to see him. It would have pleased her even more if afterwards she had seen him work as she had had to work on the kolkhoz, labouring in the fields, fine hands roughened and bruised and calloused.

And Henschke writhed and slumped alternately as the women used every wile they knew to gratify themselves and heighten his own helplessness.

"The bottle," cried Maryusha suddenly. "We'll give him the bottle."

Only Shura knew what she meant.

"The bottle!" she gurgled cheerfully. "That's it. The bottle ... Here, pass us up a bottle someone."

Two or three bottles were passed to the front while Henschke looked on with numb incomprehension, not knowing but dreading the next wave of deviltry.

Irina Tsiganka was the first to divine the plan.

"Boge moy!" she cried aloud, slapping her thigh. "That's a good one. That'll make him think. That'll be a different place for him."

Deliberately Maryusha took the big man's flaccid, shrunken organ and thrust it with coarse fingers into the neck of the bottle.

"And what good's that going to be?" Anna Turuchin demanded. "How does that hurt him?"

"You'll see, my girl. Off with your things now. Give him a bit of a show. And make it good."

The little blonde sergeant, who had been Katrina Semyonovna's secretary once, understood at last and with a shrill cry of delight began at once to peel off her clothes.

Lewdly she began to posture up and down before the bound giant.

With bulging eyes Henschke looked – and tried not to look. Frantically he tried to keep his mind a blank, to discipline his libido out of existence.

But he could not take his eyes off the girl for there walked one who in appearance could have been another of the flaxen-haired chits of his childhood. She could have been one of the ones he had hungered for when he was a boy and now she was there before him, naked and attainable – if he had not been bound, if it had not been for the bottle.

Despite himself sparks of desire flickered in his loins and blood began to pump into erectile tissue.

And as the bottle's neck pressed in with cruel restriction a new agony began for Ernst Henschke, the woodman's son.

CHAPTER 28

The Panzers were rolling east again, rolling across the pontoons over the River Don, rolling with their rumbling engines out into the great plain that still separated them from Stalingrad.

Brutally massive, their steel tracks hammered them away from Misgorod, on towards the next battle and the next victory.

General Budin's scouts watched them go – and reported back to their leader.

"And the strength left in Misgorod, Vassily? How do we guess it?"

"Perhaps brigade strength," Jakubovitsch answered. "Perhaps a little more. Two batteries of anti-aircraft guns – 88 millimetres. They're sited at either end of the pontoon bridge. Some 3.5 PAKS – though as we haven't any tanks it doesn't really matter that they've got anti-tank guns. They seem to have about six Ishaks as well as their normal infantry mortars. There are four tanks too but they seem to have been left behind for repair."

"Very comprehensive, Vassily. I congratulate your intelligence section."

His chief of staff flushed a little at the rare compliment.

"You should thank Major Kroup for a lot of the information. Those women of hers know the town inside out. They got my men in – and out again."

"The Zhenski Battalion," mused Budin. "The fighting women. We'd better be very careful or we'll find they've taken over Corps as well . . . Very good. Now let's plan the blowing of the bridge. We'll do this tonight."

Returning to the fishing village was for Katrina Semyonovna a particularly harrowing experience. The village represented the last of her old life, the last of the days of her blind folly, the final flicker of the life for which she now sought to atone.

To think, she told herself as she moved into the huddle of mean little hovels, that she had despised these people. With her haughty Party background she had had the effrontery to despise a group whose only fault was that the Party and progress had happened to ignore them.

Nothing seemed to have changed since she made her last notes in the village. Still the Don hurried on silently past in its greasy, abstracted way. Still the ancient stink of dirt and fish and faeces clung about the buildings. Kasha and fish stew bubbled on smoky fires and the fishermen and their families greeted the incursion with their usual apathetic indifference.

The Germans had not spread this far down the river and the war might never have happened so far as the villagers were concerned.

"Where are the boats?" demanded Lieutenant Mitya Gusef, the engineer officer.

"In an inlet beyond those trees," Katrina answered.

"Come on then. We have little enough time."

"But don't you want to speak to the men? Tell them what you're doing?"

Mitya Gusef was a stocky red-haired man with broad, Slavonic cheeks and blue-grey eyes. Now he looked at the woman in astonishment.

"What on earth for? What business is it of theirs?"

"The boats . . . They're the fishermen's boats."

"In time of war everything belongs to the State."

The State, Katrina thought. Always the bloody State. In the violence of her revulsion from her former views the very mention of the State was now anathema to her.

"Your men may not be able to handle the boats. You might have to use the fishermen," she said with a diplomacy that would formerly have been alien to her.

"We are engineers. We are trained in the use of boats. Now let us get to work."

He followed Semyonovna as with a shrug she headed for the inlet where the craft were moored. Once there, he began to revise his opinions.

The boats were heavy and beamy, designed to allow men to haul nets without danger of capsizing. The heavy sweeps were coarse and clumsy.

Gusef looked down at the clumsy-seeming craft in the faint light and his face fell. He called to his sergeant, a slant-eyed little man from the Altai of western Siberia. For a few moments they discussed the matter, considering the abilities of the dozen men of the section and eyeing the boats dubiously.

"All right, comrade," Lieutenant Gusef nodded. "Go back to the village and bring the men here. And quickly. The diversionary attack begins in a little while. We must be at the bridge by then."

Reluctantly the women abandoned their sport as the voice of Major Kroup sounded from outside, calling on them to fall in with their weapons.

The huge figure of Henschke, bruised now and bleeding from a score of places, slumped against the pole where he was tied, a Colossus chained and helpless.

The tears had long since been exhausted and his face was a mask of dried lines where they had run.

"Don't go away, will you?" a woman taunted from the door. "We'll have some more fun for you when we get back."

Outside, the Zhenski Battalion formed up in the darkness.

"We're going to launch a small attack to the north of

Misgorod," Major Kroup boomed. "This is only to draw away the Germans' attention from the raid on the bridge. So I want you to keep in cover and not waste ammunition."

She called Vyora Pekare and Irina Tsiganka.

"You'll scout ahead, gypsy," she told Tsiganka. "Pekare. You stay with me. I may need you as a translator. Some of these German dialects are beyond me."

Tsiganka's lips tightened at the order. Pekare, she thought, always Pekare being singled out, kept beside Natalya. New fires of jealousy swept through her.

In their felt boots the Zhenski Battalion made little sound as they moved off into the darkness.

And in the barn where he had been left, Corporal Henschke began to struggle frantically for his freedom. There were rats in the barn and he heard them scurry sometimes across the straw. Occasionally their eyes glittered in the rays of the single lamp.

The great muscles of his arms and back bulged as he threw everything into a vain attempt to burst the rope that held him.

But the rope had been tied by the deft, gypsy fingers of Irina Tsiganka. It did not give.

And though he had no more tears to shed, Henschke began to sob. Helplessly and hopelessly, his huge chest shook. The sobs were dry and harsh in his throat and his head jerked convulsively at each one.

He thought of what he had already suffered and of how much more might come. He felt drained and hollow as if all his essences had been removed.

And yet there would be more to come. Worse to come. Those devils, those she-devils in their little flirting short skirts and their flaxen hair . . .

But that was wrong. Those were different ones . . . Or the same . . . In spirit the same, the little spiteful ones, the man-haters, the man-eaters, the old enemy of man.

The rats were bolder now and one began to nibble at his toenails until a great kick sent it flying across the barn.

And as if this had been the key to a new burst of action he threw himself again at his bonds.

And this time hope sparked suddenly in his heart.

For something had begun to give. He had felt movement.

Now there was a new strength in him as he raged against his captivity, a King Kong fighting dementedly against the tethers.

He was moving. Certainly he was moving...

And now he understood how it was he was moving. The ropes were not giving – but the upright was.

The vertical beam which was fastened at the top to a cross-tie was only planted on the rammed earth of the barn floor. It was not firmly inset.

Now with his toes he began to scratch at the earth round the base of the pole. The hard clay came slowly at first but when he had scratched the surface veneer away his toes dug swiftly deeper, pushing the soil away until the upright's base was fully exposed.

Again he began to heave and as he did his mind went back to another childhood memory, the story of Samson.

Shorn, powerless, blinded Samson chained to the pillars of the temple in Gaza. They had called him Samson at school for the whole term when that story had come up. They had called him so derisively and he had perhaps consoled himself with the thought that Samson too had been derided.

Samson, he thought. Samson's strength came back at the last. So would his own.

Now his feet were set in the earth and instead of trying to break his bonds he was using them as a towrope, linking himself with the pillar, throwing all his strength into the effort to dislodge that upright, to pull it clear of the ground so that he could slip the ropes down over it, free himself.

The veins began to stand out on his narrow forehead as every muscle creaked with the effort. The sweat lashed down his whole body, stinging his wounds with fresh pain.

Rhythmically he pulled and drew back, pulled and drew back.

And the upright was moving now, moving a good inch at each tug.

In the distance he heard the rattle of small arms fire as the diversion began.

And with new energy he thrust and tugged, thrust and tugged.

Like Samson, he thought desperately, like Samson.

Then there was a creaking above him and the base of the upright was clear. He staggered as the strain came to an abrupt halt.

Now he had only to stoop, slip his ropes down and round the base and he was free.

He had to kneel to do this and as he knelt the creaking still continued above.

For this was an old barn and the cross-tie had been linked with other timbers. Pulling the upright askew had pulled the cross-tie from its place.

Above him the whole roof was crumbling into chaos.

A great, square, rough-hewn beam was pulled from its holding. And as he knelt, it fell.

The beam fell fair across the back of his bull neck and he was dead before his face was smashed into the earth floor.

Like Samson, could have been his last thought.

CHAPTER 29

The boats crept slowly towards the long line of the pontoons. There were wrappings of old rags round the thole pins and the boats had been ballasted down heavily to make them lie lower in the water. As well, branches had been laid across them to break up their outline, to make them seem only a shadow on the water.

The fishermen, not wholly comprehending their purpose, heaved slowly and resentfully at the sweeps, keeping the boats close to the banks and out of the main stream of the current.

Katrina Semyonovna was in the leading boat for the thick patois of the fishing village was almost incomprehensible to the engineers. Now she crouched beside the engineer officer, silent and watchful.

Her writer's mind was now editing subconsciously all that had happened in the past few days, the conscription to the battalion, the meeting with Sasha, her revulsion from the

Party, the attack and that nightmare of rape. It seemed very far away now, as if it had happened to some other person. In her mind it was almost as if it had been already written into a book.

Occasionally from one side of the bridge or the other a flare would be fired and in its white glare it seemed impossible that they should go unobserved. Yet there was no alarm and no sudden burst of machine gun fire to hole and sink the old boats.

The smell of fish was almost overwhelming, the essence of fish soaked up by the floorboards over generations of work.

"Can't they row any faster?" Lieutenant Gusef demanded, glancing at his watch. "In two minutes the diversion begins."

"If they row faster they'll splash. We'll be seen," Katrina answered coolly.

Abruptly the sound of the battle to the north of the town began with a snarling stream of fire from a Schmeisser machine pistol as an outpost spotted the attacking women.

Fire answered fire and the soft whistle of mortar bombs was followed by the disproportionate crash of their explosions. For a little the stroke of the oarsmen faltered and Katrina had to encourage them to row on.

"Davai, davai," she said softly. "Only a little longer."

The long, low line of the bridge was ahead now, just visible against the water. They could see the ungainly boxes of the pontoons and the tracking that linked them. Now they could even hear the splashing of the ripples against the sides of the great, floating tanks.

With a few more strokes the boats were under the cover of the roadway, hidden from sight from the banks.

Two more flares went up at that moment, as if the Germans suspected what was happening. Yet the boats were not detected and like well-drilled teams the engineers began to plant their demolition charges.

Some went to the pontoons themselves, to sink them. Others were on the track so that when they blew the whole bridge would disintegrate into its parts and float away as separate units.

Katrina could not help now. She could only watch as the

charges were taped in place and the fuses led back to the boat.

Suddenly from the far bank of the river, where one of the boats had gone, there came a burst of machine-gun fire followed by screams.

The raid had been seen.

And now, with frightening speed, the Germans counter-attacked. Troops came running out along the open-work track to fire down into the unprotected boats.

Lieutenant Gusef was striking vainly at matches, soaked somehow, which would not light. From nearby a grenade exploded deafeningly.

Katrina fumbled frantically in her pockets and found a cigarette lighter, the last relic of life in Moscow. But even while she held it out to the engineer lieutenant his face registered a sudden surprise and he fell slowly over the boat's side with a bullet through the back of his head.

The boatmen were crying aloud in fear and one of them cut adrift the rope holding the boat to the pontoon.

Now it was all for nothing. The boat began to drift downstream and the charges had not been lit.

Katrina acted then without even starting to think. With the lighter in one hand she leaped for the steel of the pontoon, landing on a ledge of angle iron and clawing with her free hand at the stanchions that held the road surface.

Vaguely she was aware of shattering rattle of small arms fire from just above her head. Grenades were exploding in the river downstream of her as she sought out the fuse where it led from the little packages of explosive.

Still clinging with one hand, she snapped the lighter into flame and touched it to the end of the fuse.

From above she heard a hoarse cry and looking up through the lattice of the roadway she saw a German soldier staring down, his attention drawn by the flash of the lighter.

At point-blank range a machine-pistol began to hammer out a stream of bullets. They ricocheted from the road girders, whined off the steel surface of the pontoon, filled the air with a devilish swarm of stinging metal.

The hand that gripped the pontoon began suddenly to grow limp. Katrina found herself looking at it in surprise, marvelling that it no longer answered the dictates of her mind.

She felt herself falling back towards the water yet it all happened, or so it seemed, with an infinite slowness.

The thoughts formed in her head: I have been hit . . . I am losing my grip on the pontoon . . . I am going to fall into the river. And between these thoughts she could wonder at her own presence there. She could savour the irony that, after losing all illusions about the regime and the Party, she was now losing her life in a desperate attempt to blow up a bridge to halt in some small way the advance of an invader who would destroy both regime and Party.

Her brain, she thought, had never worked so swiftly or so lucidly. In the second between being hit and striking the brown, chill water of the Don she even realised why it was that this should be right.

For in the ultimate analysis it was not for the Party or its grey, remote highnesses that she was there. It was for Russia. For the people. And for all people, even for the very ones she now fought.

If only, she thought, as the waters closed over her, she could transmit this clarity to paper, make the people understand.

Then the waters closed over her head and she was being borne down the turgid stream, down and away from the bridge, feeling no pain, feeling only a mild wonder that everything that was now so clear should before have been so obscure.

She was a full hundred yards away before the blast of the explosion sent great sections of the bridge sky-high, ripped vast holes in the steel of the pontoon and cut irrevocably the communications of the Waffen SS Division with its rear.

Afterwards she remembered how the clarity of her thoughts, the clarity she had assumed of death, was suddenly obfuscated by the hammer blows of the shock wave as it travelled through and tightened on her chest in the first pain she had felt since the bullet that struck her arm had made her release her grip on the pontoon.

She had thought before that she was dying and it had been a wonderful and mystical experience. Now she knew this was not so. Now, with the shock wave crushing her, she knew her first fear. And the shock wave that should have killed her startled her body into a struggle for life.

At last she began to swim.

On the river bank a little cluster of fisher women stood, staring uncomprehendingly upstream at the source of the explosions, at the direction which their menfolk had taken.

The first shattered boat drifted downstream with its cargo of dead and dying, the engineers and the fishermen, the shattered, bleeding bodies.

The wailing women rushed in waist-deep to drag the wreck ashore, to gaze down bitterly on the bodies.

And it was not only grief that was in their faces. Their men were dead now. The boats were shattered.

How would they live now? How would they live?

The clouded sky made up for their unshed tears. The bleak, inexorable rains of the plains had begun.

CHAPTER 30

"In the old days, Vassily, we would have said this is an answer to prayer. And maybe there are certain Russian church reactionaries who have been praying on our behalf."

General Grigori Budin was almost skipping through the mud as he made his morning inspection.

"It could not possibly have been timed better. We have cut the pontoon, therefore the Panzers cannot come back. The roads to the west will be impassable within two days. Therefore, there will be no reinforcements."

"Half-tracks could still get through," Jakubovitsch pointed out.

His superior smiled sardonically. "And how many half-tracks have they to spare? Their main forces are all committed to the north. No, no, Vassily. There will be no German reinforcements for Misgorod. This is only a line of communication base, an unimportant one. And since the pontoon bridge has gone, there is not even a line of communication."

He gazed with pleasure at the row of battered Studebaker lorries that had come in during the night and were now in the cover of the trees, camouflage nets in place.

"He has no prospect of reinforcement, whereas we do. Now, I put myself in the position of the German army commander. I have thrown my Panzers across the river. They are striking on to link up with the main battle. If I do anything at all it will be to try to salve my armour. If I can get them fuel, by air maybe, then I might even get some of my tanks back. But Misgorod. Pooh! What is Misgorod to me in the overall concept of the action. If it can hold on, well and good. If it fails . . . well, I will have Stalingrad."

He gestured swiftly as he spoke. He seemed a new man on this bleak, wet morning.

"For the German commander it is a very minor issue – but not for me. If I have Misgorod before the snow starts I have a base from which I can press on after the Panzers. They are caught out in the open. We have a base. We harry the Panzers in the rear just as they harry our own main southern flank. It is beautifully complex. It makes me think of chess, of the unconsidered pawn who brings about the checkmate."

He halted abruptly, scowling at four men carrying equipment from a lorry.

"What's that?"

"New radio, Comrade General. From Army headquarters."

Budin's happy mood was gone as he tugged again at the dangling lobe of his right ear. Radio. Communications. Orders from Army. Orders from Moscow. His happy independent isolation was gone again.

"Well. Carry on."

The men squelched on their way with their burden.

"What about the reinforcements from the Urals," he asked in a now surly tone. "The ones Andrienko is supposed to be bringing us. Where are they?"

"There have been no further despatches from Colonel Andrienko. The situation remains fluid to the north."

"You mean in its usual state of bloody chaos. So. And how do I take Misgorod without these reinforcements?

Send out some Cossacks to see if they can make contact. I must know when these fresh troops are arriving."

He stalked on towards the women's quarters.

Katrina Semyonovna's arm was shattered and even a good surgeon might have found it hard to save it. But here there were no surgeons, no hospitals, no operating theatre, only a vratsch, a half-trained medical orderly whose normal duties were to take temperatures and empty bed-pans.

He flustered over the agonised flesh, dark purple, torn, fragments of bone protruding through the upper arm. He swabbed away the blood and the incipient pus and shook his head.

"Oh, go to hell," growled Major Kroup. "You're useless, man, useless. Go on. Get out of it."

Katrina Semyonovna was in the major's own quarters now, on her bed. She lay very still, conscious but pale and breathing shallowly.

It was still strange to her that she was alive. She could remember nothing but the shattering explosion at the pontoon. She had no memory of swimming down the river, floating rather with feeble movements of her good arm and her legs. Nor had she any memory of being pulled ashore by the women of the fishing village.

Irina Tsiganka looked on indifferently as the Major swabbed gently at the wound, probed with her thick fingers, manipulated gently the shattered flesh. What did it matter anyway, she thought. This was the crazy one, the one who had actually wanted to be raped. Why did the Major bother? There were more important matters to be considered.

There was a shadow in the doorway and General Budin's muddy feet stumped across the floor that Tsiganka had swept twice already that day. Her lip curled faintly. That was men all over, crude, careless, uncaring of what harm they did.

Budin paused at the bed and gazed down at the wounded woman.

"So this is our heroine," he said gently.

He raised an enquiring eyebrow as he gazed at Major

Kroup. She shrugged faintly, knowing that he meant "Will she live?"

"Comrade heroine, your great deed at the bridge has been reported to me by one of the wounded engineers. But for you, this vital attack would have failed. Despite the risk to your own life you pressed home the attack, lit the fuses that destroyed the German bridge. Therefore, by the powers vested in me as a general officer commanding in the field I do now award you the Order of the Red Star and do hereby invest you with its insignia."

From his pocket he brought out his own medal and laid it gently on the woman's breast. He took a pace back and saluted, holding the salute for long seconds.

Then he stooped and kissed the woman gently on each cheek.

Major Kroup watched cynically. It was a gesture, yes. But probably an empty one. Her recollection of the regulations was that supreme battle honour could be awarded only by the Supreme Soviet. Still, if General Budin cared to overstep his powers it was none of her business. And it would certainly be good for the morale of the battalion. Probably that was why he did it.

The corps commander beckoned her outside.

"Will she live?" he demanded.

"Not without treatment, Comrade General, not without an immediate operation. Her temperature is already dangerously high. She needs a surgeon."

"I have no surgeons. You know that. Field hospital was overrun a fortnight ago. Our last doctor was left behind three days ago with a party of wounded men."

He snapped a finger and Vassily came running up.

"There were medical supplies in the convoy. See that the comrade major has all that she needs. Bring her a list of what there is."

Jakubovitsch saluted and hurried off.

"There is another matter, Major Kroup. My radio operators were killed in last night's shelling. A direct hit. Now I have a new radio and no operators. Are there any trained operators in the Zhenski Battalion?"

Kroup considered this question before answering it.

There was in fact one operator, Irina Tsiganka. Kroup had seen to her training months before so that she would not be dependent on Army signallers for her own communications.

But could she spare Tsiganka? Tsiganka was her principal source of comfort. She was also a very capable forager, a good orderly, exceptionally useful for a multitude of small tasks.

On the other hand, Irina Tsiganka had been displaying a new side to her nature recently. She had been sullen, cheeky almost. Of the cause, Kroup had no doubt. It was jealousy. Tsiganka was jealous of Vyora Pekare. It might be well to teach her a lesson.

"I think I can help you, Comrade General," she nodded. "I have one woman who can operate most service equipment. But she would be on loan only temporarily."

"Of course," Comrade Major. And may I say, Comrade Major, that your battalion has performed extremely efficiently and my commendations will be forwarded to Moscow when a channel is open. Furthermore I shall be promulgating a Corps Order today, naming our heroine Katrina Semyonovna as a recipient of the Red Star."

Damn the woman, he thought, she might at least smile. But that great stony slab of a face of hers never showed emotion. Was that what NKVD training did to a woman? Or had she been like that before.

Jakubovitsch returned with the list of medical supplies and handed it to Kroup, who studied it gravely.

"Is there anything you want?"

"Morphine sulphate – in ampoules. Bandages and dressings. I'll come and take what I need."

"You're going to set up a dressing station?"

"No. I'm going to cut off a woman's arm before she dies."

As she stumped off bulkily Grigori Budin felt again his strange mingling of admiration and disgust. So competent, he thought, so very able – and so devoid of feeling.

He turned back through the rain to his headquarters to begin the planning for the assault on Misgorod.

CHAPTER 31

In their new quarters, for the barn was now untenable since Henschke had pulled down the roof, the women were domestically busy.

The general had allocated them a stable and turned out his own headquarters company to make way for them. It was a better building than the barn though smaller and they had brought timbers from the barn to make three tiers of rough bunks along one wall. They were covered with thick layers of straw and were moderately comfortable. At any rate, the women could sleep out of the damp that trickled in through the door and the tiles of the rough roof, driven by a rising wind.

Some of them were busy with needle and thread, patching their clothes. Others were delousing their tunics and trousers, running a lighted match down the seams.

In a copper in the corner with a fire below it, Shura, the cat-burglar, was rejoicing in a bath while other women urged her to hurry so that they could cook the evening kasha which would be livened by canned meat from the convoy's stores.

There was a mutter of gossip everywhere, the tensioning of jealousies, the crystallisation of cliques as they grew to know each other better.

Some groups had been formed long before. The kolkhozniki had already formed their little alliances before they were called up and the strafniki too all knew each other.

The rest had formed and re-formed into uneasy relationships.

Anna Turuchin, despite her rank, had joined the strafniki. In their hardness, callousness and total amorality she found something to salve her bruised spirit.

Also, she had worries which she hoped they would allay.

"I've never been late before," she told Maryusha despondently. "Never. I was always most regular."

"You're up the spout then," Maryusha answered brutally.

"Not much wonder. How many did you have anyway?"

"Do you think I was counting! I tried not to think about it at all."

Maryusha laughed coarsely: "That was a mistake. When you couldn't do anything about it you should have let yourself enjoy it. Take it from me – it's easier that way. You fight and you get torn. And you get it just the same. Relax and it's almost a pleasure. Also they like it better when you fight."

"Bloody swine," Anna Turuchin groaned. "My God, I wish they'd let us really go for them! That raid the other night. I'd have liked to get in and kill them – kill them all."

"When I was a kid," Maryusha reflected, "there was a big police sergeant in the town who fancied me. And got me too, I'll tell you. The first time – that was tough. I fought. As well as taking me he bashed me up a bit. I think he liked bashing me even more than he did screwing me. There are some like that.

"Well, there was an old tart – died of the clap long ago, poor thing – and she took me aside and gave the facts. So then, when the sergeant came for me again, I'd be all soft and willing, give him all he wanted and ask for more. That foxed him good and proper, I can tell you. There wasn't any kick in it for him any more. He went off me altogether, never laid another finger on me. It worked with other men too. Half the time it's the fight they're after, the struggle. And if they don't get that, they don't get anything."

Anna Turuchin's round face remained set in its scowling lines.

"What about me though," she muttered. "That's not much help to me. I told you. I'm late. And I'm never late. Listen, I'm not carrying one of their bastards for nine months. What can you do about it?"

"Don't hit the roof. It's time enough yet to worry. If you miss twice – well that's it. You'll have to do something then. Not yet though. You could just be upset inside. It takes some that way, even after their marriage. If you're really in the pudding club, old Katya will help you out . . . or try the bath after Shura. Get it really hot and stay in it."

She grinned: "Or maybe you'd better wait till after the

kasha's cooked. If that doesn't work – well, Katya's a wonder with a knitting needle."

A headquarters messenger who had just returned from a battalion outpost and had not heard of the change of arrangements stumbled in out of the rain and gaped in wonder round the scene, at the naked and the half-naked women sprawled about the stable.

Shrill screams greeted his incursion and the clad women darted forward to thrust him out of the door while the unclad grabbed at whatever was nearest to cover themselves.

"Silly bitches," Maryusha commented. She herself had not stirred though she was wearing only a short vest that exposed all of her huge thighs while she sewed industriously at a patch on one sleeve of her tunic. "What have they got to hide anyway? You'd think they were virgins in an eastern prince's harem."

She sewed a few more stitches before she added: "Anyway, there are a dozen men outside with their eyes glued to the cracks in this old shack."

"How do you know? I can't see them," Anna Turuchin gasped. "I can't see anyone."

"I know men," Maryusha answered. "Next to having a woman what they like best is seeing one. When I was a kid I could make five roubles a night in a little cellar place just taking off my clothes and letting them look at me. And they never touched me, you understand; they paid just to look."

She sighed as she gazed round the room.

"It's a great shame. A great waste."

"What is?"

"All these women in here. All those men out there. What a lot of money we could make if we handled it right."

The sergeant looked at her with round eyes.

"But – but this is the Red Army. We are all soldiers. Soldiers do not go with soldiers."

Maryusha stared back in growing astonishment: "What an innocent little ninny you are to be sure, comrade sergeant."

Vyora Pekare had integrated with no group as yet, nor had she really tried. Looking up from the patch that she was putting over a worn part of her trouser knee she wondered how it could be that with so many women in one place she could find none with whom she had anything in common.

Perhaps, she thought, it was the torturing of Henschke that had sickened her. That there had been no protest, no overt disgust in any of them. Certainly the big German had deserved punishment. But they should not have enjoyed that punishment. They should not have shown that schadenfreude which she had regarded as a particularly German attribute.

They had been more savage and inhuman than the man. It would have been one thing to shoot him out of hand but the other . . . the memory of his sobbing and his screams was still in her ears. That and his link with Rudi.

She could not forget Rudi, not at all. He was dead and yet he still seemed alive to her, the old Rudi she had loved in Berlin.

"Pekare!"

It was Irina Tsiganka at the door.

"The major wants you."

The gypsy's face was cold, her eyes baleful as she glared at Vyora.

Vyora could guess what was in her mind. The new favourite. Kroup's new lover. And she could not even begin to explain to Tsiganka that the position was none of her seeking, that she would gladly have relinquished it at a moment's notice.

She began to pull on her trousers.

"Why bother," someone sniggered. "She'll only have them off you again in a minute."

They were jealous of her, Vyora thought. Jealous because she had caught the major's eye. If only she could tell them how ill-founded their jealousy was.

"Better hurry," the gypsy warned and trudged away angrily towards the radio post.

Vyora pulled on her coat and hurried out into the rain.

Kroup and the vratsch, both wearing clean white coats, stood by Katrina Semyonovna's bed. The major held out a bundle of pamphlets.

"The morphine is captured German stuff. These are the instructions. I want a quick translation about the dosage."

There was a box of ampoules of morphine, each with its individual needle.

"I've given her one," said Kroup brusquely. "How many more can I give her without killing her?"

Katrina looked more relaxed now but her eyes were still open a little and the pupils had begun to contract under the influence of the drug.

Vyora looked startled at the major's words then hastily began to scan the pamphlets, making heavy weather of the turgid German technical words.

"Three more would be a fatal dose," she faltered. "That is, if I understand it right. It depends on body weight, health, other factors. But I think three would be too many."

Kroup nodded brusquely and took two of the little ampoules, broke off the needle covers and injected into the wounded woman's good arm.

"How long to wait?"

"To wait, Comrade Major?"

"Until she's out. Damn it. I can't operate until she's completely unconscious. Women can stand pain better than men – but how can I cut if she's struggling. Besides, the effect of the shock would probably kill her."

It was not like Kroup to explain herself to an underling and it was a measure of an underlying nervousness in her. She was about to tackle something she had never done before and for once she was not quite sure of herself.

Katrina's eyes had closed now and her breathing was shallower but easier. The lines of pain had begun to smooth from her face.

"Right. To work."

Kroup snapped her fingers at the vratsch and he brought a petrol drum with its top cut off. Petrol fumes spilled out and scattered about the room as the can was moved. Vyora's lip began to tremble. At last she fully understood what it was that the big major was about to do.

It was absurd, she thought. The sight of blood should not affect her now. Not after all she had seen. Yet her knees were weak and she knew her face must be pale.

The instruments were the crudest possible. There was a hacksaw, a common mechanic's hacksaw taken from a workshop lorry. There was a cook's knife, sharpened to razor edge. There were two pairs of scissors, one pair was a tiny nail scissors. And there was a reel of stout linen thread and four needles, one coarse, one medium and two fine. All had been soaking in the petrol in the drum for half an hour after scrupulous cleaning. It had been the best sterilisation the NKVD major had been able to devise.

Now she took out the cook's knife and advanced to the patient.

"Hold the arm," she told the vratsch curtly.

For a moment she paused and then began to cut through the skin and into the flesh.

Her strong, stubby fingers worked slowly and carefully and when she had exposed the main artery and vein she paused and tied them off with linen sutures.

"Fifty years ago," she commented harshly, "an army surgeon would have hacked the arm off and slapped some hot pitch on the stump. Probably the patient would have died. But we live in more progressive times. We are not under the Tsars now."

But the morphine that kept the patient unconscious came from captured German supplies, Byora thought.

Then the circular cut was complete and the bone gleamed whitely through the flesh.

"The saw," grunted Kroup.

A little blood was dripping down the wounded arm but less than Vyora had expected.

"The saw, you fool," Kroup growled. "Give me the saw."

Only then did the girl understand that the order had been addressed to her. She snatched up the saw with its wooden handle and handed it to the major. The vratsch continued to hold the arm phlegmatically.

The fine teeth of the hacksaw, teeth made for cutting steel, made short work of the woman's arm bone. In a moment it was detached and in the orderly's hands.

Kroup stooped to examine the stump.

"There doesn't seem to be any infection higher up . . . But give me that tin."

Vyora was glad to drag her gaze from the raw, bleeding stump and snatch up the tin of sulphonamide powder. Kroup dusted the stump with it, powdering it heavily so that the blood almost instantly formed a cake. She clasped on a dressing pad and bandaged up the wound with deft efficiency.

"I think she'll do. I really think she'll do," she said in relief. "Yes. She'll live. She'll live maybe to get her medal again from the Hozyain himself. The Zhenski Battalion's first heroine."

She glared at the vratsch.

"What are you standing there for, you great oaf?"

"The – the arm, Comrade Major. What do you want me to do with the arm?"

"What does it matter what you do with it, you bloody fool? It's only carrion now. Burn it, bury it – whatever you like."

As he went out Kroup's huge hand fell on Vyora's shoulder.

"That showed them, eh? That showed the swine?"

The girl swayed a little, still weak with suppressed nausea after the operation.

"Showed them?"

"The men . . . Damn it, don't you see? The men."

Her obsession never left her, thought Vyora. Men. She had always to be proving herself the equal of men, their better.

The door opened again and this time it was Irina Tsiganka. Two soldiers followed her, carrying the parts of the radio set.

"Comrade Major, I thought it would be better to have the radio here in case the comrade major needs me."

She shot a flat, hostile glance at Vyora, taking in the bloody handmark on her shoulder, seeing it as a badge of affection. Kroup thought for a moment then nodded.

"Very well. You can help with the nursing of Semyonovna as well. You and Pekare can do it between you . . . Has the set been in operation yet? Any signals?"

"Not yet."

"All right. Keep me informed."

She threw off her white coat, pulled on her great-coat and stumped to the door. The rain had eased a little now and it was almost dry again. But she was under no illusions of what the weather was going to be from now on. There would be more rain. And very soon there would be the snow.

How long would it be before the general made his move on Misgorod? Surely he must act before the snow came to clog the roads and make discreet movement impossible.

And when he moved on Misgorod the Zhenski Battalion would be in the front of the attack. On that she was utterly and ruthlessly determined.

The Zhenski Battalion would lead the way. And Major Natalya Kroup would lead the Zhenski Battalion.

She stalked through the mud towards the battalion billet. A day of war, she had read, was worth a year of training in the making of a soldier. They had had their day of war. But they were still woefully weak in the matter of training. It was time to rectify that a little, to weld the battalion even more into the tempered weapon she desired.

CHAPTER 32

"Vassily, is that woman mad, do you think?"

General Budin's chief of staff maintained a discreet silence. He knew very well to whom Budin referred. He had been a witness to the last stormy scene when yet again the general had refused to use the Zhenski Battalion in the assault he was now planning on Misgorod.

"Well?" Budin plucked at the dangling lobe of his ear. "Well? I asked you a question. Is she mad? Out for glory? What goes on inside her? You know more about women than I do, from what you've said from time to time over the vodka. Let's hear how you sum her up."

"Comrade General, *that* kind of woman I have never met before."

"Come, Vassily, I seem to remember you assuring me gravely that there were two kinds of women – those that did and those that didn't."

Vassily smiled weakly. Long-Lug had him in an impossible

position. The Academy trained staff officers, not budding psycho-analysts.

"From what I hear, Comrade General – the Major is one of those that don't. Not with men anyway."

"I'd guessed that. A man would be hard pushed to go with her. And yet you know some of our simple lads think there is good luck in bedding an ugly woman – especially an old, ugly woman. Yes. We'll say she is a Lesbian. I've heard rumours to that effect."

In fact old Shiryaev had passed him the word. Though how the old devil had his information so pat Budin did not know. But Shiryaev had no doubts on the matter. Maybe he had been talking to some of the women. In fact certainly he had been talking to some of the women. Vodka and women and food had always been Shiryaev's obsessions . . . and better maybe than the promotion rat-race when all was said. When the scapegoats were sought it was not the sergeants who ended up before the firing squads.

"So she's queer," Budin murmured. "Yes, yes. We can take that as read. But why does she want to get all her women killed? If she's so fond of them, why does she want them thrown into an attack?"

"To prove something maybe," Vassily answered, coming very close to the truth. "Maybe just to prove women are as good as men."

Cleverly he seized the initiative.

"Comrade General, the point isn't so much what she wants to do as what you want to do with her battalion. Will you use them? I've been watching them training over the last two days. They're not at all bad. They're quite well disciplined; she has some good shots."

"And what, my good Vassily, would be the effect on the rest of the corps if they knew we were using women in the front line? It was one thing to put them on that diversionary attack. It would be another thing altogether to have them in an assault."

"If they can do the job, Comrade General . . ."

"It's not a matter of if they can do the job. It's a matter of the men's morale. You know Ivan Ivanovitch as well as I do. He bitches all the time. He calls his generals an ignorant pack of swine. He calls the supply elements even worse – and with some excuse. He sees himself facing superior enemy numbers with better weapons and he takes a slug at his vodka and he mutters 'nitchevo'. But he knows in the long run it will turn out all right. He knows the Red Army will win in spite of us all. Right?"

It was one way of putting it, Vassily thought. It would hardly have done for the staff college, though. But he nodded and murmured: "Right."

"But suppose he sees us putting women in to do the fighting? What's he going to think then? It hasn't been done before. Except for the Regiment of Death that the Whites used during the Revolution. When Ivan sees the women going in he's going to think things are very, very bad indeed. He's going to think maybe that if they're that bad it's time to get out the white flag."

"Surrender? They wouldn't do that. Not our men."

Budin looked at him pityingly.

"The realities, Vassily. Always remember the realities. I've seen Ivan surrender before, surrender in droves. I've turned machine guns on him to stop him surrendering. That was real, Vassily, and not a good thing to have to do . . . And where's the rest of my corps, Vassily? They didn't melt into the soil. If they haven't surrendered, where are they?"

"Little parties are still coming in. They were cut off."

"Little parties . . . But what about the big parties? We haven't lost them in platoons, we've lost them in whole divisions. Surrendered or deserted, what does that matter. When men come anywhere near breaking point it takes very little to push them over the edge."

He began to roll a cigarette and muttered round its unlit end.

"It's the little things, Vassily, that put men over the edge. You can put Ivan in a trench and shell him and starve him and feed him to the rats. He'll hold on. He'll stand mortar fire and machine-gun fire and having his best friend's guts thrown in his face by a shell-burst. He'll stand it and eat his black bread, if he's got any, and fight on like the good chap he is. But give him some little thing that strikes the heart out of him – and that's it. He has to hope, Vassily. Take away hope, and he's lost.

"That was one of the things that beat us last time. The Germans started packing a few mortar bombs with mail. Our men's mail that they'd captured in a raid. And that small thing just killed their hope. If the Germans were even getting their mail – you see what I mean?

"Right then. If they see we're having to put the women into the firing line – hope's going to die in old Ivan's heart. He doesn't know these girls. But he thinks of his own baba somewhere in the mud, fighting. He knows it's the end of the road, things are so bad they're never going to get better. Take out the hope and Ivan's finished."

Jakubovitsch was wondering just how much treason Long-Lug had spoken. Enough certainly to have him shot. But then he had listened to it and that made him eligible too for the firing squad. He was greatly relieved that the political officers had decided to continue their work at a lower level.

"I take it then, Comrade General, you have made up your mind not to use the Zhenski Battalion in the all-out assault on Misgorod?"

Budin looked at him in astonishment.

"You haven't listened to a blind word I've been saying. The realities, Vassily. The realities. If the Urals reinforcements come in time I won't use the Zhenski. If they don't come – I've got to."

The flight of Heinkels roared low over Misgorod and parachutes fluttered down from their fuselage hatches. At first it seemed as if the Germans were throwing in parachute troops as reinforcements but old Sergeant Shiryaev's eyes were sharper than the young troops around him.

"Containers," he chuckled harshly. "That's a good sign, men. It shows the roads are well and truly blocked. They can't get transport through. They're supplying from the air."

The planes swung onto a new course, over the woods, over the Russian positions. The whine of bombs filled the air and men dived for cover.

"Supplying us too," a corporal yelled.

The earth fountained up a half kilometre away and Sergeant Shiryaev, who still stood where he had been, puffed on the ragged butt of his cigarette and glared his contempt at those who had run for cover.

"By this time," he taunted them, "I thought you'd have learned where a bomb is going to land. But you'll see. It's a good sign. These are the first bombers they've put in here for days, weeks maybe. Someone has the wind-up. It's a good sign."

Katrina Semyonovna's temperature was down and that at least was a good sign, Major Kroup thought. She was not herself a superstitious woman but she knew that most of her command were. They had despised Semyonovna, reviled her as she had reviled herself for some twisted reason.

But since she had been invested with the Red Star their attitude to her had changed completely. Now she was an object almost of veneration. The Red Star had the effect almost of some divine stigmata, making her something precious to all of them, making them hate themselves for the past. Semyonovna had gained a curiously mystical significance and if she died it could have a profound effect on them all.

But Semyonovna would live now, Kroup felt almost certain. Her temperature was almost normal, she was eating, even taking a remote interest in what happened around her. Her recovery was exactly what was needed to renew the fighting spirit of the Zhenski Battalion.

Now Katrina Semyonovna slept and looking down on her Major Kroup felt an immense gratitude, an abstract gratitude. That deed on the pontoon would be the lever she needed to bend the General to her will.

He could not deny the fitness of the Zhenski Battalion for battle when he had himself decorated one of its members with the Red Star . . . whether legally or not.

He would be forced into letting them join the assault. She would force him, she would drive him on. Whatever his soft, masculine scruples, she would make him let her lead the battalion into action, into real action, into all-out battle that would prove women could take their place beside or even ahead of men in any field.

Men! Women were fools enough but they could never be such fools as men.

She swung away from the bed, pacing up and down the farmhouse floor.

It must be soon. It must be very soon. Whatever happy chance had delayed the Urals reinforcements, they must turn up in the near future. And when they arrived Budin would fob her off. He would have an excuse to, then. He would have fresh troops to his hand. He could mount his attack without the Zhenski Battalion. And if he did he would rip down the whole foundation of her ambitions. He would deny her the ultimate truth that she sought to prove.

The assault must begin before the reinforcements came.

The battalion must go into action.

She could feel within her the excitement of the charge, the sense of danger and the elation of accomplishment. She could savour in a way the onrush of her women, the merciless onslaught on the men, the pounding down of male flesh, the destruction, the killing.

A bodily heat built up in her and her nostrils dilated as she thought of the men she would kill, the dominance she would assert over those who had tried to dominate her. Her women would smash them down, kill them, destroy them.

She looked over at Irina Tsiganka, headset at her ears, fingers twiddling patiently at the dials. She strode over to the gypsy girl and her hands fell furiously on her shoulders, dragging her back from the set, pressing in the young head against her.

In her ears Irina could hear a faint signal. A touch on the dial could have brought it up to full strength. But her fingers did not reach out for the controls. This was more important. Like a great cat's, her head began to rub up and down the major's belly.

CHAPTER 33

"Katyusha is a very fine lady, no doubt," General Budin commented sourly as he examined the mortar positions, "but it's not going to help us into winter quarters if she speaks too loudly. This is a fault of fine ladies. They don't care what they say, and they do a lot of damage with their tongues. I don't want the damned town brought to ruins. We've got to live in it."

He looked across the rolling fields of rye, swaying in the wind with the feel and appearance of an inland sea, at the buildings that were so exasperatingly close.

"We could pound them out of it. I know that. Now we've got the supplies. But we couldn't live there afterwards. It has to be an assault."

Vassily Jakubovitsch had the map board in his hand with the German positions marked on it.

"It won't be easy. The Germans are very well dug in. They've got good fields of fire for all their automatics."

A mile away the usual harassing fire made a faint obbligato to their discussion.

"I know it won't be easy," General Budin exploded. "If I had the men it wouldn't be easy. Without the men, it's . . ."

He had been going to say "impossible". But this was a word soldiers did not use, not especially within earshot of political officers. The commissar was hovering close by, his nose as ever a good argument for the pocket handkerchief.

With a flick of his fingers Budin demanded Jakubovitsch's binoculars and had them placed in his hands. It was easy to pick out some of the German positions now, even to see the grimed faces of the men behind the machine guns.

It was curious in war how easy it could be to see the face of the enemy who must be destroyed – or who would be destroying you very shortly. It made an awful intimacy of the matter, worse than the actual moments of contact, of killing and dying.

Carefully, Budin began to study the map again though by

now the whole plan of the city was committed to his memory. Carefully he related the two dimensions of the paper to the three dimensions of the ground itself. Hungrily he looked towards the town.

"There's new earth behind that bunker on the left," he said sharply. "They've been deepening it."

"The company commander in that sector reported activity during the night."

"Deep bunkers are hard to take out."

His gaze swept the terrain again, the broad acres of rye that waved in the wind and would now never be harvested, the trees that made a formal frieze beyond the fields, the outline of the town on the banks of the Don.

The sky had begun to grey over, a solid, bleak grey. How long now before the snow came? They must be in Misgorod before then.

"All right," he said again. "I've seen enough. We'll go back."

And as he stumped back to his headquarters his mind was working out an equation. To take the town he had X troops. But the task really required X + Y. When the reinforcements from the Urals arrived he would have that Y he needed. But when would they come? There had been no signal at all since that first message from Andrienko that they were on their way.

The position at Army seemed to be even more chaotic than here if he was to judge from the signals now pouring in again through that damned new radio operated so efficiently for him by that wild gypsy girl.

Exhortations from Moscow, demands for advances, demands for information, even the inevitable demands for returns. The farcical signals that always came in the middle of the tensest battle seeking the obscurest information; numbers of men inoculated for tetanus, men qualified in handling live-stock – even a peremptory demand from the army laundry service about a missing consignment of socks.

And of course there was that day's signal that now burned a hole in his pocket.

"Tomorrow morning's radio will contain a communique

announcing the recapture of Misgorod from the Fascist invaders . . ."

Bluntly the signal said: "Take Misgorod this day."

"Comrade Major . . ."

Irina Tsiganka held out the signal she had just copied down on the message pad. It was from the 375th Regiment.

"Have been engaged by strong German patrol elements twelve miles north of Misgorod and badly delayed but the situation now normalised and am proceeding. Estimated time of arrival Misgorod sunset plus one hour."

Kroup read the message with lowering brows.

The reinforcements at last, she thought. The reinforcements Budin had been awaiting so long, the sinews of his assault on the town.

She thought of the news from a military standpoint first. The German patrol must have come from Misgorod. There were no other German troops anywhere near – unless by some chance a German column had been cut off. But the probability was that the Misgorod commander had sent out the patrol to harry the reinforcements. He would know about them all right. All messages were being sent in clear now, for there was no coding officer alive at Corps headquarters. The Germans would know as much about the Russian situation as Budin did.

They would know also about the ominous ultimatum that had come that day. They would know that the assault was imminent. All they would not know was exactly when and exactly where.

Kroup plucked at her lower lip thoughtfully, still reading the signal but letting the idea that had begun to jig about in her mind, back and forward, take full shape.

First, the Germans knew about the reinforcements.

Therefore, they would *not* expect an assault until they arrived, after dark. They would expect a night attack.

Second, a day attack would take them by surprise. A day attack launched through the wavings fields of rye which would provide cover for her women to the very last moment.

And the only troops available would be the Zhenski Battalion.

She felt a mounting excitement as the idea took fuller shape.

This was the moment she had waited for so long. This was the time of justification. This was the time when she would prove what the Zhenski Battalion could really do.

It would require a little manipulation but that was well within her compass. Now her foresight in taking over the radio was completely justified.

"Irina," she said softly. "I think I'll have that last signal re-written. Static is very bad today and the last words were not quite clear."

The gypsy girl looked up at her and her cat-like smile began to curl the corners of her lips.

"You mean . . . stop at the word 'delayed', Comrade Major?"

"Good girl!" Kroup's hand caressed the gypsy's neck. "You read my thoughts."

Irina's angular handwriting abbreviated the message and in its new form it read: "*Have been engaged by strong German patrol elements twelve miles north of Misgorod and badly delayed.*"

Major Kroup began to smile. To Budin she knew exactly what *this* message would mean. There would be no reinforcements. He would have to take Misgorod with what troops he now had. And those troops included the Zhenski Battalion.

CHAPTER 34

Katrina Semyonovna was still under sedation, a little morphine each day to dull the agony of her arm. She could still feel the pain of her shattered arm though that limb had since been buried somewhere in the mud.

Oddly, the fingers that were no longer there caused her the most pain. She found herself continually flexing and unflexing those non-existent fingers, the nerves that connected them to her mind not yet accepting the severance at the amputation line.

From the wound of the operation itself she suffered very little pain at all and it was only when she rolled in her sleep, pressing the stub of her arm against wall or bed that it stang her into abrupt consciousness.

The continual presence of Irina Tsiganka in the room had not disturbed her. The girl's voice in the background, indeed the soft hum of the radio itself, were soothing. She let her mind wander, hovering for hours and days between sleep and wakefulness.

She heard everything that passed but rarely heeded it. Her only moments of real wakefulness were when one of the women, usually it was Vyora Pekare, came to dress her wound or feed her or sponge her down.

For most of the time she had been absorbed in a dreamy duologue between her past and her present, her past self making excuses for old errors, her present self analysing her self-deception, criticising with a bitter ruthlessness the blind, selfish folly that had made the regime seem so perfect.

"And you helped them," she accused herself. "Your books, making the Party a picture of immaculate purity, may have kept millions from examining the truth of the situation. Your books. You even let your husband, Sasha, be condemned . . . you condemned him yourself."

It was torment, but it would not stop.

Yet now it had stopped. For it was as if her mind was a tape-recorder now on play-back. She had not consciously listened to Major Kroup and Irina Tsiganka but now she could re-hear every word they had said.

And understand what lay behind the words.

Was she mad, this Major Kroup? Why did she want to destroy the Battalion? What crazy purpose was it which drove her on?

What a theme, she thought irrelevantly. This powerful woman besotted with the need to prove her own power, to demonstrate her equality with or even superiority to men. It was a theme worthy of Dostoievsky, more than worthy.

Even now she would be with the general, pointing out to him the inescapable facts of the case – that Moscow expected Misgorod to be retaken that day; that the reinforcements would not arrive in time; that the Zhenski Battalion was the only available force for the assault.

Budin's resistance would crumble before her insistence. The attack would be launched.

And how many would die? How many other women would lie moaning with shattered limbs and broken bodies? How many? And all for the megalomania of one perverted woman.

Katrina Semyonovna writhed in a spiritual torment on her bed of straw. Only she knew what was in Kroup's mind and she was helpless.

She tried to summon up the strength to rise, to get her clothes on and make for the door. She had to reach the general, warn him.

Desperately, she got her one arm underneath her and forced her slim body upright. Even this faint exertion had brought the sweat starting out on her brow, trickling in a little stream between her small breasts.

Yet she was upright now, fighting the waves of dizziness as her blood pressure adjusted itself to the new posture. Her mind began to clear a little.

She would never get her clothes on. It was impossible. Her hand fumbled uselessly with her blouse. It could not be done. Or if it could be done it would take too long. She must get to the general at once, even if she had to go naked. Modesty was for times of peace.

And what did it matter now what other men saw her body? Enough had seen it in the German time, seen it and used it.

What man would look at her twice now anyway – scrawny, one-armed, stinking with the sweat of illness.

She slid her buttocks to the edge of the bed and propelled herself forward. Whatever happened she must get to General Budin and stop the unnecessary blood-sacrifice of the Zhenski Battalion.

Her feet hit the floor and at once the weakened muscles of her legs collapsed. She pitched forward and her hands went out to save herself. But there was only one hand, one arm, to take her weight. She had not yet learned to compensate for that ghost arm that was no longer there.

She pitched heavily to the side where there was no support, landing agonisingly on the raw stump of the amputation. Her face hit the floor and for a little time she fainted.

Like a cat that's been at the cream, Budin thought moodily. A great, fat cat swollen with triumph. She was having her way at last.

He made a frantic last search of his mind for some other way. But the realities were there. He had to take Misgorod. He had to take it now. And there were going to be no reinforcements, the message had said. The realities said it would be madness not to use the Zhenski Battalion. The realities said they were soldiers first and women only second.

The attack needed soldiers. He had to use them. Yet there was a foul taste in his mouth.

"Very well, comrades," he growled to the gathering of all his commanders. "You know the plans. Synchronise your watches and return to your units."

And pray, he thought. If any of you still know how, pray . . ."

The chill wakened Katrina Semyonovna, the chill of the floor striking up into her naked body. For a moment, dazed, she wondered what had happened, where she was. Then she remembered.

The attack! The Major! Somehow she had to stop Kroup. She tried to reach her feet and failed. Tears of helplessness began to stream down her cheeks. Everything depended on her, everything. And she was too weak to help.

But she had to help. She had to get to General Budin. She had to tell him of Natalya Kroup's duplicity and prevent the impending massacre of the women.

Now she began to slither across the floor, raising herself on her one arm, thrusting forward and collapsing again to her breasts and face.

If she could only reach the door . . . if she could only reach the door. Surely there would be someone passing, someone who could take her to the general.

Rise and thrust and fall in a dreadful parody of crawling; rise and thrust and fall . . .

And then she was passing the radio and crumpled on the floor was the original message Irina Tsiganka had written.

Katrina's eyes lit up as she read it, panting painfully. This would be better than any words of her own, she thought. This would save explanations, be complete proof of Kroup's madness.

Her hand closed on the paper and she continued on her Calvary to the door.

CHAPTER 35

Irina Tsiganka rose from where she had been squatting outside the headquarters, silent and impassive as the men passed in and out, ignoring their jokes and their crude invitations.

Now she sprang erect as she saw Kroup come out. It was going to be as they had planned. She could tell that as soon as she saw the big NKVD major. She could see triumph bubbling from Kroup at every pore and because the major was elated so was Tsiganka.

"Not much time, Irina," Kroup said briskly. "The attack's in an hour from now. I'll want all the platoon commanders for briefing though it's going to be almost exactly as I'd planned, only a little difference in objectives. Hurry them up."

She felt as if she had been drinking champagne all day. At last she would prove what she had always believed. At last the women would have a chance for equal recognition. And it did not worry her at all that all could be equal in death.

"Dumb," said the corporal. "Just struck dumb I was. Well, how would you have felt, Sergeant Shiryaev, if you'd seen a big, bare backside come at you out a door, a woman's backside, mind?"

"You've got good eyes," Shiryaev cackled through mahorka smoke. "Good eyes . . . and what did you do?"

"I stared. That's what I did. I stared. Couldn't make out what the hell was up. I thought maybe that little wild gypsy bit of the major's had come on heat and was inviting one and all to have a go."

Shiryaev spat, enjoying the story. "That sort don't. Not ever. When they get that way they stay that way . . . Well then, what did you do?"

"I went over, taking a quick look round, mind. I mean, if there was going to be any screwing I wasn't reckoning to share it. Then I saw it wasn't the gypsy at all. It was that skinny one that got the medal. The writer. She was crawling backward out of the major's place with a bit of paper in her hand."

"Looking for the latrines, maybe."

"Oh, I think she was out of her mind. 'The general' she said when I bent down to help her. 'Get me to the general.' Imagine! Take her to the General. Imagine what Long-Lug would have said if I'd brought her in, starkers."

Shiryaev wheezed enjoyably.

"Maybe he likes them that way . . . I remember . . . Well, go on. What did you do? You didn't bang her?"

"A heroine of the Soviet Union, holder of the Red Star! You're joking! Only *she* didn't think that."

"She didn't? How do you mean?"

"Oh, not the writer. The other one, the major. Kroup. The NKVD's gift to the fighting man."

The sergeant looked puzzled.

"Where does she come into it?"

"Next thing I knew I'd got a damned great boot up the backside and was flying arse over tip into the Major's room. And that pretty little gypsy was coming at me with a knife. I tell you, I didn't fancy her then. Not a little bit."

"What did you do?"

"I got out of there just as damn quick as I was able. I saw the Major pick up the heroine and take her over to the bed. And that was that."

"As a story I've heard better," Shiryaev commented. "Better give your gun a last check over. It's almost time."

The corporal worked the bolt of the Degtyaryov he was carrying and checked the magazine. All through the corp's position the first stirrings of tension had begun, the stirring that came because men were preparing their minds for the moments of decision, for the killing time.

"Put your knife away, you silly little gypsy bitch," Kroup said flatly. "Is that all you can ever think of – killing?"

Irina Tsiganka's face was sulky as she pointed to the paper in the major's hands.

"If she takes that message to the general there'll be plenty of killing."

Kroup looked scornful as she took out her cigarette lighter. The flame licked up the message form and it crumbled into black and white ash. Her massive hand closed on the ash powdering it.

"If she takes *what* to the general?" she scowled.

Helpless on the bed, Katrina Semyonovna looked up at the two women.

Small tears of frustration were running slowly down her cheeks and she felt a terrible despair in her heart. Again, she thought, again she had betrayed the innocent. Because of her the women would die. So many would die, and because she had not the strength to deliver that message. She cursed her frail body but she said nothing aloud.

Now Kroup was advancing on her, two ampoules of morphine in her hand.

"Besides," said the major softly, "we don't want to lose our little Heroine of the Soviet Union, do we? And it would cause some talk if she was found with her throat slit."

Irina Tsiganka closed her clasp knife and put it back in her pocket.

"A painless, peaceful death," she smiled wickedly. "Comrade Major, you always think farther ahead than I . . . But four of the ampoules make the fatal dose, not two."

"You are stupid, as I said before." Kroup slipped the first needle into Katrina's arm. "I think maybe you will always be stupid. And this is not your fault, my love. You think like a cat, like an animal, without logic, striking instinctively and at random."

"But afterwards she'll talk," the gypsy insisted. "When the attack's over."

"Afterwards, I doubt if she'll remember this. She'll have all the nightmares and dreams that come with drugs. How will she know what is true and what is false? Even now she is not at all sure where the borderline comes between reality and the drowsiness of unconsciousness. It will be one vast nightmare to her."

Already Katrina's eyes had closed though the second ampoule was not yet empty. Kroup straightened and smiled, one of her rare, dazzling smiles.

"Now we'll go and show those men how to win wars."

CHAPTER 36

From his command post among the trees, General Budin had a perfect view of almost his whole line, for the trees were on high ground and the town lay in the dip of the river. Beyond Misgorod, the Don, reinforced by the rain, was a swifter stream than he remembered seeing it. But it would not flow much longer, he thought grimly. The signs were in the air of an early winter. The clouds to the east gave the promise of the first snow.

"It will not do to lose this particular battle, Vassily," he said grimly.

"We'll win," said Jakubovitsch confidently. "We'll eat our supper in Misgorod tonight."

"I wish I had some tanks though. One tank even, something to crack their outer ring."

"The mortars will take out the machine guns," said the chief of staff. "They're all ranged in already."

"If all the posts have been located."

The general pulled furiously at his ear.

"I have a bad taste in my mouth about this one. It's the women. I just don't like using the women. Not in an assault."

His chief of staff smiled drily.

"The realities, Comrade General. As you told me so often, the realities. Without the women you don't have an assault."

"The bulldozers," Budin said suddenly. "We still have them, don't we? The bulldozers from the kolkhoz. They could make tanks of a sort. They could take out some of the enemy posts. Why didn't I think of the bulldozers before? Get them, Vassily. Get them!"

And as he spoke smoke began to puff up lazily along the borders of the rye. The sound of the explosions came much later, individual explosions at first and then a regular thunder as the corps mortars and close-support guns began to pound the enemy positions.

"It's too late now," Vassily Jakubovitsch shouted above the thunder. "The attack's begun."

Major Kroup felt a curious exaltation as the mortaring began. This was it, at last. This was the time she had waited for, hoped for. Now the women would show them.

On either side of her the Zhenski Battalion was spread out in a long line, prone on the ground, hidden in the waving blueness of the rye.

At the first explosion they began to move forward, elbowing along like clumsy seals, spread out, faces to the damp earth.

The rye that should have been harvested some weeks before shed its ripe grain down on them as they moved. The seeds got under collars and up sleeves, a new irritation that grew more urgent than the imminent danger from the enemy.

Major Kroup was festooned with grenades, a dozen of them, for she had chosen the centre of the line where there were at last two German emplacements for her station.

There was no counter fire at first from the Germans but after about ten minutes of the slow advance the women heard the sound of explosions behind them as German mortars and light artillery began to respond to the corps attack.

No shells at all dropped in the rye and Kroup smiled a hungry content.

Her plan was working perfectly she thought. The Germans could not see the advancing women. They had no idea of the imminent attack.

After all, it should be easy.

Vyora Pekare came to a halt in the tall rye, not knowing

why she halted, knowing only that some deep instinct made her flatten low to the ground.

By now the nearest German position was only fifty metres away, almost within throwing distance of her grenades, and the attack was almost ready to be sprung. Yet she clung to the ground, as if she would have buried her face in the black, moist soil.

Off to the flank there was a sudden cacophony of machine gun fire mingled with the quick, soft explosions of hand grenades and the shrill, wordless scream of men charging.

"Get on," she heard Irina Tsiganka hiss. "Go on there. Keep moving."

Beyond the gypsy was the major, glaring at her from her great stone face. Kroup was gesturing wildly, ordering her forward. But she could not shout now, she could do nothing since they were well within earshot of the Germans.

Beyond Vyora Pekare the others too had halted, the stoppage rippling down the line as if it were a snake on whose tail someone had stood.

But at the other side of Major Kroup the line was still moving slowly forward. The whole attack was going awry, out of balance because Vyora Pekare had halted.

"Get them going!" Kroup hissed to her gypsy.

And then Tsiganka was dragging herself towards Vyora with the knife coming from her pocket and being opened in the same moment.

She was smiling as she came, or at any rate her teeth were bared in a flat, hard grin.

Vyora Pekare would move or die, the gypsy was thinking. Maybe both. Now Major Kroup would see who was her true friend, whom she really needed.

She thought of how Pekare had wormed herself into the major's affection, how she herself had been cast out, rejected. This was the time she had waited for.

As hypnotised as any rabbit before a snake. Vyora watched the gypsy creep closer, watched the glint of the watery sunlight on the knife blade.

Her mouth fell open a little and she began to moan softly in an unutterable helplessness. Already, it seemed to her, she could feel the cold entry of the steel as it slid into her body. Already she could feel the pain.

It seemed an age as the gypsy crawled nearer with death in her eyes, but it could have been only a few brief seconds for they had been yards only apart.

Vyora felt her stomach churn uncontrollably, her body altogether incontinent in its fear.

No thought of self-protection came into her mind, of raising her own gun and blasting it into the gypsy's face. She could only lie wide-eyed, feeling as she had in Rudi's room while Henschke had stripped her; alone, helpless, terrified.

And yet she knew also that this terror could end if only she moved on, crawled a few further yards until the attack could explode into life. But the same massive instinct which had halted her kept her motionless.

Her eyes must have seen, though her mind did not comprehend the danger that was just before her, the three slender copper wires that thrust upward from the ground, almost hidden in the rye, the thin whiskers that were the outward and visible sign that a German mine lay buried just beneath.

Of mines, Vyora had been taught nothing, neither how to recognise them nor to deactivate them. This was no engineering unit trained in mine disposal. It was a women's battalion only, a hastily gathered, hastily trained, frightened group of women driving onward at the will of one woman.

And now Tsiganka was at Vyora's side, the knife reaching out.

In this last moment Vyora suddenly burst free of the paralysis that had gripped her. Fear defeated fear. Or the urge to survive drove out the terror of the knife.

Her hand clutched at the gypsy's wrist and with a jerk that could not have been bettered had she been a trained wrestler she threw Irina Tsiganka over her head.

And for the gypsy there was oblivion as the copper wires transmitted her contact to the sensitive mechanism of the detonators and the mine blew in a fury of heat and sound.

For an instant, though surely even then dead, it seemed as if the gypsy had clawed herself to her feet, her belly a red ruin of blood and intestine. But it was surely the blast of the mine that had blown her freakishly into the air to hang poised for an instant before she fell again into the rye.

The mines were one thing Natalya Kroup had not bargained for or even thought of. And the general had not warned her that any defensive troops' first thought was always to get the mines out.

For a minute Kroup was taken aback, dumbfounded. For it had been going so well. Surprise seemed so certain. The way to Misgorod was almost open.

Now surprise was gone and the hardest part was to come.

Yet while the echo of the explosion still deafened her she was on her feet, gesturing violently to all the Zhenski Battalion.

"Forward! Charge!"

And she herself began to run, readying the grenades, throwing them as she ran.

From the flanks the machine guns began to scream in reply, the harsh hammer of the Spandaus throwing down a broad cone of fire across all their front.

But the suddenness of the attack gave it a prospect of success still.

The huge figure of Kroup seemed to dominate the field as she hurled her grenades, still charging at the nearest emplacement. The grenades seemed to patter like confetti round the gunpit and abruptly there was no more fire from that point.

Along the line of charging women there rippled a strange excitement as they rose from the rye and flung themselves towards the German positions. Some had grenades and some had only sub-machine guns, rifles or pistols.

But the Germans had not been idle during the nights when they had been left undisturbed. The whole front of the position had been well sewn with mines and the deadly little boxes blasted into their brief life as the women's pounding legs struck the deadly whiskers.

It was as if the line of attackers had come unders hell-fire. Worse than the incessant chatter of the machine guns was the blast that came from under the women's feet, shattering a body, throwing its pieces over the neighbouring line.

And yet still the line went forward, following Kroup as she shouted at them, urged them on, an incredible, inviolate figure amid the carnage.

Vyora Pekare picked herself, stunned, from where she had been thrown when Irina Tsiganka was destroyed. The gypsy girl's body had protected her from most of the blast of the mine though she was deafened from the noise and could hear nothing.

Ahead of her she saw Natalya Kroup, gesturing onward, standing maniacally above a gunpit, emptying the magazine of her sub-machine gun into a trench that held only the dead now.

And Vyora Pekare too began to charge forward.

CHAPTER 37

"Oh, the fools," groaned Budin. "I thought she knew about the mines. Did nobody tell her? She should have known about the mines. Everyone knows about mines."

He looked for confirmation at his chief of staff and saw Vassily Jakubovitsch's eyes intent on the battle.

And Budin remembered that he was a general.

"The Cossacks," he said suddenly and harshly. "Put in the Cossacks."

Jakubovitsch stared at him. Everyone knew that cavalry should never be used against fixed positions, against automatic fire.

"Put them in. Now!" Budin roared. "Davai . . . Davai!"

For he had seen what his chief of staff had failed to notice. On the right of the Zhenski Battalion there was a gap in the German fireplan. Three gun positions had been altered hastily to cope with the sudden attack from the women. The flank was open.

A cavalryman's delight . . . an open flank . . .

"Davai!" he roared. "Get on with it! Get the Cossacks in while the women are keeping Fritz occupied. Tell them to charge straight into the town, to stop for nothing. Go on, before you get my boot up your hole."

He was almost chattering with rage as he gave the orders, a terrible conflict in his mind. For the women had opened up the gap he needed – the only gap in the Misgorod perimeter. Only the Cossacks could exploit it. As soon as infantry were seen the guns would be swung and the gap would be closed.

But the cavalry could burst through. They could use that gap and be in the town before the Germans knew what was hitting them.

He had been in too many cavalry charges himself in the old days to have any doubt at all about the shock effect of a horsed charge on a startled defence.

Vassily Jakubovitsch was running now, running back through the trees to the Cossack command point where men and horses were waiting with a bloody eagerness to be in the battle. Scouting and messenger service was no pleasure to the Cossack breed. And when they got the order they would surge forward irresistibly.

The town could be his within the hour – if they started now.

And if the women could keep the Germans occupied long enough.

Half of them were down already, he thought, as he turned back to the battle. But that major, that great animal of a Natalya Kroup, she was fighting on still.

"Smoke!" he cried to the Katyusha mortar battery beside his position. "Give them smoke. Give them some cover at least."

Then his binoculars were at his eyes again, watching in a numb horror, as what he had ordered began to come to pass.

"It's what they wanted," he told himself. "It's what she wanted."

Natalya Kroup was not like any woman now. Her face was a mask of blood from a small gash on her forehead. And the great slab of her face was twisted in a wild ferocity. Her hair tossed about her head, for her hat had long since gone.

And the butt of her gun was now one great smear of blood for she had long fired her last magazine and she had clubbed the gun as she leaped from trench to trench, smashing dementedly at every head and face that appeared.

Probably now, she had no thought at all but to kill, to crush, to smash whatever lived in her sight.

To the Germans she was an incredible figure of vengeance, a Valkyrie straight from Gotterdämerung, invulnerable and infinitely destructive.

For these were not Panzers or SS men, they were second-line troops, fit only for the defence of an unimportant town against an attack that probably would never come from an enemy who strategically was already beaten.

Yet there were some of sterner stuff, older men who had soldiered on the Western Front in the First World War, others downgraded by some minor physical defect.

There were old NCOs, too, who kept their heads, old sergeants who had sized up the position, who knew what kind of fate to expect from the Russkis if Misgorod fell. It was not a season for taking prisoners, not with two thousand miles of conquered territory left behind them, with Radio Moscow screaming out its daily accusations of outrage, murder and rape.

The battle seethed round the German positions. Small slit trenches were taken, re-taken and taken again by women who fired blindly at point-blank range or threw grenades without always fusing them.

Anna Turuchin was emulating the major, swinging a German rifle by the barrel, smashing with the butt, jabbing and kicking.

Vyora Pekare saw her sometimes leaping through the wreaths of smoke from the Russian mortars that had begun to plop all across the field so that neither attacker nor defender had any clear idea of what was happening.

The little blonde sergeant's blouse had been ripped down the front and her breasts seemed to lift her along as she ran, as if they had been filled with hydrogen.

Twice Vyora almost shot her, for each time she swung up her rifle it seemed as if the sergeant sprang deliberately into her sights.

In fact Vyora did not once fire the gun. Dumbly and deafened, she kept staring round her, trying to bring an element of sanity into the incredible confusion.

What was she doing there? What should she be doing?

The German mortars were now in full flood, the donkeys braying frantically and the salvoes of bombs sweeping along their own front line with reckless disregard for their own men's lives.

And yet still the women were fighting.

And still Major Natalya Kroup was leading them. A great gap had been cut in the first line of the German defences and she was leading the Zhenski Battalion on to the outskirts of the town.

One more tussle and they would be through. One more thrust into the trenches and the dugouts and the way to the town would be wide open.

"Za rodinu, za Stalina!" she cried hoarsely and heard her voice echoed from close behind.

The ground ahead looked like a flickering heath fire, so many guns seemed to have opened up. It was impossible that anyone could drive on through that hail of fire. And yet Kroup kept going, her great body impervious to anything the Germans could hurl at her.

Bullets ripped through her clothes. One pierced her left shoulder and sang on out behind her. A bomb splinter gashed her hip but she did not slow.

The terrible mace of the gun in her hands was smashing down again at new faces.

Panting and far behind, Vyora Pekare saw Kroup tower over the men in the trenches while puny flame darted up and could not halt her.

But it could halt Anna Turuchin. Vyora saw the sergeant jerk to a halt in mid-stride and then throw herself backward with her body arched.

She saw the ballet dancer fall and knew she would never go back to the Bolshoi for all her exercising. A dancer needs legs more even than exercise.

The smoke was clearing and along the line there was only a woman here and there, some still running onward as if drawn hypnotically by Kroup's magnetism, others slowing, looking round bewildered for their missing companions. And some one or two were running back to the Russian lines, hands over their ears and terror in their humped backs.

And yet it did not seem to matter. Kroup was still there. Kroup was still driving onward with a terrible elemental savagery.

Major Kroup alone, it seemed, could win the battle. There was no need for others.

Then in a trench ahead of her a sergeant glared up at the vast figure overhead and fired the pistol in his hand.

And this pistol was no Mauser or Luger.

It was a stubby signal pistol, broad-muzzled and firing a signal flare. At any range at all, it could have done little harm beyond a surface burn.

But at that range, those few feet, the flare burst through the soft tissue of the NKVD major's belly and exploded within into a million blazing particles of phosphorus.

For a terrible instant Natalya Kroup became a gigantic, glowing Roman candle, the fire within her seeming even to glow through her ribs, outlining them as her clothes flared up and she became a vast carnival figure, dying in one agonising instant of terrible heat.

And yet even as she died the Cossacks were moving from the trees, exploiting the gap that the women's attack had caused on the right flank.

Vyora Pekare turned as she saw the swift movement. At a hand gallop the sturdy ponies swept through the rye and hardly a gun was turned towards them as they raced for the town and the capture of Misgorod.

How pretty they looked, Vyora Pekare thought as she watched them. How pretty. Like a vision from the past.

And as she formed the thought the bullets began to hit her from a machine gun she could not even hear.

She felt a little shock as the bullets made a straight line across her chest but she felt no pain as she fell.

CHAPTER 38

Sergeant Shiryaev was chewing sunflower seeds and spitting out the husks in a way that was not wholly conducive to good military discipline.

"Nu kak dyela?" he asked. "A great victory, eh, Comrade General."

Budin did not answer. He was still under the trees, still looking on the battlefield before the town, though the Cossacks were already in Misgorod and he had thrown in all his raggle-taggle infantry to exploit the charge.

Now on his left wing he had only two skeleton battalions pinning down that flank of the Germans. It was dark but Misgorod was his.

Fires were flaring up in the town and despite all his hopes of keeping the buildings unharmed the Katyushas and the mortars were steadily pounding the place to rubble.

"A couple of days mopping up," opined the old sergeant. "And that's it, eh? Then who fights in the snow, Comrade General? Fritz, eh? Fritz."

"You talk too much," Budin said roughly.

Shiryaev said nothing but backed away a little from the general. He kept on chewing his sunflower seeds until his hand was empty. Then he began to roll himself a cigarette.

"Andrienko's new regiment is almost here," he said at last. "I spoke to a D.R. Going to throw them in tonight?"

Budin did not answer but Shiryaev sensed him stiffen a little at his words.

"Daylight would be better, I'd say," Sergeant Shiryaev mused. "Give them time for a look at the place. Give you time to tidy up, too."

He spat through the butt of his cigarette.

"They could take it funny, I wouldn't be surprised. Fresh and green from the Urals, got all their news from Moscow radio . . . Then they find the battlefield's covered with dead women!"

"I know," Budin grated. "Boge moy! Shut up, will you? Shut up. Or maybe you'd like to change badges."

"And you too, Comrade General," Shiryaev chuckled.

Then his satirical mood subsided and his hand clamped onto Budin's shoulder.

"Grigori. I know. It was a bloody thing to do, bloody. But . . . what else? What the hell else could you do?"

Budin made a sound that was between a cough and a sob.

"It was what she wanted, that's the trouble. From the start that's what she wanted. I don't see how I could have stopped her. I don't see it, not even now."

Fresh in his mind was the message the despatch rider had brought, the confirmation of the earlier delay – and the amplification of the new regiment's time of arrival, the time he had not known, the time that Kroup had kept from him.

Radio trouble, or Kroup's own design? Instinctively he knew the answer.

And he knew now what his answer to Natalya Kroup should have been.

Yet the Cossacks had the town now and that was what really counted . . . or was it?

Shiryaev had been going to say more but even in the faint light he could see the moisture that glistened on Budin's cheekbones and instead of speaking he gave a last clap to his old comrade's back and moved off into the shadows.

There were a lot of liberties he would take with Grigori but no sergeant should see his general weeping.

Katrina Semyonovna's head had the lightness of the after-effects of morphine. There was in her ears a faint, continuous buzzing and her mouth felt continually arid, as if she had supped on alum.

And yet she felt also that her mind had never worked so clearly, that matters had never been so perfectly in perspective as when, infinitely slowly, she dressed herself.

The trousers first, then the footcloths, then the boots, all done very slowly and clumsily with one arm and one hand. The vest was harder, with its manipulation of fabric above her head. The blouse was harder still. But at last she was dressed, swaying a little as she stood in the room that had been Kroup's, by the bed that had been Kroup's, and for which she knew now without anyone having come to tell her, Natalya Kroup would have no further use.

Swaying she went out in the crisp morning light. There had been frost and the ground crackled underfoot where before there had been mud.

From Misgorod, the sounds of fighting still came but Misgorod had no interest for her as she swayed through the now almost deserted lines. Only a few orderlies, a few cooks, a few men tidying up the remnants of corps headquarters were left there and though they looked at her curiously no one came to interfere.

She saw no women at all, not a single one as she made towards the fighting lines of the day before. A bulldozer was at work amidst the rye, driving a great trench with its blade, piling up the earth and plants in a black and green mass.

The driver was smoking and if it had not been for his uniform this could have been a pastoral scene. And if also the city beyond had not rung sometimes with the quick rattle of machine gun fire or the crump of a mortar shell.

Katrina walked unsteadily down the field, down to where the rye had been trampled and blasted by the mortar bombs. A lone infantry officer, wearing colonel's insignia, was bending over a still form that lay on the ground.

And now at last she began to find the bodies. They lay scattered in all directions, some of them sprawled on their faces as if they were asleep, others staring upwards with blank, lustreless eyes at a heaven in which so many of them had no belief. Many were terribly ripped and torn and all were dead, the stiffness of rigor mortis reinforced by the overnight frost.

Now that she saw them Katrina Semyonovna wondered why she had come. The memory would haunt her, she knew. Yet there and then, gazing at the pathetic wreckage, she could feel nothing.

Slowly she began to pace through the bodies, recognizing one and then another, pondering the identity of some maimed beyond all recognition.

She could hear someone running behind her and a hand touched her, started to halt her. He was speaking to her but she heard no words. Her mind was numbed, her senses suspended.

A very faint frown came to her forehead when she saw the face gazing down at her, saw the mouth working. Her mind would take in no words though gradually she began to recognize a face from a long time ago, a whole world ago.

Before the war? Was there ever a time before the war?

She had it now, Andrienko, Colonel Andrienko . . . Vyora Pekare's lover for a little. She remembered once seeing the two twisting naked bodies entwined on the banks of the Don.

Now there was a terrible pity on the colonel's face and the words that she was not hearing were surely words of sympathy. She did not want to hear them. He was too remote, too far apart from all that had happened this day at Misgorod.

For an instant she thought of crying harshly that he would lie no more with Vyora Pekare in the sun, that only the worms would enter that body now.

But the effort of collecting her thoughts, of making coherent words come from her own mouth was too much. Imperceptibly she shrugged his hand away and moved on slowly.

And as she walked the numbness began to pass. She felt now that she wanted to turn, to call him back, to lash him with terrible words and heap on him all the blame for the tragedy of the Zhenski Battalion. Instead, she continued walking, head down and the pangs of pain growing ever sharper, pangs that reached down deep within her being.

And she did not turn to call Andrienko back. Let him make his own search of the battlefield. Let him suffer for himself.

"Comrade, you should not have come here."

It was Budin who had paced up silently behind her, stumping through the rye. Another of them, she thought. She said nothing as she turned to face him.

"You should be in your bed. We don't want to lose our heroine."

Her mouth twisted in a bitter smile.

"You seem to have lost plenty of them."

And as she spoke she was sorry for the jibe for now she recognized the deep hurt in his eyes. Her hand patted his arm.

"I'm sorry," she said. "I know you could not have stopped her. I tried to."

"You tried?"

"The signal. You only got half the signal. She knew you would not use the Zhenski Battalion if you were aware that the reinforcements were almost here. I tried to warn you. But . . ."

Her lip twitched at the memory of her helplessness. She swayed a little and the General's hand steadied her.

"You should go to bed, Comrade. You are not well enough yet."

"I've got to know it all, see it all . . . Is she . . . ?"

Each felt a terrible reluctance to use Kroup's name, as if somehow the very word might conjure back the avenging spirit of the woman.

"She's dead," Budin said harshly. "Don't look for her. You won't like it. She was one of the worse ones."

Katrina shrugged and eased her arm from his grasp.

"There's nothing worse than death and there's plenty of that to be seen. Please show me, Comrade General."

It seemed a long walk through the rye and around the scattered bodies.

"I have to tell you this also," Budin said abruptly. "That pit . . . it's for them. Now. Today."

"Clear up the rubbish from the battlefield!"

"It's more than that. These new troops. They mustn't see a thing like this. All these dead women. Very bad for their morale."

Behind them the bulldozer had already begun to lever bodies into the pit, the massive steel blade rolling them over unceremoniously, breaking the broken bodies still more.

"You're wrong. Surely you're wrong. Would it not inflame them, drive them on for revenge?"

Abruptly Katrina Semyonovna began to laugh, a low, terrible, almost hysterical laugh.

"Revenge! What a fine emotion too. You know, I think I

may very well carry within me the seed of one of these Germans who took me when I was a prisoner. So maybe at last I will have a son and what will he be? How will he seek revenge? On whom? Will he want to kill Germans or Russians? Or maybe those that make wars possible.

"Maybe me, Comrade General, with my books that told everyone that all was for the best in the best of all countries. Maybe I'm the one he'll blame."

Now they had come to where Natalya Kroup lay at the edge of the German trench with her terrible wound crying out to the skies.

Yet, strangely, she had died with a smile on her face. No doubt it had been a terrible rictus of agony but the relaxation that death brings to the muscles of the face had turned it to a very happy smile now, a broad, cheerful grin as if she greeted the two with "I told you so".

"I always said to her she should smile more often," Budin remarked sombrely. "Maybe she would have been a different woman then. Maybe she would have wanted something else."

"I think she got what she wanted," Katrina answered, also sombrely. "Za rodinu, za Stalina . . ."

Abruptly and shockingly in that place of death she made a coarse, derisive sound.

"What a lot of nonsense," she said fiercely. "The Romans, the ancient Romans, had a saying: 'Dulce et decorum est pro patria mori.' – 'It is a sweet and seemly thing to die for the fatherland.' None of them here look too sweet or seemly. They look butchered and dead and soon they'll be stinking. You bloody men, oh, you bloody, bloody men."

And at last she began to cry, shaking helplessly, tears streaming down her thin cheeks and her mouth wide. She was bawling like a hurt child at the total terror and incomprehensibility of a men's world of pain and suffering and death.

Budin stooped to lift her from the ground and carry her back to headquarters. He was appalled at how light the body had become, as small in his arms as a child's.

But as to what she was saying, that was a lot of rubbish. Every old soldier knew there had to be wars. And people were killed in wars. They always had been, they always would be. If there were no wars how would the soldiers live?

Katrina felt a great comfort in the general's embrace, in the rough, male, paternal smell of him. Her tears died and she began to think as she was carried onward.

She would write again, she thought. And this time there would be truth in what she wrote. There would be no more pandering to the Party shibboleths. It would be a book against all that, and against war. If unpublishable in Moscow, then perhaps in the West? Somewhere.

Maybe that was the real point of what Kroup had done – that Katrina Semyonovna should write a new book.

She fell asleep while she was still being carried and she did not hear or see the approach of Vassily Jakubovitsch.

"The new regiment," said the chief of staff. "They're still in their bivouac from last night. Colonel Andrienko wants to know if they can come on now?"

Budin looked back across the rye field. Already the bulldozers had done most of their work. By the time the new troops came there would be nothing left to see. There would be only a wonderful and heroic legend about the battalion of women, an inspiring legend which would grow from year to year.

"Yes. They can come on now," he nodded. "There's work for them in Misgorod."

THE END